THE RULES *of* MATCHMAKING

THE
RULES
of
MATCHMAKING

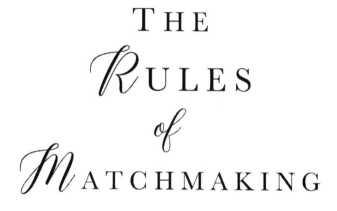

Castles & Courtship
Series

REBECCA CONNOLLY

To Miss Rebecca Clare, my most fabulous and beautiful goddaughter. May you find yourself a friend as eerily crazy and witty as your mom and I did, and may you grow to be the perfect combo of sweet and salty. You're my only hope.

And to you. May your life be far less complicated than mine. (Name that movie!)

CHAPTER ONE

"Jane, darling, I have a proposition for you."

Those were not words that were welcome to any of the relations of Anne-Marie Richards, let alone the one to whom they were addressed, but Jane Richards knew better than to ignore her elderly aunt under any circumstances. Her cousin Phillip had done so once and found that his favorite horse at her estate had been sold off before his next visit.

Jane did not have a favorite horse, nor a favorite painting, book, or mattress within the control of Aunt Anne-Marie, but she would not put it past the woman to find some way to make Jane pay, should she ignore the summons.

Thus, she must reply.

Sighing as silently as possible, for no sigh would ever be deemed acceptable as a response, Jane turned towards the room she had hoped to pass unnoticed and forced a would-be fond smile on her lips. She was truly fond of her aunt, just not her summons.

The details were important.

"A proposition, Aunt?" she asked in a tone she hoped would pass for intrigued.

Aunt Anne-Marie, aged somewhere between seventy-three and one hundred four, raised an impertinent brow, her wrinkled lips pursing in a manner that showed the exact inner line of her lip paint. "I saw the pause in your step, young lady. There is no need to be so hesitant to respond to my words. I am not about to suggest you become my companion while I await the arrival of my deathbed."

It was a task indeed for Jane not to show abject relief upon her features at those words, though she could not say she had feared that particular situation. Ought she begin to fear it in the future?

Jane moved more fully into the room and stood herself before her aunt, clasping her fingers in what she prayed was an elegant fashion before her. "No, Aunt. I am sorry." She paused for the distinction between statements, wet her lips, and smiled further. "What is the proposition?"

"A house party, dear." Her aunt's painted lips curved to one side, pulling the skin opposite tight enough to smooth her lines. "In the Cotswolds."

Was that something about which Jane ought to be excited? She knew nothing about the Cotswolds, other than that they existed, and was not immediately aware of any particular members of Society who called that place home. But Jane generally enjoyed house parties, so there was at least one element about the proposition that would hold amusement for her.

Wait.

The proposition was from her aunt, not from an invitation.

A house party with her ancient and unpredictably vindictive aunt. In the Cotswolds. Where she knew nothing and no one.

This sounded rather like the plot of a particularly garish novel of fiction where a ghastly murder took place under suspicious circumstances.

Jane made a mental note to write a revealing entry in her diary the moment this interlude with her aunt was concluded.

"Your reaction is hardly encouraging," the aunt in question said in a flat voice. "To what do you object?"

"Nothing," Jane replied quickly, though it was impossible to remove the hesitation from her voice entirely.

Aunt Anne-Marie made an attempt to raise a single brow at the remark, but only succeeded in adding a notable strain to her features before cocking her head to make it seem as though one brow rose above the other. "And yet . . ."

Jane said nothing at first, uncertain as to what she could safely say.

"I know you adore house parties, child," her aunt reminded her. "Last year, you went to Hampshire to visit that flowery estate. The one your friend Harwood insisted you come to. And you always attend Harwood's dreadful soirees at Battensay every year. So if it is not the prospect of a house party, what is it?"

"I do not know the Cotswolds," Jane admitted finally. "Nor anyone who lives there."

"You *think* so," her aunt corrected, wagging a wrinkled and ring-laden finger at her. "But how many members of Society have country houses, the location of which you actually know?"

That was a valid point, much as Jane hated to admit it, and she moved to a chair in the room, sitting to endure what was destined to be a lengthy explanation of why she ought to look forward to this occasion.

"Where *are* the Cotswolds?" she asked her aunt, the question sounding ignorant even to her own ears.

Aunt Anne-Marie rolled her eyes, sputtering. "Janet Catherine Rose, are you telling me you do not know the geography of your own homeland? What sort of education and accomplishment did you even receive?"

Jane winced at the horrid use of her full name, as all indi-

3

viduals must. She *hated* being named Janet, which was why she had always been Jane, but when her family was particularly displeased with her, Janet came out, and her defense of whatever had occurred vanished into thin air.

She could not argue with anyone when she was Janet.

"I will study the Atlas in Father's library from the moment I get home until the day we leave," Jane assured her, not entirely apologizing, but contrite all the same.

Aunt Anne-Marie huffed, but looked slightly less put out than before. "It is in part of the Midlands, if you must know. Gloucestershire and Oxfordshire, mostly, though I don't believe it is restricted to them alone. Lovely area. Rich history. You ought to study that as well."

"Yes, Aunt." There was no point in refuting her claims at this point, so Jane would simply be biddable and indulgent. So long as her aunt did not find her patronizing, it would work out beautifully.

"Do you not wish to know who is hosting this soiree I wish you to attend?" her aunt asked, her tone turning particularly imperious.

Jane blinked at her. "If you think it will help."

Aunt Anne-Marie sputtered again in the way that only elderly ladies were permitted to. "Well, do you want to accompany me now? Without knowing who is hosting?"

Not particularly, Jane thought to herself, biting the inside of her lip to keep from expressing any such thing. "I would certainly consider the idea."

"Would?"

"Am," Jane corrected quickly. "I am considering the idea."

Her aunt did not believe her, and that was evident. Still, she was not about to take it back. There was nothing Aunt Anne-Marie detested so much as taking things back.

She considered it spineless, and nothing was more intolerable than spinelessness.

But anyone with a spine in her presence had a battle to end the world on their hands.

What was between spinelessness and the reverse? That was where Jane needed to be.

"Lord Cavernaugh is hosting," Aunt Anne-Marie told her with a faint sniff. "And his mother."

"The dowager Lady Cavernaugh?"

Aunt Anne-Marie rolled her eyes again. "If there is no *wife* to Lord Cavernaugh, which would create a *second* Lady Cavernaugh, then there can be no *dowager* Lady Cavernaugh. Honestly, Jane, do you know nothing?"

"Apparently," Jane muttered before she could stop herself. "She's old, Aunt. How can she not be a dowager?"

"Watch yourself, Janet," her aunt shot back. "Age is relative."

Jane held up her hands in surrender. "Of course. But if Lady Cavernaugh is of a certain age, how is it that . . . ?"

"A woman's age is no indication of her bachelor son's willingness to wed!" Aunt Anne-Marie groaned, rubbing at her brow. "I should have invited Alexandrina to join me."

Now that was a laughable idea. Alexandrina was recovering from the loss of her dreadful husband and dealing with the fallout from such a loss, which meant she was in no state to go anywhere with their provoking aunt, and she had not been in good humor for many years, so it would have been a dreadful idea to *take* Alexandrina anywhere.

Aunt Anne-Marie knew that all too well, which meant she was simply grasping at straws in exasperation.

A strange tingle began at the back of Jane's neck, and she barely avoided attempting to crack her neck at its sensation. She cocked her head slightly, eyes narrowing at her scheming aunt. "Are you trying to match me with Lord Cavernaugh, Aunt?"

Her aunt scoffed dramatically. "Of course not. The man is as dim-witted as a pigeon and lacks the ability to say anything of the remotest interest to anyone who does not fixate on the subject of horse racing, horse breeding, or gambling on either of the aforementioned subjects."

"How exactly does one gamble on horse breeding?" Jane wondered aloud, folding her arms.

That was summarily ignored by her aunt. "Enough hemming and hawing," she snapped, waving her hands. "The house party is in two weeks. Will you come with me?"

Jane pursed her lips, now surveying her aunt carefully. "What is in a house party for you, Aunt?"

Aunt Anne-Marie mirrored her expression, her own lips pressing forward in apparent thought. "Lady Cavernaugh is an old friend, and she has invited me. I have it on good authority that other friends will also be attending, and spending time in the countryside of the Cotswolds sounds like bliss at my age."

The argument was losing its speed, Jane could tell, which meant she would have to commit to one side of it rather soon.

Truth be told, she liked spending time with this particular aunt. She spoke freely and maintained her dignity in the midst of it, though she might bruise a few individuals in her wake. But she was surprisingly gentle and generous when she needed to be, and Jane knew that she had sent a supportive letter to Alexandrina after the death of Lord Lawson, as well as a significant donation of funds.

No matter how the woman bristled, she was in possession of a warm heart and family devotion.

As well as a very acute and sharp sense of humor.

There were worse companions for a house party.

"I would be happy to attend with you, Aunt," Jane finally told the woman with a smile. "It sounds like it could be an amusing and worthwhile enterprise for us both."

Aunt Anne-Marie smiled broadly and with real delight, which was enough for Jane to feel reinforced in her decision. Who knew how many true smiles her aged aunt would have left in her life? She was in good health and as hearty as she had ever been, but after a certain age, the slightest chill could take a person down without warning.

Jane could not risk disappointing her with that possibility hanging over them.

"Marvelous!" Aunt Anne-Marie exclaimed, her wrinkled visage creasing with the force of her smile. "I heard from Lady Cavernaugh that there will be at least a dozen eligible bachelors in attendance, so you will have your chance at any of them. And your silly friend, Lord Harwood, won't be there, so you will not have him as a distraction or excuse. But so help me, if you try and make a boring match of convenience to shut me up, I will make your life miserable, Janet."

There was nothing surprising in that statement. In fact, Jane had expected it, to be honest. The addition of excluding a convenient match was a trifle surprising, but Jane's family had always had feelings about feelings being involved in their matches. Love matches were not expected, but any marriage had to be one of affection and respect, if nothing else.

Jane was not yet at an age where marriage was of ultimate concern, nor was her fortune something to sniff at. But there was very little for a young woman to do in her life but make a match, so it was always a topic of conversation when one was old enough to warrant such.

It would have been useless to refuse to entertain the idea of making a match at this house party, so she said nothing.

She did, however, roll her eyes.

"Mm-hmm," her aunt said when she caught sight of it. "So long as we know where we both stand, my dear."

Jane folded her arms. "Are you going to be harping on me about matches the entire time, Aunt? I will warn you: I have learned from your venerable example. I will match you to any suitable gentlemen of relative age who are in attendance."

Aunt Anne-Marie barked a rasping, throaty laugh. "What in the world would marriage do for a woman like me? Not to mention everything attractive is withered and shriveled, apart from my fortune."

"I did not need to know that," Jane announced, making a face.

"And I've already been married once," her aunt went on. "I have a son. I'm independently wealthy from him and enjoy the widowhood life. You go right ahead and match me with an elderly gentleman close to death, but nothing will come of it but some short-lived entertainment."

Jane grunted once. "For me or for you? Or for him?"

Anne-Marie shrugged. "Perhaps all of us, depending on the man. I've had vast amounts of entertainment in my life from surprising and unexpected sources."

This was unbearable, and Jane covered her face with her hand, torn between laughter and exasperation. "Aunt . . ."

"But I digress," her aunt said on a sigh. "The point of the matter is that we may now prepare for attending the house party hosted by the delightful Cavernaughs at Dewbury Castle."

Jane blinked, forcing herself to swallow the cough of surprise that rose. "Castle?" she managed to repeat.

Her aunt sniffed very faintly. "Did I neglect to mention that? Oh, how silly of me. Yes, the Cavernaughs' country estate is a castle. Quite a masterpiece of architecture and design, if you are interested in that sort of thing. Thirty guest bedrooms in one wing alone, and the grounds are immaculate. I believe there is even a set of ancient ruins somewhere, which I have no doubt will be utilized for some sort of romantic entanglements. Delphine will not be pleased unless there are at least three matches made from her party, and would be positively delighted if one of them were scandalous. Don't be that one, Janet. We are not so desperate, and you are not so silly."

There was nothing else to do but throw up her hands and leave the room, which Jane did in that moment. She had endured a great many schemes at the hands of Aunt Anne-

Marie over the years, but this one was reaching for new heights. Or plumbing deeper depths. Whichever seemed the most appropriate.

Jane's father had always preferred Anne-Marie to the wives of his other brothers, and even to his own sister Catherine. She spoke freely and took the trouble to be involved in the lives of her nieces and nephews, which were plenty. Her husband had passed several years ago, but she had not let widowhood remove her from the Richards family fold.

She had never been the favorite aunt of the children growing up—more for her intimidating ways and no-nonsense manner than anything else—but she had always been respected, or feared.

It was only in adulthood that Jane and her cousins had grown to truly appreciate the dry wit and extraordinary antics of this woman. She was excellent company, if one could withstand occasional barbs of raw honesty. She saw both people and situations clearly, her understanding and foresight one of near brilliance.

But she had also forced Jane, specifically, into excruciating dinner sets with bores for partners, into singing duets with far superior vocalists, into parlor games she detested, and so on—whatever awkward and moderately embarrassing situations arose. It seemed that Jane was her favorite pawn in some social chess game for her own amusement.

Perhaps she knew that Jane recovered from embarrassment and awkwardness easily. Perhaps she knew that Jane would not hold a grudge for such things. Perhaps she wanted Jane to be more independent of her own volition.

Perhaps she was simply bored, and Jane was a convenient option for entertainment.

Whatever her reasoning, whatever her thought, Jane had grown accustomed to being her aunt's favorite, for better or worse. Most of the time worse.

But a house party at a castle in the Cotswolds? That was

certainly a new endeavor on Anne-Marie's part. She had never once shown interest in participating in social activities outside of London and had frequently complained against all such things. She had adamantly refused to engage in them, turning down invitations from even the highest families. The only thing to get her out of London, she'd always said, were her grandchildren in the countryside and family Christmases in Hampshire.

What should suddenly change her mind now? What was it about Lord Cavernaugh—or his mother—that should convince her aunt so strongly that they ought to go? Despite what she had said, Jane did not, for one minute, believe that she was persuaded to see friends, to see the castle, or to see the Cotswolds. She had some certain ulterior motives, though what, Jane could not see.

Possibly Jane's future marriage; that was the most obvious choice. And yet, if the woman had a favorite among Society that she wished for Jane, it would have to be a relatively new one. And how would she know who would be in attendance at the house party?

There were far more questions than answers at this point, and Jane wasn't entirely comfortable with that. There were no options open to her, as she had agreed to attend, but it was uncomfortable all the same. She would simply have to spend the next two weeks preparing herself for whatever Aunt Anne-Marie was planning.

Jane had persevered through the Marriage Mart thus far, and one house party in the Cotswolds wasn't going to upset her streak now.

In fact, she was determined *not* to find her future husband at this house party. She was not going to find her match at Dewbury Castle. She was not going to engage in any romantic ramblings, wanderings, flirtations, waltzes, or promises of courtship. There would be no contrived dances or walks requiring an escort, no accidental grazes of hands or schemed partnerships on lawn games.

She was going to disappoint her aunt, Lady Cavernaugh, and any man who thought he might have a chance with her.

And she was going to have a most excellent time doing so.

CHAPTER TWO

Simon Appleby was irritated.

And that was a mild description.

"You did what?" he asked again, as his companion had not answered him the first time the question had been posed.

Intentionally. She had intentionally not answered him.

She liked doing that.

"I accepted an invitation to a house party in the Cotswolds," his great-aunt Louise told him, batting her lashes like a silly girl trying to appear attractive over tea. "For both of us."

Simon closed his eyes, pressed his tongue to the front of his teeth, and shook his head. "Why would you do that? First of all, on my behalf. You know how I feel about my personal agenda and my business, and about invasions into my privacy. And secondly, for a house party out in the middle of nowhere. I don't like house parties that are in known locations, and I might add, neither do you!"

His aunt—technically his father's aunt, despite there being only three years between them—raised a carefully painted brow. "I maintain my ability to change my mind and my tastes at any time I deem appropriate. Upon receiving the invitation from Lady Cavernaugh, I deemed it appropriate on this occasion. Dewbury Castle is one of the last remaining fixtures in England from the Norman times, and the Cavernaughs are stubbornly against visitors to their very own fortress. You did not expect me to refuse such a chance when it may never happen again, did you? And as I could not possibly attend a house party alone, I selected you as my escort."

Did she actually think this made sense? It was an even more ridiculous idea than it had been four minutes ago!

It took a few gaping moments for him to find words, and even then, he was not certain if they were the right ones. But Aunt Louise had never had a problem with waiting for responses.

She had spent a great deal of time doing so when it came to her family.

"What if I refuse to go with you?" Simon demanded, sitting back in his chair and folding his arms moodily.

His aunt was entirely unruffled. "You won't."

He cocked his head, more with curiosity than anything else. "How can you be so certain?"

One side of her mouth curved into a knowing smile Simon recognized all too well—she wore it often. "Because the alternative is remaining here and engaging with the remaining Marriage Mart. It is the Season, my dear Simon, and you will be even more in the sights of the mamas if you remain here instead of joining me in the Cotswolds."

Simon opened his mouth to argue the point, but found there was nothing to argue.

She was right. She was absolutely right, and while that was maddening, it was not the worst of the two options.

Remaining in London and becoming more prominent in the views of the mamas and misses not invited to join the house party was the greater evil, without question. It was always the greater evil, and if he could have avoided participating in the farce at all, he would have done so.

Having fewer candidates to deflect attention away from himself on the occasions when he must attend sounded like throwing himself into a den of ravenous and angry lions.

He was not about to do that.

"Fine," Simon grumbled, shifting his weight in his chair and scowling. "I don't like it, but fine."

Louise smirked at his response, practically dancing in her seat as her shoulders seemed to bounce with unshed giggles. "You don't have to like it, darling. You simply have to come along and endure."

He gave her a dark look. "Are you going to foist me off on any chit in residence at the house party for your entertainment?"

"Of course not!" She leaned forward, her pale eyes going almost unnaturally wide with her earnestness. "Do I throw you at misses when we are in London?"

"No," Simon was forced to admit. "No, you are very good about that."

Louise nodded once. "Unlike your dear mama, for instance." She raised a brow and harrumphed softly.

Simon chose to ignore that jab. It was true, but it served nothing to reinforce that point. Plus, he was almost certain his mother had the ability to hear anything that was said about her by any of her children from any corner of the world, and then somehow make that knowledge the fodder for her next awkward topic of conversation at a family supper. He had only just gotten out of the realm of her motherly grudges, and he was not about to subject himself to another.

"I have no intention of marrying you off to anyone, let alone at this particular house party," his aunt assured him, looking as though she was going to cross the room and pat his knee. Thankfully, with the trouble she had with her knees and rising to her feet at any given time, she remained in her seat. "I trust you to make your own choice of wife when you are ready to do so. I trust you to make one of affection, not just convenience, and to make a match of love, if it is within your power."

Now Simon heaved an irritated, heavy sigh. "Aunt Louise . . ."

"I know, I know," she broke in before he could say another word. "You aren't the love-match type and you do not believe you will find such a thing, nor are you looking for it, and so on." She made a rolling motion with one hand, her expression full of derision. "I have let you live in that delusion all this time, but that does not mean I have to accept it. If I could love my husband and he could love me, then you are not even remotely close to hopeless in that regard."

"But I am not your late husband, Louise," Simon reminded her as gently, and playfully, as he dared. "By your own admission over the years, I am far more stubborn than Bartholomew ever was."

Louise nodded very firmly, tugging at the rim of the lace collar at her aged neck. "You are. But Bartholomew was more challenging to love. The point is, darling, that you can be as difficult as you please and still fall victim to love. I hope you do, but I'll not push you."

Simon grunted softly, shaking his head. She might not push him in the physical sense, or even in the verbal sense, but she would make her feelings known without question. She would try to sway him without doing anything directly. Louise knew how to best use her influence to direct others and did so effortlessly.

It was not uncommon to find oneself doing exactly what Louise wished without meaning to, purely because it felt natural.

It had been the subject of much discussion among Simon, his siblings, and his cousins.

Aunt Louise was crafty, and they all had to be on edge constantly.

Simon exhaled slowly. "I'm not falling in love, Aunt."

"Well, to be fair, no one is until they are." She shrugged and rose, moving to ring for tea. "It can be very sudden, you know. Very little preparation goes into it."

"Aunt . . ."

She turned with remarkable speed and agility for one who so often complained about her joints. "Of course you aren't falling in love. With whom would you be falling in love? Until someone strikes your fancy in a way that no one has before, you won't believe it is even possible. No one starts falling in love before that. No one."

"Can we please stop talking about this?" Simon asked with an exasperated fling of one arm. "You just said we are not going to this house party for matchmaking! Why does it matter if I love or do not love or want to love or do not want to love? I don't even have to marry!"

"I know!" Louise exclaimed, the near-screeching nature and volume of her voice startling him.

He blinked at her, his eyes darting from the suddenly dislodged gray ringlet to the right of her face to the raised color in her cheeks, to the skewed way her beads hung against the ruffles of her bodice. He had never seen her look so disarrayed, and the look in her eyes as they skewered him was one of determination and utter superiority.

It was on the tip of Simon's tongue to ask if she was quite well, but prudence told him to remain silent and let his great-aunt speak in her own time.

If she would.

Louise took in a breath, her eyes fluttering closed. She looked down, her hands moving to her beads and adjusting them before smoothing back her hair, neatly tucking the loose tendril behind one ear. She inhaled again, then looked at Simon once more.

"I know," she said again, the color in her cheeks fading into her natural, if cosmetic, complexion. "I don't agree with you, but I know. I know you feel that way. I know you hate discussing love, for whatever reason. I know you don't want to be pushed or forced, I know you hate Society, I know you have no interest in courtship or any relationships that were not presented to you at birth."

There was a hint of spite in that last grouping, and, he wouldn't lie, Simon felt stung. To say that the only relationships he cared about were his family? He certainly cared about them most of all, but he had friends. Sort of. He cared about other people. For the most part. He wasn't a complete curmudgeon.

Not really.

His cravat seemed a little tight, but he avoided fidgeting against it. She was more right than he would allow himself to truly admit. He would fight against it and argue the point until his dying breath.

But in truth . . .

"It doesn't matter, Simon," Louise went on, her voice now carefully controlled. "You are you, and I will let you be you, however wrong you are about yourself."

If she truly thought he was so wrong, though, would she be content to let him be?

Simon stared at his aunt, the woman who had taken a particular interest in him from his youth, unlike so many of his other relations. He narrowed his eyes, more in playfulness than in sincerity.

"What?" Louise asked, returning his look with confusion. "Why are you looking at me like that? Your eyes get less blue and more stormy, and it is terribly disconcerting."

"Good," he grunted. "I want to be disconcerting."

Louise huffed in irritation, looking away. "Impossible man. Why?"

"Because I need to ensure you will be true to your word," he told her. He sat forward and rubbed his hands together slowly. "I need you to mean it when you say that I can be myself and that you will not force me into complicated situations in an attempt to implement romantic ideals at this house party."

"Define complicated," Louise muttered, her eyes flicking to him.

Simon raised a brow. "Aunt Louise."

"I am not going to force anything at all," she relented as she moved back to her seat. "At all. Other than you coming to this house party with me. Everything else is up to you. I would ask that you do not embarrass me, but as that is not usually your manner, I don't believe I have anything to worry about."

"Thank you, I think." He smiled at her at last, wondering if this house party might be the most entertaining event he had ever attended purely because Aunt Louise would be there.

She smiled back and adjusted her skirts about her lower legs. "Impertinent boy. Now, how well do you know Lord Cavernaugh?"

Simon sat back, crossing one leg over the other. "Well enough. Decent shot, not particularly intelligent or well-spoken, but from an ancient family, obviously. He needs a wealthy wife to maintain the family property, though I doubt that is well-known."

"Does he, indeed?" Aunt Louise brightened at the prospect, her mouth curving into a deep smile. "Well, well . . ."

A groan welled up in Simon's chest and he covered his face with one hand. "Oh, good heavens."

"Stop that," Louise scolded with a flick of her hand. "I am only interested in the ladies that will be invited to the house party, if that is Lady Cavernaugh's secret intention for her son. Why else would they be opening up Dewbury? She's hosting a wife hunt."

"Do they use hounds for that?" Simon asked her in bemusement.

She ignored him. "And you are going to be there for sows that aren't worth the blue ribbon at the county fair. You and all the other gentlemen in attendance shall have the pick of his unimpressive castoffs. The dogs that cannot hunt. The horses that do not jump."

Simon barked a laugh. "Should I be insulted now or wait until we get there?"

"Delphine will be particularly selective," Louise murmured, seeming completely oblivious to his presence now. "Particularly if her son has little enough to recommend him. If he's no rake to be reformed and he's not a popular bachelor of the Season, he's likely a bore in the middle of the pack."

"Which means what for the selection criteria?" Simon inquired as she began to pace. He had no interest in the subject, but he might as well join in his aunt's ridiculous rambling, if she would not take his commentary into consideration.

"Dumb chits with more money than sense," she replied, somehow hearing him that time when the others hadn't had any sort of impact. "Pretty butterflies with plenty of color who don't know to avoid the net. Clueless kittens who will pounce on any creature they can. Biddable blossoms blowing in their mama's wind."

Simon grimaced. "I have so many images in my head now. All unfortunate."

Louise began making a tsking sound as she paced. "Could she include *any* intelligent females in the group? I suppose it would depend on the size of the fortune, but she would certainly not want a woman who would outshine her son. Unless, of course, that is exactly what she is aiming for. Ohhh, that could change the game entirely. How many brilliant heiresses do we know?"

"From this century?" Simon pretended to muse on that. "One, two . . . three, if her father has corrected his ways . . ."

"Delphine loves breeding," Louise went on.

"Who doesn't?"

"Pedigree," she corrected in a loud voice, glaring at Simon for the first time. "Pedigree and family breeding."

Simon held up his hands in surrender. "Apologies. My mistake."

His aunt shook her head and resumed her immersion into her own world. "We need to know more. I need to know Delphine's aims and schemes. If only I could get my hands on the invitation list . . . That would change everything."

"To what end?" Simon cleared his throat, wondering if it would bring her back to the real world they inhabited.

"Thirty guest rooms," she murmured. "Minimum. Chaperones included. She'd want even numbers to avoid being blatant. No exceptional gentlemen, as her son needs to be the focus."

"I beg your pardon?"

Louise swept her skirts behind her as she turned, her eyes on the path she had just trod rather than on her objecting nephew. "I need the plans for Dewbury. I need to know where the rooms are and just how many in all usable wings."

The maid entered with the tea service then and Simon nodded at her, gesturing towards the small table before him despite his aunt continuing to wear a steady pattern into the rug across the room. She set the tray down and started to pull cups and saucers off, but he shook his head, smiling as he waved her away. She curtseyed quickly and left the room, sparing his aunt a curious look.

There would almost certainly be talk below stairs now.

But in Louise's house, there was likely always talk below stairs on something or other. The servants saw and heard everything, after all. The only question every homeowner had to ask was if the staff could be trusted to keep that talk among the household alone.

Nobody in Society needed to know that Lady Clarke paced and muttered to herself on the subject of matchmaking.

"But," Louise continued, her tone almost sharp, "she will

likely be just as strategic with which guest goes into which room as well. So I will also need her housekeeper's plans."

Simon shook his head as he poured tea into a cup. "Before you decide to remove yourself to Dewbury and take over Lady Cavernaugh's house party for whatever scheme you are concocting, will you take some tea?" He held out the cup and saucer, flicking his eyes to it pointedly.

Louise stopped and looked at it, then at him. "How many sugars have you added?"

"None yet. How many would you like?"

Her jaw moved from side to side, then she marched back towards her chair. "Two. And a splash of milk."

Simon nodded and made the tea according to her specifications, handing it to her the moment he was done. "I will ask you again, Aunt. To what end would you need the invitation list, the plans for the castle, and the housekeeper's plans?"

"To anticipate Delphine's actions and intentions, of course." She scoffed, taking a small sip of her tea. "I want to judge her matchmaking schemes and watch the reality unfold. Nobody likes to guess at these things."

"You are not throwing me into this mix, correct?" He poured tea for himself, trying to meet her eyes while he did so. "We just discussed this—you aren't going back on your word already, are you?"

Louise shook her head and reached for a biscuit. "You are only a name on an invitation list at this time, Simon. If you are not a threat to Delphine or Cavernaugh, a match for yourself is utterly irrelevant."

"And so, the blows continue," he grumbled, widening his eyes and dropping a cube of sugar into his cup, stirring quickly.

"No," she went on, "I don't care who they relegate as dregs for your cup of tea, darling. I want to know who the biscuit on the top tier of the tea stand is. And what makes her so very top tier."

CHAPTER THREE

Complain as she might about traveling with her aunt in general, Jane had to admit that Aunt Anne-Marie's carriage was far preferable to any other form of transportation she had ever taken into the countryside. She knew nothing about the construction of carriages, the business of axles and springs and the like, but she could appreciate when one was particularly well constructed for comfort and conveyance. She had slept for at least an hour perfectly undisturbed and without any sense of the condition of the roads, as comfortable as she might have been on any settee at home.

This carriage must have cost a fortune.

She would not ask her aunt about that, of course. Discussions of finances were uncouth, even within a family.

But Jane was suddenly more interested in making an advantageous marriage, financially speaking, if it meant she could ride in such carriages for the rest of her life.

She would not inform her aunt of that either.

Jane had only just managed to convince her this morning that there would be no matchmaking schemes during this house party. Even hinting that she might seek a match of any kind at some point in her life might negate the restraint she had so recently instilled in her aunt.

It would be a boon to attend a house party where she was not part of some scheme. Where she could simply enjoy herself and enjoy the company. Where she would not have to over-think or over-prepare. Where nothing would be seen as more than it appeared, and nothing would need be discussed after the fact.

Where Taft—Lord Harwood—would not influence her to do something silly, bold, or entertaining in ways that only he would appreciate.

She would certainly miss Taft, as she rarely attended house parties or events where he was not also invited, but he did have a way of taking over whatever social setting he was in purely by his good nature and pleasing manner. Only last year, they had attended a house party of a friend of his in Hamp-shire, and it had ended badly. Not because of anything they had done, but because Mr. Roth's mother had become dread-fully unwell. But before that, the party had been an extraordinary event.

She had even convinced her cousin Alexandrina to come, though her mourning period had been perhaps too fresh for that.

Not that she truly mourned her husband. But the techni-cality must be observed in polite society.

Taft was like a rambunctious brother to Jane, and to her sisters. They'd grown up together, and, should they have wanted a convenient marriage without fuss, they might have considered marrying each other. But neither of them had ever discussed the idea, and Jane was certainly not in love with Taft. He was handsome enough, it was true, but he was too much a sibling to be a suitor.

Besides, they were so free with their opinions and barbs with each other that they might actually do each other an injury should they be wedded. Imagine trying to raise a child with a man one already knew how to strongly argue against!

Jane shuddered in the carriage, feeling more than a little ill and unnerved at the suggestion. No, she needed to find her own way and her own match at a time that was right. When that would be and how it might come about was not at all clear, and she was not in a hurry.

A young woman, or one on her way to no longer being referred to as young, had no real occupation during the Season other than seeking the perfect match for herself and her future. Or being volunteered by eager and enterprising parents. Or being instructed by ruthless and formal guardians. Whoever was doing the managing, there did not seem to be another option for spending one's time than planning for a match, scheming for one, securing one, or in some cases, avoiding one. That was it. That was all that happened and all that anyone seemed to think about.

Every event was for matchmaking. Every outing was for matchmaking. Every gown was for matchmaking. Every conversation, every stroll, every ride, every ribbon in one's hair —all was for matchmaking. It was demeaning, it was stifling, and it was exhausting.

Jane was a bit of an oddity in her lack of concern for her so-called success in the Marriage Mart, and reaching the age of three and twenty without a single proposal hadn't affected her mood for one second. She was rather proud of it, actually. She had no designs on reaching a particular age before marriage or for being known as a woman who resisted such, but she was proud not to have been one of the tens of other women who married before they had developed any sense of self.

Surely any respectable man wanted to marry a woman who knew who she was.

But then, she rarely met a man who actually wanted a woman to think.

Another reason not to marry young. That was a truth that

took a little wisdom and experience to learn, and most women learned it through disappointment, if not heartbreak.

Not Jane. She had never experienced her heart breaking or bursting or blooming or whatever sort of whimsical notions one used to describe romantic sensations. She had quite simply always been a part of Society without being at the center of it.

She rather liked it that way.

The carriage turned at a fork in the road and began to climb, the upward progression growing just the slightest bit bumpy compared to the rest of the journey thus far. Still not jostling, by any stretch, but it was enough that Anne-Marie woke herself up with a loud snort.

Smacking her dried lips together, Anne-Marie blinked slowly exactly twice. She turned her head from side to side, looking out each window with wide, bleary eyes. "Where are we?"

Jane shook her head, biting down hard on her lips to keep from giggling. "I'm not entirely certain, Aunt."

"Of course you're not," her aunt retorted, her voice slightly clogged with the remnants of sleep. "What are you, a map?" She mumbled something under her breath and focused on their surroundings. "Hmm. Gloucestershire, I'd reckon. We're nearly there."

The impulse to giggle faded at once. "How can you tell that?"

Anne-Marie looked at her with utter superiority. "Because it looks like Gloucestershire, Jane. Why else would I say so?"

"Why, indeed," she muttered, craning her neck from side to side.

"I will not insult your age and maturity by giving you a list of expected behaviors during this party," Anne-Marie announced, suddenly perfectly awake and alert. "I will only remind you not to embarrass me or give me reason to regret having you accompany me. I was the one who was invited, not you."

Jane managed a smile. "I am not likely to forget, Aunt, with how frequently you have reminded me over the last two weeks."

Anne-Marie raised her painted brows. "Not off to a particularly promising start, my dear."

"You prefer me when I am impudent," she shot back.

"True." Her aunt hummed softly, seeming bemused, if not outright pleased. "You're always a well-behaved girl, Janet, even when you are impudent. There are no expectations for engagements or courtships coming out of this event, so use it as an opportunity to enjoy yourself. It is so rare to be in your position during the Season. I hope you will take advantage of it."

Jane nodded, understanding all too well what her aunt meant. "Believe me, Aunt, I intend to. Is there anything I can do for you during this house party? As your companion, of a sort, I feel it only right to be at your leisure, in many respects."

Anne-Marie waved her hand rather dismissively. "Oh, tosh. I am not a doddering biddy, dear. Unless being a doddering biddy means I may have breakfast on a tray in my room at my request. I only ask that you tell me any delicious gossip you hear in your young people gatherings. If I require something more specific of you, I shall ask at the time."

"Are you certain?" Jane smiled at her aunt, trying to appear as genuine and affectionate as she truly felt. "I don't mind."

"Well . . ." Anne-Marie looked out the window, her high brow creasing in thought. "If I remember correctly, Delphine has cultivated a marvelous garden at Dewbury. I would not say no to you escorting me on a morning walk in them on fair days."

Jane nodded and folded her hands in her lap. "I can do that. I love a morning walk myself. We are to stay for a week, yes?"

Her aunt nodded. "One week, unless there is a very good

reason to remain." Her expression suddenly turned rather dubious. "The only reason that would be is if you should find yourself in an understanding with Lord Cavernaugh, and I would never see you again if you were that stupid."

Laughter erupted from Jane at the statement, and she fell back against the seat in her mirth. "Aunt Anne-Marie! He cannot be so bad as all that."

"No, he is not," her aunt returned. "But he is also the most unremarkable young man of my acquaintance. And you shall not marry a boring, unremarkable, entirely forgettable man just to become a wife. You are better than that."

"I have no designs on Lord Cavernaugh," Jane assured her. "I don't even know the man. And you know me better than to believe I would marry a man simply to have a wedding and become a wife."

The smile on her aunt's lips told Jane that she did know this, and there was a strange comfort in that. It seemed such a small thing for a relative to be certain of, but it said something much deeper for Jane. Her aunt knew her, knew her personality, knew her values, knew her nature and her goals. She would never be flighty or silly like other girls, and she viewed marriage as something more sincere and important than an improvement of status.

It was not the most popular view of matrimony, but there it was.

"Wiser girls than you have made dumber decisions under a certain influence," her aunt said gently. "I have seen it. Just remember that for yourself, Jane. Remember the real world outside of the walls of this castle. That is all I ask."

Jane felt the moment grow heavy and somber, which was a strange experience in this woman's presence. She wasn't entirely certain that she liked it, but there wasn't exactly a way to escape it.

"Do you have the gift of premonition, Aunt?" she asked

slowly, wondering if there was something she ought to know about this woman she thought she had known her entire life.

Her aunt scoffed and sputtered so loudly, Jane jumped. "Of course not. Can I not simply be a voice of warning? Honestly, you do say the most extraordinary things sometimes."

The mockery was more comfortable than where she had been moments before, but there was something about her aunt's manner and quick defense that made Jane uneasy all the same.

Of course, she did not actually believe that her aunt had some sort of mystic power to predict the future. But it was absolutely like her aunt to have some plot or scheme up her sleeve, so to speak. Very like her, in fact.

Jane would have to watch out for that while they were at this house party. Or castle party, as it were.

But all she had asked of Jane was that she not marry Lord Cavernaugh, which she hadn't thought of doing in the least, and that she enjoy herself, which she had hoped to do anyway.

If there was a trick or scheme in that, Jane couldn't see it.

Unless Lord Cavernaugh was actually a remarkable man of exceptionally good looks and impeccable manners who would make any woman of sense and taste the perfect husband.

She'd have to keep an open mind about that one. If she had ever met Lord Cavernaugh in London, she could not recollect doing so, which would not bode well for her if he was such a man, and would not bode well for him if he was as her aunt had suggested.

Well, now her mind was positively spinning, and it was entirely her aunt's fault.

She would not take the blame for thinking the reverse of her aunt's statement. Aunt Anne-Marie was just the sort of difficult personality to do such a thing, and it was perfectly reasonable to leap to such conclusions. Any of her siblings or cousins would have done so without shame, and they would all support her thoughts on the subject. And it did not matter if she happened to be wrong about Lord Cavernaugh. She was perfectly right to suspect her aunt was up to something.

The only real question was that of her aunt's aim, and how soon into the house party Jane would be able to figure out what it was.

She did enjoy a challenge, so there were certainly some benefits to having an ulterior motive in attending the house party.

Determining her aunt's plans and thwarting them would be a delicious form of entertainment for herself. And Aunt Anne-Marie *had* suggested that Jane spend the house party enjoying herself, had she not?

She felt her mouth curve to one side as she looked out of the window, letting her eyes trace across the landscape of Gloucestershire, if her aunt was to be believed. It was a beautiful county, with its lush, rolling hills of green and the endless expanse of sky above. Of course, Jane knew the sky was the same size no matter where she was, but when in the countryside, it seemed to loom so much the grander above the land, and the colors of it just the slightest different in shade. The clouds seemed a puffier sort of white, and the trees a richer hue of green.

It was a lovely view, there was no mistaking that.

"How old would you say Dewbury Castle is?" Jane inquired as the carriage took another fork in the road. "Tudor age?"

"Older, my dear. Norman, if Delphine's boasts are to be believed."

Jane glanced at her aunt in surprise. "Truly?"

Anne-Marie shrugged. "Parts of it, at least. You know how such things go. Expanding wings as needs be, reconstruction where waste or decay has occurred, refurbishing as tastes and fashions change . . . There are probably ruins of an ancient monastery on the estate, given the propensity of the times to have a castle and monastery in close quarters."

"Do you think the ruins are something that can be explored

by guests?" Jane struggled to hide her eagerness, her fingers clenching together and her throat tightening. She was, if she were to be frank, a bit of an explorer when opportunities arose. Climbing rocks and hills, ruins and remnants of ancient structures, wandering cemeteries, clambering up trees . . .

Her sisters had complained of her antics and her mother had despaired of her.

She kept most of those impulses in check now, as she was so often in Society and London, where opportunities to indulge were limited at best. But when she was out in the country or with comfortable and trusted friends . . .

She'd had to explain more than one pair of ruined stockings in her adult life, that was for certain.

Aunt Anne-Marie chuckled knowingly. "I have no doubt that anything on the estate Delphine can use to attract attention to their fortune and status, she will. She might even claim that Henry VIII himself stayed in the castle so often, he had a favorite bedchamber or mattress. Or had a child off one of the family maids, for heaven's sake."

"Aunt!" Jane protested with a laugh. It was not altogether that shocking, considering her aunt, but it was not exactly a topic of conversation for polite company.

Unruffled, Anne-Marie nodded as she looked out of the window. "Aha, I do believe we are arriving. See the village of Dewbury here?"

Jane leaned to view out the same window, smiling at the simple, quaint village they were passing through. It could not have been less like London if it had tried to be so. The buildings were no more than two stories tall, every other roof appeared thatched, and the streets were more dust than cobblestone, though a few of the buildings had stone at the threshold of their doors. Apart from the contemporary clothing the villagers wore, one might have been transported three hundred years back in time by the village itself.

It was the most adorable place Jane had ever seen.

"I dare you to ask one of them who the king is," Anne-Marie teased, her voice rife with laughter.

Jane threw a scolding look in her direction. "Aunt . . . I am certain they are perfectly modern people, despite how the village appears."

Anne-Marie shrugged, jostling her beaded necklaces. "I have no doubt they are, even if they do believe Henry VIII is king."

Rolling her eyes, Jane returned herself to her seat and eyed the passing structures with a fondness her aunt seemed to lack. "It will be a lovely place to take a stroll, if we have the time."

"And to hear the latest news about the latest queen."

Jane ignored that. "I see a very pretty modiste shop there, and a milliner shop beside. That is perfectly situated."

"Stop trying so hard, Janet, you will strain yourself." Anne-Marie sighed and tapped her hand against the window lightly. "There is the tower of the castle above the trees, look!"

Jane returned to the window and glanced out, her jaw going slack when she caught sight of it. "That? My heavens, it's huge!"

"Well, what did you expect when I told you a castle?" Anne-Marie gently pushed her back into her seat. "Stop gawping. We're going up the drive in just a moment, and we must appear perfectly composed."

"Trying to impress Delphine?" Jane suggested dryly.

Her aunt speared her with a dark look. "I will be entirely *un*impressed for Delphine, thank you very much. It is only a castle, not a cathedral."

"And one sees castles nearly every day," Jane continued, her tone turning positively dismissive.

"Quite." Her aunt sniffed, picked up her walking stick, and propped it up before her, both hands resting elegantly atop it.

Jane could only shake her head and wait for their approach to begin, however her aunt imagined that going.

CHAPTER FOUR

"Simon, you do stride so. Kindly remember to temper your paces with your aunt, would you?"

Simon glanced down at Louise on his arm, offering a wry smile. "I am not striding, Aunt."

"Don't be impertinent. If I say you are striding, you are striding." She tsked loudly, jabbing her walking stick at the air ahead of them. "Look at Delphine. Standing there in the archway like she's queen of the court. And what is she thinking with those silk skirts? The ground is so dry, and the breeze so light, she will be coated in dust and dirt before the last of the guests arrive."

"I have no doubt that Lady Cavernaugh considered her ensemble quite carefully," Simon told her with polite deference.

Louise made a noise of disgust. "Delphine considers one thing and one thing only: her appearance. She has never been accused of having any degree of intellect, Simon. Kindly do not give her more credit than she deserves."

Simon barely avoided a snort of amusement. "You are harsh. Are you unwell after our travels?"

"Never," his aunt retorted. "Only tired of the carriage. And your presence."

"I can go," he offered, leaning away.

She seized his arm more tightly against her. "Do be quiet, boy. You know what I mean. Now, do you spy anyone you know?"

Simon glanced around the courtyard they were all disembarking in—at least six carriages parked within or in the process of turning about once the luggage was removed. A line of more carriages were stopped along the drive outside the courtyard to be directed in.

It was an impressive number of guests, even he would admit that.

And the castle was beyond impressive.

Simon took the opportunity to look up and around him. The walls were tall and majestic, built with speckled stones in varying shades of tan, brown, and gray, and there were turrets and parapets and pinnacles as high as the eye could see. The windows were glinting in the brilliant sun, neat and clean squares in the tall windows, and brilliant colors of stained glass and arches in others. It was a beautiful example of medieval architecture, and Simon was just enough of a little boy on the inside to imagine soldiers and archers and knights lining the walls and ramparts in preparation for battle.

And he was just enough of a scholar to appreciate the structure and design of the place while not recollecting much about the styles or exact names.

Really, it was an amazing building, and if he could find a way to explore the nooks and crannies of the place, he would do so without shame.

"Simon! The people!" his aunt hissed, nudging him hard as they moved toward the entrance to the castle itself, where the host and hostess waited.

Simon shook himself and focused on the people flocking elegantly and gracefully in the same direction they were. "Let me see. There is Miss Beacom, she is generally thought to be good company and a good match."

"How can a young woman be generally a good match?" Louise snapped. "No one is a good match for everyone."

"I don't know," Simon admitted. "I am only telling you what is said, not that I say it myself." He continued to look around. "Miss Prescott. She is silly and unrepentant about snide remarks."

"Now that is more like it!" his aunt cackled, patting his arm. "This is the sort of information I want to know!"

Simon chuckled and covered her hand with his. "I will do my best to satisfy your insatiable need for blatant truths others might consider gossip."

"Good lad."

"That there is Mr. Young," Simon went on, gesturing faintly to the man greeting the Cavernaughs at the moment. "Bit of a bore, but nothing to fault."

"Boredom is a fault, to my mind," Louise muttered.

Simon bit back a laugh. "Miss Dawes there will say whatever needs to be said to make a favorable impression, and as far as anybody knows, has no personality of her own."

Louise chuckled darkly at that. "She is not alone in Society in that regard. No one teaches their daughters to be an individual. What a horrid thought!"

"Indeed," Simon concurred in a pompous voice. "Heaven preserve us from such." He glanced behind them, leaning close to his aunt. "Miss Cole falls into that category as well. Mr. Jenkins is a toad, but he is well connected, so he gets invited everywhere. Miss Rawlins is very accomplished and keeps her opinions to herself. Mr. Gideon needs a wife and isn't all that particular. Mr. Drake likes the cards, but they do not like him. Miss Lyle is an enigma to me, but I know nothing to her discredit."

"That sounds encouraging," Louise whispered. "Now do shut up. Our time is almost here."

Simon nodded in all due obedience, though he was fighting laughter. "Yes, Aunt Louise."

The young lady and her companion ahead of them moved into the house, and Simon led his aunt forward.

The elderly, but not necessarily old, Lady Cavernaugh beamed at Louise, her face and features stretching to an almost unnatural degree. "Lady Clarke! How lovely to see you again!"

Louise inclined her head, her status not dictating any sort of actual deference to the woman. "Lady Cavernaugh. Thank you for the invitation. Dewbury looks as lovely as you have always said it was."

"I am not usually prone to exaggeration, as you well know," Lady Cavernaugh said in an almost tinny voice, "but it is a pleasure to hear all the same. This is my son, Lord Cavernaugh."

The tall younger man with a long face and a fixed smile bowed. "Pleasure to meet you, Lady Clarke. Welcome."

Louise nodded and stepped a little away from Simon to present him. "This is my nephew, Mr. Appleby."

The men nodded at each other, and Lady Cavernaugh seemed to see something in Simon that she approved of, her lips pursing in a strange sort of smile. Was he, perhaps, not as impressive to her as her son? Less of a threat to the young ladies she had invited? Just the sort of title-less man she wished to have as competition for her heir?

Whatever it was, she seemed pleased to see him.

"What a grand addition to our party here!" Lady Cavernaugh gushed. She gestured for Simon and his aunt to proceed past them and into the house. "The footman there will show you to your rooms, and your bags will be brought up forthwith. We will have a gathering before supper to make necessary introductions for everyone, so we are all comfortable and ready for the schedule of events here."

"That sounds lovely, thank you," Louise told her, smiling in her most polite manner. She tugged on Simon's arm, which propelled him forward at once.

"Schedule of events?" he complained once they were out of earshot. "What the devil have you gotten me into, Louise?"

She dug her nails into the fabric of his coat, which did nothing to deaden the feeling of them. "Do you think I enjoy the prospect either? Trust Delphine to control every aspect of this entire spectacle. It would not surprise me if she wanted us to ask permission to remove ourselves to any retiring room to refresh and relieve ourselves."

Simon coughed in surprise, his face heating at the suggestion. "Aunt!"

"Tosh, everyone does it, don't be such a goosecap." She nudged the footman to go ahead of them with her walking stick, shaking her head. "Utterly ridiculous. This glorious building and all its furnishing reduced to a boarding school for unmarried idiots."

"I beg your pardon," Simon protested half-heartedly.

She ignored him as they started up the creaky wooden stairs, the rug running along them doing little to deaden the sound. "Look at the woodwork, Simon. They don't make houses like this anymore. The carvings are extraordinary!"

He looked up, smiling to himself at exactly what she was describing. The dark wood running along the wall where it met the ceiling was carved with images of vines and leaves, as well as the occasional flower, and there was the faintest sheen of gold within it. The railings along the stairs were not carved, but the balusters were all elegance and curves, shined to the fullest extent that wood was capable.

Then they reached the landing and turned to go up another set, the back wall now entirely of wood that was carved into an artistic scene of a joust.

"Aunt," Simon whispered, gesturing to the wall. "Henry VIII?"

Aunt Louise snorted softly. "Probably a gift from the man

himself. Delphine will know. We may hear about it at supper, in fact."

"Right this way," the footman said suddenly, indicating the hallway at the top of the stairs.

Simon smiled at the young man and made a bit of a show of escorting his aunt the rest of the way up and moving down the hallway with her in his care. "What a lovely wing this is!"

Louise laughed at his polite praise, enthusiastically given. "Indeed! Such a marvelous display of tapestries. One might wonder if there are tapestries anywhere else in the house!"

The number of tapestries lining the walls really was excessive. There were at least a dozen, each of them seeming to be reproductions of classic works of art. Murals of gods and goddesses from ancient lore. Celtic influence was evident in a few of them. And not a one of them seemed to be faded with any kind of age. They might have been woven last week, for all they knew.

It made this particular wing look almost like a country cottage rather than a suite of guest rooms in a castle.

"Don't put me by an ugly tapestry," Louise whispered under her breath. "Don't put me by an ugly tapestry."

"Stop that," Simon instructed amid his restrained laughs.

To his relief, for his aunt's sake, they went to the end of the corridor and rounded a corner, which opened to a new corridor where no tapestries could be seen.

"Her ladyship will have you here, madam," the footman indicated. "The windows face onto the garden courtyard on this level. It can be accessed just at the corner we've passed."

"Marvelous," Louise said on another sigh, this one heavy and relieved.

"Your maid should be up any moment, madam, as well as your trunks. And sir," the footman continued, turning to Simon, "if you will follow me, I will escort you to your room."

"Fair enough," he replied, releasing his aunt's arm. "Will you be all right here, Aunt?"

She all but shoved him away. "I am perfectly capable of spending ten minutes alone in my own company without shriveling or shrinking, thank you. Go away now. I will see you at the infernal supper gathering."

Simon chuckled and nodded. "Shall I escort you down?"

"For heaven's sake, no. Go now and give me peace." Louise turned away from him and entered her room without looking back.

Simon grinned, turning to the footman. "Show me the way, then."

He nodded in response and began down the corridor.

"Do you have an elderly female relative in your life?" Simon asked him.

"I do, sir," came the careful reply.

"Ah," he said with a slow bob of his head. "Then you understand my pain."

There was a hint of a laugh from his companion, and then came his response. "Quite, sir."

Simon laughed to himself. "And how do you cope with yours?"

"Self-preservation, sir," the footman told him. "Do what she says and stay out of her way."

"Perfectly said," Simon praised with a quick smile. "You will go very far in life, my man."

The footman nodded and stopped in front of a room. "Thank you, sir. This is your room."

"Is it, indeed? Marvelous." He winced, glancing at the footman. "Don't tell my aunt I said the same thing she did. She'll be ever so pleased, and I can assure you, it was quite on accident."

"Not a word, sir. Your man should be up to assist you shortly."

Simon nodded and entered his room, looking around the tidy space for a moment, then moving to the window. He did not have the benefit of the elevated garden for his view, but he did see the vast expanse of the estate and a glimpse of a lake. It was a lovely spot of land, and he could spend a great deal of time walking those grounds quite happily.

Alone, if he had anything to say about it.

He did not suspect his aunt would wish to join him, but he would very much appreciate any chance to avoid spending a quantity of time with other guests at the party.

Yet he could not exactly be rude enough to completely disregard the schedule his host and hostess had set up for them. Some things, of course, depending on the particulars, but he would have to be some sort of reasonable guest—for his aunt's sake, if nothing else.

Gads, what would they be doing for those unending hours of scheduled time?

He knew full well that remaining aloof would be an excellent deterrent to the more eager misses looking for any husband who could set them up in a decent household, with a certain income. He had employed the tactic at nearly every social gathering he had ever been part of. It would not stop all, of course, as some of the young ladies were more determined than any soldier he had ever met, but it would stop a great deal of them.

And that was all he needed, really.

And perhaps that was what Lord Cavernaugh wished for with this elaborate occasion. For the landscape and the castle to tempt the mass of young ladies to flock to him and leave the other men alone, or at least leave them to a scant one or two who were unimpressed.

Simon would leave any or all of them to the other guests. He'd never yet been impressed enough to court a young woman, and he wasn't certain he ever would.

He'd been asked once or twice in his adult life about what *would* impress him, or what he was looking for in a woman to become his wife. And the truth of the matter was that he didn't know.

He truly didn't.

He wanted an accomplished wife, but he didn't have particular expectations or preferences as to specific areas in which she was accomplished. He wanted an educated wife but wasn't sure how educated he preferred. He wanted a pretty wife but had no favorites as far as features went. He wanted an agreeable wife but wasn't certain in what way. He wanted . . .

Basically, Simon didn't have any idea what he wanted.

He only knew he hadn't found it and wasn't in a rush to do so.

He'd never been wholly captivated by the idea of marriage or finding a wife, though he was certain that he might do so someday. He just never thought much of it. There was no title to secure with an heir, no inheritance hinging on a wedding, and no need of a large dowry to fill his coffers.

And he had never been in love.

He wasn't sure he believed in love, actually. Not in the heady, nonsensical, lose oneself to insanity, wholly devoted to another person at the risk of one's own life or happiness sort of way. His parents had a healthy, affectionate marriage, and he believed in that love. He believed in the love between family and siblings and even, of a sort, between friends.

But the sort of love that poets waxed effusively on?

Not really.

Until he felt it himself, he would not believe it. He would only believe that others fancied themselves in such love because they had a lack of understanding of their own emotions or a lack of vocabulary to properly explain them.

Or they were simply delusional.

Or all of the above.

"Planning your first ride out on the estate or plotting an escape?"

Simon turned in surprise at the voice and quickly grinned at the sight of one of his oldest friends, George Ellis, leaning in his doorway. "Ellis! I hadn't thought you'd be here!"

"Why not?" he asked in a bemused retort. "You don't think I'm capable of being worthy of Cavernaugh's castoffs?"

"So you feel that way, too, eh?" Simon barked a laugh and went over to shake his hand and thump his back. "It's good to see you."

Ellis returned his smile, nodding almost proudly. "It is good to be seen."

"Anyone else we know going to be here?" Simon asked, folding his arms. "I hadn't thought to ask, since I was dragged here by my aunt."

"Louise?" Ellis threw his head back on a laugh. "Now that is perfect. I've missed her."

"Then you can entertain her," Simon grumbled. "I'm expecting her to throw a young woman at me, despite her promises to the contrary."

Ellis nodded very sagely. "Indeed. Very like her. Well, I had thought that Palmer would attend, seeing as how he needs to embrace his fashionable new title of Lord Huxley, but it would seem that the man has gone and gotten himself married."

"He *what?*" Simon openly gaped at that, his heart sinking ominously. "Daniel Palmer. Earl of Huxley. Amiable chap from Northumberland with good sense and a bit of wit who got himself a place in Lancashire with his title. That Palmer?"

To his credit, Ellis didn't react to Simon's disbelief with his usual mockery. Instead, the man only nodded slowly. "That is the one."

"What the devil did he do that for?" Simon shook his head and ran his hands through his hair.

"He fell in love, man. Apparently, there's no arguing with that."

Simon glared at his friend as darkly as he dared. "Oh, yes there is. Perhaps not with him; it's too late. But I'll spend this entire house party arguing against it. Mark my words."

CHAPTER FIVE

"What about that one, Jane? He'd be a fine catch."

"Beatrice, I am not interested in catching at the present."

"But he is mightily good looking. Far better than your sister's husband, and wouldn't that be something for people to talk about?"

Jane rolled her eyes heavenward, smiling against her will at the antics of her good friend, Beatrice Wyant. "What people say or do not say as regarding Hannah's husband is none of my concern, nor do I care how my future one stacks up."

"Now that is not true and you know it," Beatrice insisted with a laugh. "You would love it if your husband bested him in some way."

Laughter erupted up Jane's throat and she glanced at her friend, a dark-haired beauty with equally dark eyes. "You're right, I would."

Beatrice toasted her with a glass of lemonade and surveyed the room before them. The supper had been rather good, and now that it was finished, a sort of casual soiree was taking place. There were a few couples dancing as some young woman played at the pianoforte, while others simply chatted in small groups about the room. No games of cards had started up, but it would not surprise Jane if that should happen.

Her aunt, on the other hand, was deep in conversation with three other elderly women over by the windows in the room. Whether they had known each other before today or had simply bonded together over something or other wasn't clear, but she was pleased Anne-Marie would at least have some others to commiserate with.

There weren't that many elderly ladies about, most of them being middle-aged mothers or companions or the like, which made Jane wonder if Lady Cavernaugh had wanted to show off for friends and/or rivals such as Anne-Marie.

It was certainly something she would need to consider as she got to know their hostess a little more.

"What do you make of our host?" Beatrice murmured, swirling her lemonade just below her mouth as she blatantly stared at the man in question.

Jane glanced over at him, shrugging a shoulder. "Seems nice enough. A bit plain for my taste, and not much of a conversationalist as far as I can tell."

"I yawned during dinner," Beatrice admitted bluntly. "Twice."

"But you were sitting right next to him!" Jane cried with a laugh. "How did you manage that?"

Beatrice smiled smugly. "I was very polite with my serviette. My manners are impeccable."

Jane scoffed and hid the sound with a sip of her own drink. "For heaven's sake, Bea," she managed after a swallow. "Your fortune makes you a prime candidate for Lady Cavernaugh. How are you going to let her down?"

"I am quite certain I will think of something," Beatrice assured her. "If nothing else, I may yawn with less manners in his presence. She'll not like me then."

"He is not all that bad," Jane said with a bit of a wrinkle to her nose as she looked back at him, standing against one wall and talking to a bevy of young ladies with varying levels of interest. "He does have a very nice castle."

"Oh," Beatrice drawled slowly, the sarcasm nearly dripping from the single word, "and that is certainly something one ought to marry for, don't you think?" She huffed and shook her head. "I despair of the silly ones, Janie. I really do."

She nodded in agreement, wishing there was something to be done about them. But until the culture around Society and London changed, nothing else would. It would be all marriage and money and status, and very little else.

"I thought Harwood would be attending this sort of thing," Beatrice mused, frowning a little. "Isn't this exactly his sort of scene?"

"Taft?" Jane asked. "Oh, it absolutely is. But he was not invited. Probably too much competition for his lordship over there."

"His bore-ship, you mean." Beatrice sipped her lemonade again, emptying the glass. "There are infinitely better men all about the room, I have no doubt. Take that one there, for example." She gestured toward a tall, fair-haired man almost exactly opposite them. "He is smartly dressed and not with any silly girls. A few gents in his company, and not a drunk or rake among them. I already approve."

Jane raised a brow at her. "Really? That's all you require?"

Beatrice gestured helplessly. "Not much, is it? Now, I do not say he is my preferred candidate or perfect match, of course. Only that he is already a better prospect than Cavernaugh. Nothing more."

"Fair enough." Jane looked at the group in question a moment more and smiled slightly. "I think you may find a decent match for yourself among them, though, Bea. Look at the man to his left."

She did so, and a guttural sound of appreciation poured from her lips. "Oh yes, please. He is precisely my type. The strong jaw of a marble statue, the chocolate hair with a hint of curl, the perfect cut of a fashionably colored weskit . . . If the man can handle a team of horses with just one of those hands, I will beg him to marry me this instant."

Jane scoffed and covered her mouth with a hand to stifle her giggles. "Well, should we ask Lady Cavernaugh if a team of horses might be brought in so we can check? Then we might have all this done forthwith."

Beatrice heaved a long sigh. "No, you are right. Politeness must be maintained. I must wait and be demure."

"You *are* demure," Jane reminded her. "You may say shocking things to me and to our other friends, but you would never be as brash as you claim. You're as modest and retreating from any true suitor as anyone else."

Her friend smiled a little hesitantly. "What can I say? My private bravado hides a public insecurity I may never fully be rid of. I may never be comfortable enough with a man to share who I truly am, and that is my failing. It is not out of fear, but simply . . . out of the desire to be liked. My brothers have always told me that no man likes an outspoken woman, and that statement is in the foremost portion of my mind whenever I speak to a gentleman with whom I find potential."

"And so you think everything and anything you could say might be considered outspoken?" Jane tsked very softly. "Beatrice, you don't have to be biddable to be liked either."

"I know," her friend insisted. "But it is more than that. I seem to do the most awkward things, Janie. It is so embarrassing! I can hardly face whoever the man is again once I realize in retrospect what I have done. I cannot seem to find a pleasant middle ground between the two, nor the proper expanse of time to develop the comfort necessary to feel like myself in a man's presence."

Jane sighed softly in sympathy. "I should have you spend more time with Taft. He is a master at putting people at ease, and there would be no danger of your needing to consider him as a candidate. I know for a fact that he is not seeking marriage at this time, so it would be excellent practice for you."

"Perhaps," Beatrice murmured. "But it might not help. Taft is a fair-haired and popular sort of fellow. I have never been attracted to that sort. Poor Taft, he is too pretty for me."

"And he knows it," Jane replied with a fond smile. "He is pretty, he is silly, and he is good. He really is."

"Oh well." Beatrice looked at her glass and hummed in thought. "I shall need more lemonade. Would you like some more?"

Jane shook her head, smiling. "I am perfectly well with what I have, thank you."

Beatrice nodded and moved away, walking towards the refreshment table with the sort of singlemindedness with which she did everything else. Except, it seemed, converse with eligible gentlemen.

She would never have suspected that of her friend. Beatrice had always been rather like Jane in so many ways, especially with her easy manner, her openness about her feelings, and her lack of concern for all things matrimony. That she might secretly have wished for it had never occurred to Jane, and that she might not always be as easy with herself as Jane had thought was beyond imagination. She had never known a more confident woman than Beatrice Wyant. And yet all that fell away when in the presence of a man in whom she was interested?

How could such a thing even be?

As though the very idea needed to presently be tested, Jane saw, in a mixture of horror and amusement, the very man her friend had admired from that circle walking to the refreshment table at the same moment. Beatrice had not reached it yet, but would shortly, and unless they completely ignored each other, they would be forced to interact in some way.

Well, well, how would this scene play out?

Smiling to herself, Jane watched as her friend approached the table, and the handsome man who was Beatrice's type did so as well. It was too far away for Jane to hear a single word, but she could watch the expressions of each.

It started out rather well, she thought. Beatrice beamed at the man, and his smile was as perfect as one might hope it would be. There was a bit of laughter, a bow, a curtsey . . .

And then . . .

Well, and then it seemed to not be going quite as well.

Indeed, it was no longer going well at all.

And yet it was not exactly . . . *not* going well either.

Jane frowned as she tried to make sense of what she was witnessing, but the only thing that came to mind was that it was dreadfully awkward.

Beatrice was looking down at her hands an extraordinary amount, the lemonade entirely forgotten. She was smiling, but the smile flickered by degrees every second it was on her lips. When her lips moved with words, the man with whom she was speaking seemed to be as obsessed with the table as she was with her hands. Yet neither was moving away from one another. They stood exactly as they were, talking. Or not talking. And smiling.

What the devil?

How could something be adorable and awkward all at once?

Beatrice had managed to remove her right glove just enough that her hand was no longer in its proper position, though it was still encased in the white fabric. Was she . . . was she sliding her hand in and out from the tip of the glove?

And the man . . .

The man was winding his watch. This way and that. Over and over and over.

Jane could only shake her head at the both of them.

"He's going to break the deuced thing."

"My thoughts exactly," Jane murmured, despairing of the both of them. She turned to glance at her new companion, startled to see the fair-haired man from the group who Beatrice had initially pointed out.

He was shaking his head at the sight of their friends, just as Jane had done. "I've never seen Ellis like this in my life. He is . . . he is utterly pathetic at this moment."

Jane laughed once without humor. "And you think my friend Miss Wyant is a model of her best attributes at the moment? I want to crawl under the floorboards of this room watching her like this."

The man looked down at the floorboards, testing them slightly with the tip of one shoe. "They don't seem to be too secured, so you might be able to manage that, if you are in earnest." He offered her a small lopsided smile before bowing. "We have skipped the introductions. Simon Appleby, friend of the pathetic Mr. Ellis at the refreshment table."

Jane curtseyed quickly. "Jane Richards, friend of the suddenly awkward Miss Wyant at the same destination."

"Pleasure."

They returned their attention to their friends, and Jane heard Mr. Appleby hiss as Mr. Ellis actually rocked on his heels, his mouth moving as though he was speaking, though Beatrice did not seem to hear him as she secured her fingers back in place in the glove.

"This is actually painful," Mr. Appleby groaned.

"Isn't it?" Jane agreed, holding her glass of lemonade to her cheek. "What is she even doing? Forgive my frankness, Mr. Appleby, but she expressed her interest in your friend only moments before going for refreshments. She could want nothing more than to speak with him, and now . . ."

"Believe me, Miss Richards, your friend is precisely the sort of young woman Mr. Ellis likes." He exhaled roughly. "By appearances, anyway. I doubt he's getting to know anything about her in earnest if she's like this with him."

"And the same for him," Jane pointed out. "He could be offering a sonnet to the lemonade for all we know."

Mr. Appleby seemed to choke on a laugh. "Gads, I hope not." He was silent for a moment, then asked, "What is she really like? Your Miss Wyant."

"With me?" Jane asked. At his nod, she smiled at her friend. "Beatrice is warm and loyal. Perhaps a trifle outspoken for fashionable tastes, but all good humor. Witty, too. Accomplished enough, excellent fortune, dreadful at lawn games, passable rider . . ."

"Exactly his type," Mr. Appleby said again, this time with some finality.

Jane slid her eyes to him, wondering at his thoughts. "And Mr. Ellis? What is he like?"

"Affable," Mr. Appleby told her at once. "Humorous. Dry wit, wise, well-informed, bit of a tease, protective of his sisters, surprisingly fond of dancing, doesn't mind being second in a horse race if it's fair . . ."

"Second to you?" she asked dryly.

Mr. Appleby shrugged. "Sometimes. He's a terrible liar, and that includes cards. He cannot bluff worth a . . . well, he cannot do it. And his Latin is dreadful, quite honestly. He'll never be a scholar."

Jane looked at the pair of their friends, now not even looking in each other's direction, but not leaving the table whereon the lemonade sat.

They just . . . stood there.

Together.

"This," Jane announced only for her companion, "is ridiculous."

"Absolutely," he echoed.

"They are better than this."

"Agreed."

"They need help."

"Without a doubt."

"So we are going to help them."

"Couldn't have said it better. We are . . . wait, what?"

Jane snorted softly as she looked at him. "We are going to *help* them, Mr. Appleby."

His blue eyes went wide, his expression incredulous. "Help them what?"

She rolled her eyes and turned to face him fully. "You told me Beatrice is exactly Mr. Ellis's type. True?"

"True," he said slowly, uncertainty etched into his features.

"And based on what you have told me of Mr. Ellis, it seems as though he would be perfectly suited for my friend, when he is himself," Jane said quickly, feeling her energy and enthusiasm for the idea rise. "Yes?"

"If you say so . . ."

Jane gestured with one hand, indicating that the solution was obvious. "Then you and I, as their friends, need to *help* them to be themselves with each other."

Mr. Appleby looked as though she had grown a horn from the top of her head. "How in the world do you anticipate we do that? I don't know about you, but I am not willing to host a conversation between the two of them when it would plainly be a one-person conversation. I can hear myself talk to the open air anytime I wish without anyone else present."

"How you spend your leisure time is of little concern to me," Jane retorted in exasperation. "All I mean is that we are at a house party. There are a limited number of days in which guests of this party will be in each other's company before we all return to our various locales. There is no better time for our friends to get to know each other well because of this forced proximity, do you follow?"

"Certainly," Mr. Appleby replied easily. "That is normally how a house party goes. I have been to a few."

"Congratulations," Jane snapped, flicking a hand as though she could toss his retort over her shoulder. "We only need to ensure that they spend this time at the house party together in any way possible, in any ways we can contrive, so that they can become comfortable enough to *be* themselves *with* each other."

Mr. Appleby's chin suddenly lowered, his eyes narrowing as he looked at her. "You want to play matchmaker for them."

There was no accusation or mockery in the statement, but there was something . . . distasteful about the sentiment.

Jane grimaced at the suggestion. "Well, I think it would be up to them to make the match, but we would be . . . enabling the idea."

"Match enabling," Mr. Appleby mused, looking above her head and seeming to taste the phrase like one might a wine. "I like it. Far more pleasing an idea."

"Glad you approve," Jane grumbled, turning to look at their friends. "But it will be a better occupation for me than coming up with excuses to avoid my aunt's machinations, whatever they are."

"Ah, I have an aunt here as well, and I am convinced she will believe I am proposing to you at this very moment."

"What?" Jane recoiled and looked him up and down. "How in the world would she . . .?"

"Excellent," he praised, his words running right over hers as he seemed to glow with delight. "That expression will completely throw her off the idea. Would you mind continuing to hate me as much as possible for anyone to see? She'll be so cross, it will be utter perfection."

Jane blinked at the madman, wondering if this might not be the worst idea she'd ever been part of. "I've never been accused of hating anyone, but if you insist that I must . . ."

"Don't *actually* hate me," he told her, his smile becoming more amused again. "Unless I find myself earning it. But pretending you cannot stand me when she is around would be quite fun. And then she won't suspect anything."

"She really thinks you're that perfect?" Jane asked in disbelief.

Mr. Appleby shook his head. "No, she knows full well that I'm hopeless, but it doesn't stop her from thinking I'm wrong about love and such nonsense. It's only by sheer luck that I've convinced her not to make a match for me here."

"Ergh, mine as well." Jane shook her head. "Why must we all be obsessed with matches and marriage and the like? Why can we not simply exist and enjoy existing and worry about longevity and the future and connection and anything else when it is actually relevant to our needs and wants?"

"You could not be speaking a more welcome truth if you tried, Miss Richards." He held out his arm. "Shall we dance?"

Jane eyed him suspiciously. "Have I won your favor so easily?"

"No, not really," he said without any hint of apology. "But our friends need to dance, and I think they might if we are. Besides, our aunts won't be able to accuse us of being unsociable if we've danced, so it should serve us both to do so."

"Your logic is surprisingly sound," she allowed. "Thank you, I will." She downed the rest of her lemonade and took his arm. "If we don't bring about their dancing together, should we dance with them ourselves?"

Mr. Appleby nodded as they took up their positions. "That seems appropriate. But I must say, if they are unable to discern that necessity for themselves, given their present infatuation, they are less intelligent than we give them credit for."

"Oh, utterly," Jane agreed. She curtseyed with the other ladies and began to move towards Mr. Appleby with the light, skipping steps required of a country dance. "Tomorrow morning, we could ensure that our friends are paired together for the estate walk. Was Mr. Ellis planning to attend?"

"I haven't the foggiest," Mr. Appleby admitted as he

mirrored the steps she had just done. "We were both fairly ignoring the schedule description. Remind me what is happening."

Jane snickered and turned about with the other ladies before moving forward to take Mr. Appleby's hand and turn with him. "It is a walk . . . about the estate . . ."

"Oh, well, in that case . . ." He widened his eyes and took her other arm while they stepped together to opposite sides. "Care to expound?"

"There is an excursion," Jane explained, trying not to smile. "Led by Lord Cavernaugh, if you please. We are to go by horse, by carriage, or by foot, based on our tastes, to explore the lands of the estate, including the village, the ruins, and the lake."

Mr. Appleby made a sound of consideration. "By horse and by carriage seems to take away from calling such an excursion a walk. And given the extent of the estate, the carriages will be used to take the ladies back to the castle when they are too exhausted to continue on foot, but I am not the host of such a place and event. Perhaps the Cavernaughs have planned for such a thing." He turned them both about once more and proceeded with Jane about the short line of couples before looping back around to their new position.

"Regardless," she said, once in her new place, "we should contrive to have them together."

"The only way to do that," Mr. Appleby replied, waiting for the other couples to take their places, "would be to go ourselves and to walk with them the same. Are you willing to do that?"

Jane shrugged, nodding. "I don't mind a long walk. I may be a London miss most of the time, but my time in the country is not wasted on me."

"And your friend?" he asked, nudging his head towards the refreshment table, where the pair still, impossibly, stood.

Not looking at each other.

"I will drag her kicking and screaming if I must," Jane said darkly, wondering if Mr. Ellis was, in fact, a great idiot for not bringing Beatrice into the dance.

"And I him." Mr. Appleby seemed to sputter an exhale. "That idiot."

Jane smiled at that, looking back at Mr. Appleby as the motions of the dance repeated themselves. "I was just wondering if he was an idiot myself."

"Normally, he is not," Mr. Appleby assured her. "I have no explanation for the man you see tonight."

She nodded to the music as he and the other gentlemen skipped towards them, then moved back to their line. "The walk is supposed to include luncheon, and then I imagine there will be time for a respite for the ladies, as we are so very delicate and must retreat from the public eye in order to restore our true orderliness."

"Naturally," Mr. Appleby allowed, nodding in deference.

"And then," Jane continued, pretending he hadn't spoken as they met in the middle and turned, "after supper, there is a ball at the local assembly rooms."

Mr. Appleby groaned, half of his face contorting in a grimace. "Would now be a completely inappropriate time to confess that I do not particularly enjoy dancing?"

"It would." Jane smiled as she took both his hands and continued in the dance. "But you would not be dancing for yourself, Mr. Appleby. You would be dancing for our friends."

"This had better be worth it, Miss Richards," he warned, though he smiled fairly easily. "It is a great sacrifice on my part to be more engaging than my nature allows."

Jane raised a brow. "And a great sacrifice on my part, sir, to act as though I hate anyone. But I am willing to do so in order to see my friend happily situated."

"You are more selfless than I, Miss Richards," Mr. Appleby told her, leading her once more down the row of couples. "I can only hope to be your match in appearances."

"Not in actuality?" she asked him.

He shook his head, frowning playfully. "No, not at all. I rather enjoy being a heartless curmudgeon, and I am already looking forward to returning to that."

"One week, Mr. Appleby. Just one week, and we can both go back to who we are without any ties to this party."

"One week, Miss Richards. It's a deal."

CHAPTER SIX

The estate at Dewbury was massive.

Simon had known that from the moment he had looked out of the window of his bedchamber, but walking the thing this morning had solidified the truth of the matter.

It was honestly, impressively, and exhaustingly massive.

And he was not in the sort of physical shape that allowed him to walk the entirety without some strain. Hiding that strain was growing more and more difficult the farther they went.

But if Lord Cavernaugh, great bore that he was, would not show strain in doing so, neither would he.

Especially if Ellis wasn't showing strain either.

Was he the only one who was inwardly begging for a chance to rest his feet and his legs? Or was every other guest here, including the ladies, somehow built for the extensive excursion they were engaging in?

Still, Simon would happily admit that it was a lovely estate, and he had gleaned some ideas he would take home to Stringham Park to improve his own lands.

Not the ruins, though. He needed no ruins on his lands,

and there was something awkward about faux ruins in a place. Even if guests would not know the truth, how could the host explain their presence?

Dewbury was ancient enough for the ruins to be legitimate, and as they walked around them at the moment, Simon had to admit that they were rather fascinating.

He wasn't listening to Cavernaugh's explanation of them, as the sound of his voice alone was something rather humdrum and sleep inducing, and the words themselves were excessive. Longwinded *and* boring. Not an excellent combination for any man seeking a wife.

A pointed throat clearing sounded from behind him, and Simon mentally winced. It was not the first time he had forgotten that he was at the head of the little group he and Miss Richards had arranged, and he turned with the most apologetic expression he could manage, offering a hand.

Miss Richards took it and allowed him to help her up onto the tiered foundation of the ruins, the soft leather of her gloves rubbing against his palm. "They're talking, at least," she murmured when she reached him.

Simon looked beyond her to Ellis and Miss Wyant, who presently appeared to be listening to whatever Ellis was saying with some amusement. Her gloves, Simon was pleased to say, remained firmly on her hands.

"That's the least awkward we've seen them yet," he told Miss Richards with some satisfaction. "You could still stand between them with room to spare, though."

"Proximity will come," she insisted, smiling brightly. "It's a natural thing to move closer to the one with whom you wish to speak most."

Simon looked at the minimal space between them at the moment with a pointed expression. "You are closer to me than they are to each other. What does *that* signify to you?"

Miss Richards rolled her eyes. "Yes, but you and I are not awkward."

"Thank you?" Simon released her hand and sighed as he took in the sight of his friend. "I can see that he is pleased, and she is as well, but what are they saying that is rendering them so pleased?"

"Does it matter?" she quipped.

Simon lifted a shoulder and tried to listen in while appearing to observe the trees across from them.

"And it was the sourest apple I have ever bitten into in my life," Ellis was saying, laughing to himself. "You would never have guessed it from the look of the thing, nor even from biting into it. Crisp and juicy, and perfect, but then so very sour once it could be tasted!"

"I have never had such an experience with an apple," Miss Wyant replied, her voice sounding truly curious. "They are almost always perfectly sweet when crisp."

"That is what I thought!"

Simon blinked, then focused his attention on Miss Richards, whose expression was now as flat as an expression could physically appear.

"Unbelievable," she muttered for him alone. "Utterly unbelievable. Apples?"

"I suppose . . . a connection can form over any topic they have in common?" Simon winced, looking up at the sky as though it might hold answers. "Apples, though. Not even pies or tarts with apples, but apples themselves. I feel less intelligent by even listening."

Miss Richards rubbed at her brow, sighing. "Walk with me, Mr. Appleby. And really, I don't want to say your name right now, given their chosen topic."

"Call me Simon, then," he said at once. "I don't even want to hear my surname. And please, don't think anything of the familiarity. I don't want to form a connection."

"I don't intend to do so," Miss Richards said quickly. "Heaven forbid."

"I will try not to take that personally," Simon replied, turning from the others and walking beside her.

"It isn't personal, I assure you." She fidgeted with her gloves and exhaled slowly as they walked along the low rock formation that had once been an outer wall of the monastery. "I don't want to form a connection with any man for the present. It is simply not a priority for me. Which should take the pressure off you."

Simon smirked. "I feel lighter already."

Miss Richards flicked her wrist at him, her fingers lashing against his forearm. "Stop that, I am serious. It ought to be a relief to be able to converse with a woman without wondering about ulterior motives or schemes."

"Truthfully, it is," he told her, sobering. "I avoid Society for the most part because I grew tired of the Marriage Mart. I don't mind balls or the theatre or the parks or exhibits, only the expectations surrounding them, and the stilted conversations I am forced into with those who only see me as their means to a settled future."

"Yes, that is the worst!" Miss Richards groaned, shaking her head. "I have had to turn down proposals from perfectly amiable men because they had no true interest in me, nor I in them, and they only wanted a convenient match to have done with it. And I do not claim those proposals with any pride, I can assure you. Low-hanging apples are never the most delicious, but they are reached for all the same."

Simon pulled up short, exhaling in disgust. "Apples, Miss Richards? Again?"

To his surprise, she clapped herself on the forehead. "Curse me for being a dunce! Apologies, Simon. It was quite unintentional." She grinned quickly. "Also, if you allow me to call you Simon, it is only fair that I be Jane." She glanced back towards Ellis and Miss Wyant, her expression growing almost despairing. "If today is any indication, you and I are going to have to scheme even more to get those two in any sort of position to behave normally. That is going to require familiarity with each other, at the very least."

"Likely very true, Jane," Simon allowed, finding it surprisingly easy and comfortable to refer to her by her given name. For a man who did everything in his power to avoid familiarity with young women, being instantly comfortable with the given name of one was a strange phenomenon. Not a fearsome experience, only a strange one.

And as she had said, Jane was not interested in him in that way. And he was not interested in her. They were only helping their friends, who *were* interested in each other, to stop making a muck of their perfect chance.

And that made everything easier.

"If those two feel more comfortable talking about apples than anything of substance," Simon began, keeping his voice down so the people behind them and the people ahead of them wouldn't overhear, "then we are going to struggle to ever get them to discuss feelings."

"One step at a time," Jane reminded him. "Romance can be built on strange foundations."

Simon made a face. "Romance at all is a strange foundation."

Jane looked up at him in surprise. "Not a supporter of the idea?"

"Not a believer in it," he corrected without shame. "It is quite simply daft."

She hummed a little, seeming more thoughtful than disapproving. "Being daft doesn't erase it from existence. And how can you not believe it when you are helping your friend to find it?"

"It is a connection," Simon explained, taking Jane's arm to steer her around a loose part of the foundation she was headed for. "Nothing more. A connection with affection and mutual interests and attraction. But people lose their heads when they find themselves in it and cannot express themselves with any clarity. So they claim love and romance when it could simply be described as an inability to comprehend themselves."

"You take the scholarly approach to life, don't you?" Jane suggested, laughing to herself.

Simon did not laugh, but wasn't perturbed by the idea. "Not scholarly. Only logical."

"Love is not logical, if I understand it right."

"Everything is logical if you view it right."

"What is right and what is not right?" She gestured to the ruins they were milling about. "Take this structure. Once a monastery filled with devout men of faith, serving God and man, and living in a building that ought to have been protected because of that goodness. But then someone who believes differently and has power comes along and orders it destroyed. All that goodness, all that faith, all that service erased from this place because it was no longer right. Nothing had changed about what they were doing or how they were living except for the person in power, who decided they were wrong." She paused and stooped to pick a flower growing from a patch of grass, then held it up for him to see. "And a generation later, it was right again. But the damage was done."

It was a simple explanation for a complicated part of history, but her point was made efficiently enough. And more to the point, he could not argue it. She had chosen a rather apt illustration for her side of the argument, and had eloquently and intelligently expressed it without defiance, without anger, and without defensiveness.

It was the best response to an opinion he had ever heard in his entire life.

And he had to smile at that.

"Let us hope that the damage of my opinion is less permanent than what happened to this poor monastery," Simon said, taking the flower from her and tucking it into the buttonhole of his coat.

Jane laughed and nodded at his gesture. "Gallant and

evasive all at once." Her eyes focused on the flower a moment, her smile fading.

Simon hesitated, looking from her expression to the silly flower and back to her. "What?"

"I have an idea," Jane said slowly, biting her lip ever so slightly.

"Which is . . .?"

She shook her head. "It needs percolating. And I need to know if the schedule will allow for it. Once I know that, I can tell you."

"Very well." He sighed and continued walking, glancing ahead at Cavernaugh and the ladies vying for him. "Surely he will run out of facts to share on this place soon and we will be on our way again."

Jane grunted softly. "I would not count on that. Interested females of a silly nature will ask the most ridiculous questions if they think it will earn them favor. Cavernaugh does not have the imagination to spin stories about the monastery, but he might just have prepared enough to know a few true ones."

Simon moaned as though in agony. "Lord spare us . . . Do you think that's why the others have gone ahead?"

"Undoubtedly. And if our friends would walk with a little more haste, we might have been able to as well. But now . . ." She turned to look behind them, taking a few paces backwards. "They are so intense in their conversation, there is no hope of a change of pace."

He snorted softly. "Apples still?"

"I don't know," she admitted. "Pause at the corner to point out a tree to me, and let's see."

"Ah, Miss Richards," Simon said at once, his voice at a volume just slightly above normal as he gestured towards a tree. "Do you see? I believe that may be an elm tree just there by the stream."

"Do you think so, Mr. Appleby?" Jane replied in a similar

tone, pretending to peer where he indicated. "Surely not, sir. That must be a beech."

"A beech?" he repeated with faux indignation. "In this part of the country?"

They both fell silent as Ellis and Miss Wyant walked behind them, paying no mind to whatever their friends were doing.

"But how do you get the nib of the quill so sharp and precise?" Miss Wyant was asking. "I have tried and tried, but a fresh feather does seem to go dull so very quickly."

"It is all about letting the feather age before cutting it," Ellis explained. "And then about using a remarkably sharp knife for the cut and trim. When we are in the village, it will be my pleasure to help you select a feather to demonstrate on. Not that you would be incapable of selecting a perfectly adequate quill, of course. I would never presume to know more than anyone else."

"I would welcome your insight, sir," Miss Wyant said in a surprisingly high voice. "I always falter in such choices and doubt myself."

"Sweet merciful heavens," Jane groaned, putting both hands to her face and exhaling slowly. "Am I in hell? Tell me truthfully. I am in hell, aren't I?"

Simon tsked, unable to find the humor in the situation. "I think we might be, though I expected more fire and brimstone. And ash. And sulfur, come to think of it. Hell shouldn't be so green; it is most off-putting."

Jane rubbed at her cheeks and pressed her hands together at her lips. "Feathers, Simon. They are talking about feathers."

"Quills, technically," he offered, knowing it wouldn't improve the situation.

His companion ignored him. "I realize that people can speak about anything . . ."

"They can," he concurred.

"And topics of conversation vary widely from person to person and time to time . . ."

"They do."

"And it is difficult to judge a situation correctly when only a portion of private conversations are overheard . . ."

"It is."

She paused, a few muscles in her jaw seeming to twitch with the break in her speech. "But how the actual bloody devil can people so taken with each other honestly spend their time intently talking of apples and quills?"

It was evident, even to Simon's untrained eye, that Jane Richards was struggling with her patience, and her understanding of her friend was stretching and changing from moment to moment and breath to breath.

He quite understood the conundrum. He had never seen George Ellis be more of a nincompoop than he had been in the last twelve hours or more and would never have believed it possible of him. Yet here he was, earnestly speaking of apples and quills with a beautiful woman.

What did that say about Simon and his taste in friends? Or, indeed, his knowledge of them?

"I don't have an answer for that," he told Jane as he indicated they begin walking again, more to catch up with the group than anything else. "I really don't. I have never spoken with Ellis on either subject, which leads me to believe he has no strong feelings upon those topics."

"Beatrice detests letter writing," Jane declared. "We have talked about it for years. If she expects me to believe it is all due to a dull quill, she is sadly mistaken."

"Which means they are lacking in topics of conversation about which they really could speak as their true selves," Simon finished thoughtfully, almost squinting ahead at the couple in question. "We can help with that, I think."

Jane looked up at him, clasping her hands behind her back.

"How's that? Do you plan on interjecting yourself into the conversation on quills?"

Simon grinned and gave her a playful look. "Not quite. I plan on interjecting *them* into *our* conversation."

"On what?" Jane asked with a laugh. "We are talking of *them.*"

"What is something upon which Beatrice would actually like to speak?" Simon asked. "Anything. Anything at all."

Jane opened her mouth, then sputtered as she looked away. "I don't know. Erm . . . history. Royal history."

Simon reared back a little. "Truly?"

"She loves the queens of England," Jane admitted with a hint of a shrug. "When we were girls, she insisted that she was going to be one. Not as wife to a king, but as queen in her own right. It was a truly dreadful day when she realized it would not happen."

"Heaven help her," he uttered without much sympathy. "Right, I don't know what Ellis feels on that subject at all, but he has education enough to carry some sort of conversation there. So, my only question is, can you?"

Jane lifted her chin and met his eyes squarely. "I can indeed."

Simon quirked both brows, warming to the game of his idea rather quickly. "Then let us pick up the pace." He took her arm and they hurried ahead, lengthening their strides and closing the distance between them and the others rather neatly.

They had nearly reached them when Simon all but pulled Jane to a stop, gesturing for them to act calm and take on a more sedate pace.

"I don't know, Miss Richards," he said, giving her a quick wink. "I think Queen Mary was acting in the manner in which she had been raised. It is not any less bloody for it, but considering her parents . . ."

"I cannot excuse her influences for her actions," Jane over-rode quickly, nodding in approval as they reached Ellis and Miss Wyant. "Her father was a tyrant against the Catholics purely out of his personal vengeance; it was nothing to do with faith."

Simon looked at Miss Wyant with all due politeness. "What do you think, Miss Wyant? What are your thoughts?"

"On Queen Mary?" she asked him, her dark eyes wide.

He nodded. "Miss Richards and I were discussing the destruction of the monastery and the faith conflicts that led to it. There is no question that Queen Mary was the more brutal monarch, but I think . . ."

"Brutality aside," Miss Wyant interrupted, her eyes flashing, "her mother was the more devout Catholic. She never turned from her faith for the convenience of infidelity. And if one had led a devout life, what sort of betrayal would leaving that faith and forming a new one present?"

"I had not considered that," Ellis mused, his expression turning perfectly thoughtful. "And then for Elizabeth, who was raised in that new faith, it would be much the same."

"But without the same passion," Miss Wyant added. "A new faith was still finding its footing, and all she knew was that she was not Catholic. But she would know full well what strife between the two faiths existed and the turmoil it created."

Ellis nodded and lowered his head, his brow creasing. "I have always felt sympathy for Mary, Queen of Scots, personally."

Miss Wyant gaped, a near-audible gasp escaping her. "How can you? She contrived to steal the crown from off Elizabeth's head!"

"But who put her in that position?" Ellis countered, his voice the most natural that Simon had heard him use yet in company. "Who taught her that the throne of England rightfully belonged to her? She was not raised to leave the Catholic faith, and the battle over such an apparent betrayal was picked up by those using faith as a weapon. What influences pressured her views on the subject? Do you see what I mean?"

"Yes," Miss Wyant said slowly, nodding to herself. "It all becomes a rather sad story of leaders being influenced by their courts, doesn't it?"

"What if," Ellis went on, "there had been less rivalry and more cooperation? What would our history look like then?"

Simon gave Jane an impressed look and she gave him a smile in return. He nudged his head in the direction they were moving, and she nodded, as the pair of them continued to walk without consideration for the others, their pace naturally taking them ahead.

"That should keep them talking for a while," he murmured in satisfaction. "Speculation on history. Who'd have thought?"

"Beatrice can get quite impassioned," Jane confided, glancing over her shoulder. "Mr. Ellis deserves to see her when she gets like that."

Simon chuckled at the idea. "I have no doubt he'll enjoy it. But will it last them through the village tour that is coming up?"

"Until they find the quills, I would reckon." Jane snickered.

"Well, naturally, there is that," he allowed, grinning easily. "They do so care about their quills."

She nudged him a little. "How would you feel about a little joke for this evening, Simon?"

"I am for it, naturally."

She nodded once. "Tell me: Do you know of any particular color of weskit Mr. Ellis owns? I am wondering if Miss Wyant and I might be able to coincidentally find a ribbon to match in the village."

CHAPTER SEVEN

"And you are certain that the red ribbons look well with this? I don't want to be labeled as some sort of scarlet woman."

"Beatrice," Jane scolded, sitting on her friend's bed and swinging her legs like a child, "your ribbons are red, not your gown. And even if your gown *were* red, the neckline is so demure and your manner so charming that you would never be labeled anything of the sort. The red ribbons perfectly complement the rosebuds embroidered on the bodice and hem and make the details stand out more. It is a beautiful gown, and you know cream heightens your complexion so well."

Beatrice grinned in the looking glass at Jane, her cheeks coloring. "I only want . . . well, I only want to look well."

"As opposed to . . .?" Jane chuckled lightly and leaned back on her hands. "Bea, are you taking a fancy to Mr. Ellis?"

Her friend's cheeks flamed on cue, nearly matching the ribbons and roses in shade, and her eyes lowered at once. "I don't know. It is far too early to say. Of course, he is very handsome. Particularly when he smiles. He did not seem to mind my slow pace of walking at all today, which was rather gentlemanly of him."

"Rather, yes," Jane echoed, hiding her amusement behind her carefully listening facade.

If Beatrice heard her, it was not evident. "And there is . . . I don't know. There is something pleasant about his voice when he speaks. It does not even matter what he is speaking about, really. He just has a voice that one wants to listen to."

"That seems a rather good thing, too." Not wanting to go too far and show her hand, Jane sat up straighter. "I won't push you, Beatrice. You know that. And it is perfectly fine not to know your own feelings yet. It is only the first day, after all. I give you permission to like someone without any good explanation, or to not like them for the same, just as you please."

Beatrice turned, toying with the end of a curl dangling from her coif. "Permission?" she repeated, her tone full of laughter even if her words were not. "Do I need permission for such a thing?"

Jane shrugged playfully. "I could not possibly say, but just in case you were harboring any sort of worry or guilt for such a thing, I wanted to absolve you of it."

"Consider me absolved." Beatrice looked Jane over quickly, her smile softening. "Don't you look lovely? I do envy what that shade of green does for your eyes."

"What? Make them more feral?" Jane bared her teeth before laughing and scratching at her scalp. "I only agreed to this one because my maid wanted to use white flowers and green ribbons. And it seemed appropriate for an assembly ball, compared to the rest of the gowns she brought."

Beatrice giggled as she stared at Jane in disbelief. "Didn't you give her any indication of what gowns you wanted to have here?"

She shook her head very firmly. "Not at all. I told her to use her judgment and I would wear whatever she thought best."

"Janet Richards," Beatrice scolded, placing her hands on her hips in a very maternal way. "I don't care how much taste or skill your maid has, do you know what kind of pressure that puts on her? What if you hate something she has selected? Technically, that would be her fault for not anticipating your tastes! Anyone else could have her dismissed for not having more foresight or talent there."

"Then anyone else can dismiss their maids for such a stupid reason," Jane told her without hesitation. "And why would I own a gown that I hate? That's an even more stupid reason."

Beatrice rolled her eyes and picked up her gloves from the toilette. "You are incorrigible. I don't want to hear you complain about a single article of clothing this entire week."

"Fine with me." Jane pushed herself up from the bed and took her own gloves, slipping them on easily. "Do you know, I don't think I've been to an assembly ball in three years?"

"That long?" Beatrice tugged on her gloves and grabbed her reticule, heading for the door. "How is that possible?"

Jane followed, her own reticule swinging easily from her wrist. "We've barely been to our country house at all of late, and never when assemblies were held. Mama has recently developed a taste for the more refined events, which means all formality and little fun. I haven't really minded, but until this moment, I'd forgotten. Is it even worth having a dance card?"

Beatrice chuckled at the idea and gave her a look. "You get rid of yours, and I'll get rid of mine."

"Don't tempt me," Jane warned. "Aunt Anne-Marie has insisted on accompanying me tonight, and any hint of impropriety will likely add an additional mile to our morning garden walk."

"In those gardens, that would be all too easy." Beatrice glanced over the stair railing as they approached, biting her full bottom lip. "Do you suppose the gentlemen are waiting below for the ladies? Are we all going together in procession? Might some have already left?"

Jane took her hand and pressed it gently. "I am quite

certain that it will all be nicely arranged by the Cavernaughs so that no one feels pressured or abandoned."

Beatrice gave her a shy look. "I must confess . . . Mr. Ellis asked if he could escort me to the assembly. I hope you don't mind enduring Mr. Appleby again."

On cue, Jane sighed heavily. "If I must, I must."

"You seemed to be getting along a little better this morning," Beatrice suggested, her tone turning hopeful.

"Better than what?" Jane retorted under her breath, remembering her pledge to pretend to hate him. "The man thinks himself a wit, but he is only tolerably droll at best. I am good company, but even I have my limits."

"I am sorry," Beatrice half whispered.

Jane smiled at her and patted her hand. "It is fine. If it gives you more time to decide if you like Mr. Ellis or not, I am happy to endure his company. It is better than being left alone with Aunt Anne-Marie, at any rate."

"And that is not saying very much," Beatrice agreed with a crooked grin. "Much as I like your aunt."

"At least I am used to my aunt and can anticipate her thoughts and actions." Jane smiled as they reached the bottom of the stairs and turned into the nearest drawing room, which was nearly full of fellow guests. The ladies all looked suitably dressed for an assembly ball with their ribbons and muslin, and the gentlemen were as fashionable as anyone could hope for. There were a few longsuffering expressions already, which did not bode well for the evening ahead of them, but not everyone was as tolerant and accepting of the simpler nature of an assembly as opposed to a ball.

The entertainment of such an evening would be lost on their stuffiness, and that was fine for Jane. She would never turn down the opportunity to dance if she could help it, no matter if it was in an assembly room, a drawing room, a music room, or a ballroom. She'd even dance in a pasture with the tenants of an estate for a harvest celebration, if the invitation arose.

Let the haughty turn up their noses. She would not do so.

A few more ladies swept into the room, perhaps a little grandly dressed for the occasion, but at least they were not unfashionable about it.

Only then did Lord and Lady Cavernaugh enter, as though they had been watching their guests file into the room one by one.

Jane looked around, wondering if her aunt had found a seat somewhere or simply had yet to make her appearance. If Jane did not take note of her, or left without her, there would undoubtedly be hell to pay.

"Ladies and gentlemen," Lady Cavernaugh intoned with all the grand somberness a matron might wish for at Almack's, "if you will kindly proceed out to the carriages, we will be transported to the Assembly Rooms in Dewbury for the evening's entertainment."

Scattered applause filled the room and Jane looked at Beatrice in surprise. "Are we applauding the hostess for arranging our transportation? Or for hosting her house party when an assembly ball was organized?"

"Knowing her?" Beatrice murmured. "She probably orchestrated the assembly ball herself."

"More than likely," Jane agreed with a quick nod, avoiding the needless applause. "Now have you seen Mr. Ellis? If he is your escort, then he should . . ."

"He's there," Beatrice interrupted in a tight voice. "By the window."

Jane looked where she indicated, hiding a smile. The man was all but gawping at Beatrice, and was rather shameless in doing so.

There would be no mistaking the man's interest for anyone with eyes.

Simon stood behind him, one hand covering his mouth, his eyes crinkled with mirth.

Jane met his eyes, then pointedly rolled hers.

He nodded once and nudged his head towards Mr. Ellis before tugging once on his own weskit.

Jane looked, and bit back a laugh. As they had planned, Mr. Ellis was wearing a red weskit that near perfectly matched the ribbons she and Beatrice had purchased in Dewbury that day.

And there was no possible way Jane could know what Mr. Ellis, or his valet, had planned for him to wear that evening. Not in the least.

It would be a sight to see when Beatrice noticed their coincidental matching.

If she was as distracted this evening as she usually was around Mr. Ellis, it could take a while before she did so. Of course, she did notice many things about him, and could recount them almost absently when removed from his presence, so perhaps she would catalogue his ensemble more quickly than Jane anticipated.

Jane almost jumped in surprise when she saw Mr. Ellis moving in their direction without much of a sign he would do so. She cleared her throat and pretended to look at the art on the wall beside her.

"Miss Wyant," he greeted, bowing perfectly and speaking in a low, gentle tone. "You look lovely this evening."

"As do you, Mr. Ellis," Beatrice told him, her voice almost breathy. "I-I mean, you-you look well. Well, of course. You look well. Not lovely. Although lovely is well, if you think about it, though it is not usually ascribed to gentlemen. Not that it cannot be, but generally speaking, it is not. Even though it could be."

Mr. Ellis laughed once, the sound rich and deep. "Quite, Miss Wyant."

Jane covered her mouth with a hand, acting as though she was peering intently at the artwork. Studying it, even. Like an expert or an artist. Analyzing it, really. That was what she could be doing.

In truth, she wasn't seeing much of it.

She was just laughing.

"Red," Beatrice said then. "You . . . you're wearing red."

"I am," Mr. Ellis agreed. "As are you."

"Did you know? That I bought red ribbons in Dewbury today?"

"I had no idea. None at all. What are the chances, Miss Wyant?"

"My . . ." Beatrice swallowed audibly, her breathing not quite steady. "My grasp of mathematics does not extend quite that far."

Jane snorted suddenly and pinched her nose in response, her laughter growing harder and harder to control. She exhaled slowly, silently, through her mouth to steady herself.

"Nor does mine," Mr. Ellis admitted, his laughter less of humor and more of delight. "Is it still agreeable if I accompany you to the assembly rooms?"

"Yes," Beatrice said at once. "Very."

Jane bit down on her lip hard, needing to keep herself from bursting into hysterical laughter at her friend's rather prompt response.

"Beatrice, you need a chaperone," a familiar voice chirped. "Your mother is not coming, so I will ride with you."

Jane turned at the sound of her aunt's voice and stepped forward. "Shall I come with you, Aunt?"

"No, dear, find your own way there. There is no need for a crush." Anne-Marie waved at her, smiling ever so slightly. She leaned closer and whispered, "You are not the one babbling like an idiot in the presence of a handsome fellow, so I trust you will not shame yourself over the course of twenty minutes in a carriage."

"Aunt!" Jane hissed, her eyes going wide. Still, her lips curved into a smile all the same.

Aunt Anne-Marie winked and tapped Mr. Ellis's boot with her walking stick. "I'll take your arm, Mr. Ellis, if you can spare it."

"Of course, ma'am," he said quickly, though he looked rather lost.

Jane took pity on the poor man. "My aunt, Mr. Ellis. Mrs. Richards."

He nodded his head in deference, in lieu of bowing, which he could not do now that she had his arm. "A pleasure, madam."

"I'm sure it is," Anne-Marie quipped. "Now let us go, or we will miss the reels, which one should never do."

Mr. Ellis nodded and gently offered his arm to Beatrice as well, his smile particularly adorable in her direction. They moved from the room, along with a few others ready to depart.

Well, now. Find a ride to the assembly rooms? So long as she was not stuck with the Cavernaughs themselves, she would do fairly well. And if she understood the situation correctly, she was not one of the key candidates for Lord Cavernaugh at this time, so she would likely not be given the option of their carriage anyway.

All the better for her.

"It would seem that you are without a chaperone, Miss Richards," came the wry voice of Simon from somewhere nearby. "Might I offer a solution for you?"

Jane smiled and turned to face him. "You may offer, but I may not choose to accept."

The elderly woman at Simon's side cackled at that and thumped the ground with her walking stick. "Wise response, Miss Richards. I like you."

Jane blanched ever so slightly at having Simon's aunt hear her quip and curtseyed quickly. "I beg your pardon, madam. I was not aware that . . ."

"No pardon necessary," the woman said, raising her fingers from the handle of the walking stick. "As I said, I like you."

"High praise," Simon informed her. "Miss Richards, my great-aunt, Lady Clarke."

"My lady," Jane greeted, curtseying again.

"Miss Richards," Lady Clarke replied with a nod. "As my nephew has not made his offer yet, I shall do so. May we take you to the assembly rooms in our carriage?"

Jane smiled at her. "Certainly, my lady, if you are willing."

"I am, or I would not have forced my nephew in this direction to offer," she retorted. She nudged her graying head towards the door and pursed her lips. "Now let us go, or there will be no chairs left for these elderly legs of mine."

"Don't talk about your legs, Aunt Louise," Simon pleaded as he led her out, not bothering to hide the plaintive note in his voice. "Miss Richards may never recover from the imagery."

Lady Clarke scoffed loudly. "I know Miss Richards's aunt, nephew. Trust me, she is a worse prospect."

Jane barked a laugh before stifling it with a hand, grinning in spite of herself. "I can honestly say I have never considered the prospect. She prefers to discuss the state of her back."

"An even worse notion, all things considered." She rapped Simon's wrist. "Take Miss Richards's arm, Simon. Don't be ungallant."

He looked down at his aunt in exasperation. "You are on the side that Miss Richards is, Louise. It is difficult to offer an arm already taken, and rude to turn about in such a way. Once we are out in the entry and affixed with our cloaks, I will happily do so."

"Not that happily," his great-aunt grumbled. "The prospect of an assembly ball has put him in a sour mood all evening, Miss Richards. Would you take pity on the man and save one of your dances for him? That way he might not blend in with the footmen for the entire evening."

Jane nodded as soberly as she dared, avoiding meeting Simon's eyes. "I will do so, my lady, for your sake."

"Such a nice girl, such a sweet creature. Thank the lady, Simon."

He exhaled, shaking his head. "For pity's sake, Louise. She has not done so yet, and I am not a child."

"And yet, your petulance is astonishing." Lady Clarke winked at Jane and gestured for the waiting maids. "Get your cloak, my dear. We'd best be off before the ninnies behind us have a chance to."

Jane grinned and did as she suggested, securing her simple brown patterned cloak about her while Simon and his aunt procured their own. She hid a smile as he flipped a portion of his great-aunt's cloak down, straightening it for her without her notice.

What would his aunt have said if she'd have noticed? Would she have scolded him for interfering? Would she be genuinely touched by his simple gesture of care? Would there have been a simple thanks and nothing more?

It was an interesting relationship, this one. Only a scant few minutes of observation, and already Jane was curious about it.

Lady Clarke did not seem nearly old enough to be Simon's great-aunt. Jane would have put her a full generation closer than that, more of an age with Simon's parents than his grandparents. But the affection between them . . .

Well, it was unusually affectionate for extended relations. And that was remarkable.

But then, Jane and her aunt Anne-Marie had a familiar relationship at times. When Anne-Marie wished for it. And she liked to be especially outspoken with her, just as Lady Clarke was doing with Simon.

Perhaps there were more similarities between Simon and Jane than she'd previously thought.

Not that she'd actually thought of their similarities. She barely knew the man, really. All she knew of him was what they had discussed in attempting to match their friends.

Still, it was something to consider.

Simon looked over at her, smiling as he adjusted his cloak. "Ready, Miss Richards?"

Jane nodded in response. "Ready.

"Then so is my arm." He extended it out to one side, tipping his head.

Shaking her head, but smiling with a newfound fondness for the man, Jane came to his side and looped her arm through his.

"Are you two quite finished?" Lady Clarke barked. "At this rate, there will be no dancing left when we arrive!" She strode for the door, almost tugging Simon along as she clicked her walking stick with each step.

"Is she really so eager for dancing?" Jane whispered to him as they exited the castle and moved to the carriage.

"To watch it, yes," Simon murmured, rolling his eyes a little. "She enjoys offering a commentary. Really, if you are not dancing, it is worth a listen. She's almost never wrong."

Jane was impressed, in spite of herself. "Really? Well, well . . ."

They loaded into the carriage and were on their way almost at once.

Lady Clarke turned to Jane the moment the carriage pulled away. "So, Miss Richards, what is your dowry?"

She immediately coughed in surprise.

"Aunt Louise!" Simon exclaimed at once, his fair eyes going round across from them. "For shame!"

"What?" Lady Clarke retorted, sparing him a quick look. "Is it a miserable sum?" She looked at Jane with sympathy. "Is it, dear? It is quite all right if it is. There are always qualities that make up for that."

"No," she choked out, one hand going to her throat. "No, it's perfectly respectable, I believe. Seven thousand pounds."

"There, now," Lady Clarke praised, patting Jane's knee.

"What a pretty sum! You can pick and choose, my dear, can you not?"

"I am not hearing this," Simon grumbled, rubbing his temples.

Lady Clarke tsked loudly. "Ignore him, Miss Richards. As I said before, I know your aunt Anne-Marie. You are the daughter of Thomas, yes?"

At Jane's affirmation, Lady Clarke sat back with a satisfied nod. "Always the most handsome and intelligent of the Richards brothers, I say. Your mama is Mary Burke, then. Sweet creature and a very pretty girl. You've got her coloring."

"Thank you," Jane murmured, barely over the surprise of the question of dowry now.

"Not her complexion, unfortunately," Lady Clarke went on without stopping, "but her coloring all the same."

"Lord, give me strength," Simon seemed to pray, looking out the window and up at the sky.

Jane, however, could only smile, warming to this woman in a very strange way. "No, I am afraid my elder sister Hannah is the beauty."

Lady Clarke raised a brow, her lips curving to the same side. "And you the wit? Tush, I won't tell her she's dim. We'll keep that between us."

A series of giggles threatened to escape, but Jane clamped down on her lips hard, only nodding.

"This is why we don't take you anywhere, Aunt," Simon announced.

The woman cleared her throat and scooted closer to Jane. "It is perfectly right to acknowledge your situation for what it is and your qualities for what they are. I refuse to believe that a young woman must be stupid as well as modest about who she is. You have a brain, my dear, so I suggest you use it."

"And what of my mouth, my lady?" Jane asked before the subject could close. "What should I do with that?"

Simon began laughing across from them, but Jane continued to keep her attention on the woman beside her.

Lady Clarke smiled very slowly. "Use that as often as you use your brain, my dear Miss Richards. In your own particular voice and at whatever volume you choose."

CHAPTER EIGHT

His great-aunt was going to either be the death of him or the death of his reputation—Simon was really not entirely certain which.

Perhaps she would be the death of both.

He was going to have to do something extraordinary to apologize to Jane for the complete lack of restraint Louise had shown in the carriage, and something even more extraordinary to atone for putting her in that situation in the first place.

To her credit, Jane did not seem to be particularly upset about what had happened, as she and Louise had soon begun laughing together about various subjects. Jane had held her own against the woman and expressed herself rather freely, which his aunt had, of course, been delighted about. Even Simon had been relatively delighted by her stance, but he was fairly certain Jane had all but fled their carriage when they reached the assembly rooms.

He couldn't blame her. What had possessed Louise to immediately ask about Jane's dowry? What did a dowry have to do with anything? Simon wasn't marrying the woman, and he could afford to marry whomever he wanted, no matter the dowry, anyway. She had known almost nothing about Jane, and she had thought her dowry a good first question to ask?

The woman was growing more senile by the moment, and he was going to write to every member of his family to warn them.

Until he could do so, however, he was going to have to find a way to endure her as she was.

At the moment, she was sitting along one wall with Jane's aunt and some local women of roughly the same age. There was no doubt as to their particular topic of conversation.

The leaning close, the whispering, and the barely concealed looks at this person or that all pointed towards gossip, plain and simple.

One could only hope it would occupy the women for the rest of the night to keep them out of trouble.

"Are you going to play nanny to your aunt all night?"

Simon downed whatever remained of his drink and turned to face George Ellis, who seemed rather smug for a man who could not manage to find better subjects than apples and quills for conversation with the woman he fancied.

Grunting softly, Simon set his glass aside. "Do I seem to be playing nanny now?"

Ellis shrugged. "Not particularly, but you're watching her like a hawk. What did she do?"

"Tonight?" Simon shook his head. "She asked Miss Richards outright what her dowry is."

The sound of his friend's shoes skidding on the floor beneath them in surprise was oddly satisfying. "She did *what?*"

Simon smiled very tightly, fluttering his lashes like a ninny. "Indeed. And then told her she has the coloring of her mother, but unfortunately, not her complexion."

Ellis covered his eyes with one hand, then slowly drew it down to his mouth. "Merciful days . . ."

"It's deuced lucky," Simon told him in a low voice, "that I

am not courting Miss Richards, Ellis. I could be called out for a relative behaving that way."

His friend nodded with all sincerity. "You could, it's true. Some families take insult very personally. How did Miss Richards respond?"

Simon waved a hand. "She did brilliantly, all things considered. She's got her own aunt, whom you've met."

"Indeed, but she did not question me as to my income on the ride over." Ellis whistled low under his breath. "She didn't say much of anything, really. She just sat there, blessedly, and let me speak with Miss Wyant without interruption."

An impish streak lit into Simon's chest, and he fixed a polite smile on his face. "And what did you speak with the very pretty Miss Wyant about?"

Ellis grinned in a way that Ellis rarely grinned. "I haven't the faintest idea."

"How is that possible?" Simon demanded with a laugh. "You were there!"

"I was," he confirmed, still grinning. "But I cannot recall the topics in the least."

Simon frowned at him. "That does not speak well of your ability to converse, nor of the level of intellect involved."

"I know." Ellis laughed as he looked utterly bewildered by the situation. "I know. I have no idea what she and I have talked about, Appleby. Not a jot. But I love talking with her. She always has something to say, and we can just talk. It doesn't even matter what the topic is. I daresay we could discuss cheese and speak for three days straight."

"Might I kindly suggest that you do not attempt to?" Simon offered, wincing ever so slightly. "Just because you are incapable of remembering does not mean that she is also thusly inflicted. She could be cataloguing every conversation and reporting on each to her friends, which could make you look like a right imbecile."

Ellis shook his head, his smile remaining unmoved. "She wouldn't."

Simon lifted a suspicious brow. "So certain of that, are you? Perhaps you should try actually courting her instead of boring her to death on the subject of paper."

Finally, Ellis looked less than giddy, his eyes widening and his jaw dropping. "Have I spoken to her about paper? Did you hear me do so? I wouldn't recall, I've been so captivated by her presence and her beauty and her wit . . ."

"I have no idea if you've spoken about paper, man," Simon told him in exasperation. "It is not a favorite occupation to monitor your conversation to ensure you aren't embarrassing yourself. But if you actually want to pursue the young lady, do try to be present for the occasion. And if you are just amusing yourself for the house party, then it doesn't actually matter."

Ellis's thick brows lowered in thought. "I think it does matter, Appleby. It is not just amusement. Not for me."

Simon managed a bemused smile for his friend and cocked his head a little. "Then why are you standing here talking to me at an assembly ball? Surely you have better things to do."

"You're quite right," Ellis mused, his expression turning far more easy. "I do." Without another remark, he strode away from Simon, straight in the direction of Miss Wyant, who had just finished a dance, it seemed.

She'd likely continue dancing for the rest of the night, if Ellis had anything to say about it. Did the general rules for number of dances between couples still stand if it was a local assembly without the same number of guests as one might have at a ball?

Not that the numbers were necessarily diminished here at the Dewbury assembly rooms, but it would be foolish to compare the two occasions, given the variety of stations and status among the guests. There were tradespeople of all sorts in attendance here, and Simon highly doubted Lady Cavernaugh would have invited them to a private ball at the castle.

She was too focused on fortune and status to lower her standard of guests in such a way.

But an assembly ball was supposed to be quaint by comparison, and it would serve the castle well to support the village, so she could hardly exclude the locals entirely from the entertainment.

She would be taking note, though, on which of her guests were more comfortable in this arrangement than in the private balls to come later. She would want a wife for her son who shared her tastes and sensibilities. Lord Cavernaugh had likely not given much thought to the subject himself and was only doing as he was told. Why exert his own mental function when someone else was all-too pleased to do so for him?

There had not been a private ball to judge the guests against as yet, but if Simon were a betting man, he would have taken note of Miss Wyant, Miss Cole, Mr. Talbot, Mr. Crew, and Miss Watkins not matching up to her ladyship's standards. They were enjoying themselves far too much at an assembly ball, and only time would tell if they found the same pleasure in a private ball.

Or would match their reserve to the occasion.

And then there was Jane, of course.

Jane had danced twice so far, her steps as light and easy as any other dancer in the room, regardless of their station. She smiled prettily, moved about with grace, and made no distinction between the guests. She would most certainly be on her ladyship's watchlist.

Simon had not danced at all yet, which her ladyship would also have taken note of. He supposed it was a good thing there was no eligible Cavernaugh daughter, or he might have been a person of interest there. As it was, he was neither above the assembly room ball nor beneath it.

He was simply indifferent one way or the other.

Still, he did find himself smiling as he saw Ellis take Miss Wyant to the floor, both of them beaming for all to see.

"You're smiling. That must be a strange experience."

Simon gave a wry look to Jane, who had come to stand beside him. "Yes, my face does not quite know what to make of it."

She nodded sympathetically, her lips curving in the slightest of smiles herself. "Poor face. You must take more care, Simon, or it could become a habit."

"Never," he vowed in all seriousness. "I am only amused, and it will soon fade."

"Ah, I see. And what amuses you presently?"

He indicated their dancing friends with a pointed nod. "Them, of course. They have managed to dance, at last."

Jane hummed almost to herself, folding her hands in front of her as she watched. "They have, indeed. Any insight from your man?"

"Not much," he admitted, lowering his voice a touch. "He has apparent lapses of memory when in her company and cannot recall a single topic of conversation. He doesn't seem to mind, but it would make recollection difficult, to my mind. He would not know if they've already discussed a topic, and I'd hate for him to look a fool if he is sincerely fond of Miss Wyant."

"And is he?" Jane asked him. "Sincerely fond of her?"

Simon found himself smiling again, remarkably. "I think so. He thinks so, too. But it is quite early in their knowing each other, so it could all change tomorrow."

"Hmm. That is too true, unfortunately. I've seen it happen." She laughed very softly at the same moment that Ellis and Miss Wyant were laughing about something or other. "But they seem perfectly happy at the moment."

"They do, indeed," Simon had to admit. "What of your man? Or woman, I suppose. Has she given you any indication on her feelings?"

"Oh, she's all giggles and blushes at the moment," Jane told him candidly. "Getting a single word of sense is a trial."

Simon glanced down at her, noting the delicate white flowers interwoven with pale green ribbon in her chestnut tresses, reminding him of an elegant garden maze, in a way.

What a perverse thought.

"For those of us who don't understand such reactions," he said, focusing his attention on the portion of her expression he could see, "would you translate into plain English?"

Jane laughed once and met his eyes rather impishly. "She likes him. Plain and simple."

"Excellent. And their conversation?"

"She likes his voice," Jane confessed, looking back at the couple. "Doesn't matter so much what they speak of, so long as they speak."

Simon's brow creased as he considered that, watching the jaunty dancing with the same impassiveness as before. "So what happens when the rosiness of attraction becomes normal, and they pay attention to their conversations? They'll have spent so long speaking of nothing that there will be no substance to their relationship."

"You're overthinking this, Simon."

"You're underthinking it," he insisted. "It is all well and good to have them walk and talk, Jane, but they cannot walk and talk forever."

She shook her head. "But they can certainly walk and talk while they get to know each other."

"They *aren't* getting to know each other." Simon grumbled under his breath. "Stupid conversations about nonsense don't help anything."

"On the contrary, they seem to be allowing them to grow more comfortable in each other's company. If my friend will no longer awkwardly slip her hand in and out of her glove and your friend will not study table linens when they are together, I am willing to let them talk about nothing."

Simon folded his arms and turned to face her fully. "Who

are you and what have you done with the Jane Richards I was walking with this morning?"

She rolled her eyes and gave him the most longsuffering look he had ever received. "I am not saying they should *always* talk about nothing. But we don't need to intervene on every single conversation they hold. We are helping them to shape their own courtship, not scripting it ourselves."

"It might be easier and more efficient if we did," he grumbled, wincing as he heard a cheery yell from the dancing.

"But then it would not be them courting as themselves, but as us," Jane told him with surprising firmness. "And Mr. Ellis would not fall in love with my version of Beatrice as easily as he could with her own version of herself, I can assure you. I highly doubt Beatrice would fall in love with your version of Ellis as she could his own version of himself, either."

Simon adopted a rather sardonic look, not needing to falsify the sourness he was feeling. "You've just confused me rather neatly. Well done. Try to untangle yourself and explain with a hint of clarity next time."

She scowled, the color in her eyes shifting markedly with the expression. "Don't be a troll. You know very well what I mean."

"Do I?"

"You are intentionally being cross, and it is contagious." She sniffed and tossed her head. "I am going over there to find someone pleasant to dance with. Should you find yourself not caught in a bramblebush later, perhaps I will allow you a dance as well."

She started away, glaring over her shoulder at him.

Simon stared back without shame, completely unrepentant. It was a fool's errand they were on together, and he was not going to pretend otherwise. He was committed to it by this point, there was no question, but he was going to act according to his conscience where his friend was concerned. And his conscience was telling him that his friend needed a great deal of help to avoid making a total hash of this.

The man had turned into a bleeding idiot. Anybody could see that. Imagine not recalling a conversation with a pretty girl just because she was pretty. How could anyone lose their sense of self so wholly as to lack memory? Ellis could tease Simon about something he had done at the age of twelve, but he could not recall a topic of conversation from an hour ago?

He was either suffering from some mind-altering disease or was temporarily mad.

At least, Simon hoped it was temporary.

He wasn't sure he wanted to be friends with someone who wouldn't recall the details of said friendship.

And he was utterly positive that Miss Wyant, sweet creature that she was, would not always be so tolerant of Ellis's lack of recollection.

In fact, it could rather become a great source of contention, should they wed.

How could Jane not see that?

Overthinking, indeed. It was because Simon *was* thinking that he could see the disaster looming without their intervention!

Perhaps Jane was more of a hearts and roses woman than he had originally taken her for. It would be an unfortunate discovery, should that be true. He wouldn't enjoy being in cahoots with someone so full of whimsy and keen on giggly flirtations between people. There would not be a single moment of sense between them, no matter what had passed before. He could list any number of silly girls of his acquaintance; he'd have run the other way before entering into any understanding with them, romantic or otherwise.

As though he could feel eyes upon him, Simon looked over at his aunt and her coterie of elderly ladies, only to find all of them staring his way.

He blinked, wondering what in the world he had done to

earn their attention, or their ire, should that be the case. All he was doing was standing here.

Ah . . .

Right.

His aunt hated when he simply stood there and endured occasions. It made her act on his behalf, and that almost never worked out well.

With just a hint of a nod to his aunt in the distance, Simon moved from his position without any particular destination. Perhaps if he lost himself in the gathering of eagerly dancing guests, she wouldn't know what he was doing or where he was. He could simply find another corner to stand in, and no one would be the wiser.

To his surprise, almost the moment he found such a spot, conveniently located near a column in the room, Miss Wyant appeared, smiling rather brightly and giving her complexion even more of a sheen of perfection than she already had.

Simon bowed quickly. "Miss Wyant. You seem to be enjoying the dancing."

"I confess, I am," she laughed. "There is something very enjoyable about being free from the formality of a private ball and being able to embrace the entertainment fully."

"I will take your word on that," Simon offered with all due politeness. "I am not easily entertained, and almost never embrace it when I am."

Miss Wyant narrowed her eyes at him, her lips pursing playfully. "Would you consider trying to be entertained just this once?"

He raised a brow, smiling just a touch. "Whatever for?"

"Mr. Ellis has charged me with getting you to dance the next, for whatever reason, and seemed rather certain I would fail in doing so." She glanced over her shoulder, then stepped closer to Simon. "I would much rather prove him wrong, wouldn't you?"

"Ah, now," Simon told her, seeing what dance was forming

and immediately catching Ellis's plan. "You neglected to mention what *does* entertain me easily: a healthy dose of competition, wagering, and surprising one's friends."

Miss Wyant brightened so radiantly, Simon almost found himself captivated to within a shade of what Ellis had been.

Almost.

"So you'll do it?" she cried.

Simon nodded and extended his hand to her. "Will you dance the next with me, Miss Wyant?"

Giggling, she placed her hand in his, her dark curls bouncing in delight. "With pleasure, Mr. Appleby."

Leading her out onto the floor, Simon eyed the position of his friend, who had selected Jane as his partner.

Even better.

He took up position on Ellis's left and gave Miss Wyant an acknowledging inclination of his head. "You could have warned me," Simon murmured for him alone as they waited for the rest of the couples.

"I didn't know what was next until they called it," came the tight reply.

Simon glanced over, noting the forced smile through which Ellis had spoken. "Well done, I must say. Does Miss Wyant know she'll be dancing with you more than me in this dance?"

"I bloody hope not," he replied through his smiling teeth. "That would defeat the entire purpose of my present scheme to do so." He looked at Simon quickly. "You don't mind my choice, do you? I know you two have been sparring, but at least she's not silly."

Simon cast his gaze to Jane, who was noting the positions and the leading music striking up. She knew exactly what was happening and could not have designed the occasion better herself. Her eyes raised to him, and though her mouth was tight, one impish brow quirked.

"No," Simon assured his friend, finding a smile spreading across his lips. "I don't mind at all."

CHAPTER NINE

"Where the devil is he?" Jane muttered to herself, rubbing her arms against the chill of the morning as she paced in the corridor.

The walls and artwork had no response for her, but it was likely too early for them, as it was for her.

She turned on her heel and paced further still, her feet aching from the excessive dancing the night before and an inadequate amount of sleep between said dancing and her present pacing.

That could not be helped.

The moment she had known the schedule for the day, she'd had to send a note to Simon. There was too much room for error and distance in the day, and if they wanted their friends to make any progress whatsoever on the promising start to their relationship, they had to act fast.

Of course, Simon had not responded to her note, but she had not anticipated he would. All she had asked was that he meet her at the corner of the guest wing at this time, and unless she was mistaken, he was four minutes late.

If she'd attached a watch to her dressing gown, she would

be able to know for certain and give him an accurate measure of his tardiness.

She shook her head as she turned once more. "Insufferable, stubborn, rude man."

"Says the woman who sent him a note to meet her at an ungodly hour of the morning," growled a low voice.

Jane whirled, defenses raised, glaring darkly.

She was entirely unprepared for the slightly rough and rumpled state of the fair-haired, tall, impressively broad-shouldered man.

Why was she noticing the width of his shoulders at the moment? He was fully and properly dressed for the day, apart from missing a cravat and needing a shave . . .

Fair stubble was an interesting sight. Her cousins all had darker hair, like she did, and so dark stubble was all she had known from them. But fair stubble . . .

"Well?" Simon barked, breaking the spell of her unnatural focus on him.

Jane blinked, scowling quickly. "You're late."

His brows rose. "That's what you want to talk to me about?"

"No, of course not," she spat as she folded her arms tightly. "It only wants saying."

"Can we make this quick?" he asked. "It's rather early, and you're not dressed. Suspicions might arise."

Jane groaned dramatically, shifting her weight to her right leg. "Uncomfortable about a plait of hair over my shoulder, Simon? That's about all the difference there is between now and in three hours."

He smiled the most patronizing smile known to man, his blue eyes perfectly frosty. "That and the structured garments you wear beneath your perfectly altered gowns, Jane. What you wear at the moment is shapeless and was in your bed with you."

Her cheeks began to heat, which was probably what he had

intended by the comment. "I won't be shocked by you, Simon Appleby. Or your aunt, for that matter."

Something twitched in his features, and he looked away. "I apologize for her behavior last night. She won't see the need to do so, but it was tactless and in very poor taste. She's lost her ability to filter her speech as she's aged, so I'll thank you not to judge her harshly for it."

"I think she possesses the requisite filter," Jane told him, sensing she'd actually hit a rather tender point unintentionally. "I think she simply chooses not to employ it."

His eyes darted back to her, his mouth curving ever so slightly. "Noticed that as well, did you?"

Jane nodded easily, relaxing her stance. "Oh yes. My aunt is the same. She no longer cares if what she says is proper or not. She just says it. At any rate, there is no need to apologize. I took no offense."

"I meant to apologize last night at the assembly ball," he admitted. "I simply forgot to do so when you were around. I was . . . cross, I believe you said."

"I did say that," Jane confirmed. "Do all social occasions make you cross? Or is there something about dancing that brings about the mood?"

He shrugged those broad shoulders she had noticed and set his hands at his hips. "Most social occasions make me cross, but dancing does seem to be a usual one. I don't even mind dancing, as a rule, but there is never a chance to do so without someone inferring meaning where none ought to be."

"Is that why you only danced five times last night?"

"It is, though I cannot believe you counted." He laughed softly, without humor. "And don't worry, my aunt fairly castigated me on the drive back for being so aloof."

Jane made a face, recalling her own return journey the night before. "Mine told me I had been a silly chit who would draw comment and shame the family."

"You aren't serious."

"I'm afraid I am." She smiled and tilted her head, trying to indicate that it made no difference to her.

Simon dropped his head, scoffing softly, then met her eyes once more. "For whatever it is worth, I don't think you were silly at all last night."

"Thank you," Jane quipped with a teasing curtsey. "And you . . . Well, to be fair, you were aloof, but it seems to me that it is simply part of your nature, so I cannot see why your aunt would find it worth comment."

"Exactly so." Simon nodded once. "I will accept that. Now . . ." He stepped a touch closer, his expression turning only slightly more serious. "What brought on the early summons? The others will begin rising soon, and I doubt you wish to be seen by anyone like this."

Jane pretended to shudder. "No, thank you. Right. The men are off to a hunt this morning, yes?"

"We are," he confirmed. "The moment breakfast is cleared."

"Lord Cavernaugh," Jane said quickly, "is planning on an extended hunt. My aunt spoke with Lady Cavernaugh, and she mentioned it. You will be gone the entire morning and well into the afternoon."

Simon groaned and put a hand to his brow. "Are you in earnest? What could possibly be gained by an extended hunt? He wants a wife, not a group of new friends to go to White's with."

"To impress you all, of course." Jane snorted softly at the idea. "Because hosting a house party in a castle isn't enough to impress anyone."

"Apparently not." He exhaled roughly and looked at her. "Are you worried it will be too much time apart for our friends? Or too much introspection?"

She bobbed her head, nodding over and over. "I am. I don't know Mr. Ellis, but I know Beatrice. She is going to pick apart every detail of every interaction and ruminate until she is paralyzed over any future decisions. She'll become convinced that Mr. Ellis finds her ridiculous or intolerable or something, and we will be starting over from the very beginning tonight."

Simon said nothing as she finished, staring at her, seemingly without blinking.

After an extended silence, Jane gestured with one hand impatiently. "What?"

"That . . . sounds intense," he murmured, his mouth barely moving.

She smiled quickly. "Welcome to the ways of the female mind. I have no idea how Ellis will respond to almost an entire day away from Beatrice, or if it will even affect him."

"I have no doubt it will," Simon murmured, a faint line forming between his brows, "but as to *how* . . ." He hissed, shaking his head. "I will have to keep my eye on him and try to guide his expressed thoughts, but I cannot pretend to know Miss Wyant better than I do."

"No, you cannot . . ." Jane began to pace again, much slower this time. "And I cannot have any insight into Ellis. We've only danced once, and you know what his aim was there."

Simon chuckled, folding his arms and leaning against a wall. "The only person who does not know what he was about is, hopefully, Miss Wyant."

Jane grinned and pointed a finger at him. "I'll find out if she knows today, mark my words."

"They're marked," he replied, holding up his hands for just a moment. "But what do we do in the interim?"

"I don't know." Jane clicked her tongue a few times as she paced. "The evening entertainment is music. She's not especially gifted there, so she won't perform unless forced."

"Ellis is incapable of musicality," Simon offered as though it would help. "Completely hopeless. He usually prefers to sit near my aunt so he can hear her criticisms."

Jane paused, looking back at him in thought. "Does your aunt mind other company while she does so?"

Simon straightened up. "Not usually, no. Why?"

She turned back to face him completely, grinning easily. "We cannot fully contrive to have them sit together, much as we might wish to. If Lady Cavernaugh has not made seating arrangements at supper, we can have some luck orchestrating that. But if I focus my efforts today, while all of the ladies are trapped indoors, to improve my friendship with your aunt . . ."

"Then she could invite you to sit near her, and Miss Wyant would easily join," he finished, nodding in understanding. "It is not a perfect arrangement, but it is likely the best we've got. Anything to improve proximity on a day without proximity will help."

"Precisely." She craned her neck and looked up at the ceiling. "If tomorrow is fair, we should be doing lawn games and a picnic, followed by a ball." She flicked her eyes to Simon briefly. "Try to contain your excitement."

He grimaced in distaste and shuddered.

Jane smiled and returned her attention to the ceiling. "Pairing them together as partners is the simplest thing for it. Natural encouragement to remain together for the day, so long as they don't grow upset with each other."

"Ellis does not grow upset easily. He'll be all encouragement and good sportsmanship. Unless he is competing against me, and then he will become vicious."

"Remind me to suggest the very thing." Jane closed her eyes, sighing heavily. "We should place the thought of partnership in their minds tonight. Any ideas?"

"I suggest," Simon said, his voice drawing closer, "that you stop thinking on preparation for tomorrow and go get some sleep for today."

She lowered her head and opened her eyes to look at him, surprised that he had come to lean against the wall at which she now stood. "Why? Would it not help to be fully prepared?"

Simon chuckled softly, the sound feeling like warm ripples across her body. "You are the most prepared person I know. But I cannot possibly consider preparing something for tomorrow that will take place more than twelve hours from now without experiencing a little bit more of today. It may very well be that we need to prepare nothing for tomorrow because our friends will prepare it all themselves."

"I suppose we must allow for independent thought and the use of their own intellect," Jane said, smiling almost sheepishly as she realized how controlling she had attempted to be.

"That is generally wise, yes." Simon's smile in return was gentle and amused and, she would admit, very handsome.

Handsome smiles before breakfast? What an idea.

Jane rubbed her hands over her face. "I just want this to work for them. I think Beatrice could be very happy with Mr. Ellis, and she has bemoaned the strain of the Marriage Mart for ages."

"You're a very caring friend, Jane Richards."

She lowered her hands to beneath her chin and curved her lips into a wry smile. "Not too silly or interfering?"

Simon slowly shook his head. "Not at all. Just loyal, caring, and a little bit devious."

Jane tossed her head back on a quick laugh. "All the best friends are."

"Well, perhaps we may be friends yet," he suggested, leaning a touch closer. "If devious is part of the combination."

Jane stood her ground and chose not to lean away. "And what of caring, Mr. Appleby? When does caring come into play?"

His smile faded just a little, but the intensity in his eyes increased. "I'm not certain, Miss Richards. I'd say that I will let you know, but I have a feeling it may just sneak up on us."

Her throat went dry suddenly, which begged for an immediate swallow.

She could not manage one.

At all.

A door opened nearby, the sound lighting a fire in the soles of Jane's feet and her knees. She sprang away from Simon, gripping her wrap with one hand and her plait with another.

"Right," she said in a low, rapid rush. "H-have a good hunt. We should . . . we should speak before supper."

"Yes, of course," Simon replied, clearing his throat. "I will have a note sent when I am returned from the hunt. We can compare notes. Perhaps in the garden?"

Jane's nod was almost painfully quick. "Excellent. My aunt adores walks in the garden—it will provide the perfect excuse."

"Right, then. Good morning, Miss Richards." He bowed and turned down the hall, striding away at a clip.

Belatedly, Jane curtseyed, watching him go, acutely aware of the buzzing sensation in her stomach. "Good morning, Simon," she murmured to nobody at all.

She shook herself and hurried off to her room, dashing within and shutting the door firmly behind her. Then she leaned herself against it, slowly untying the sash of her dressing gown and letting it hang loosely.

Simon Appleby was an interesting individual. Aloof in public, witty in private, handsome at all times. And he had a particularly pleasing smile.

He was also maddening, opinionated, critical, cynical, inflexible . . .

But he was a good friend to Mr. Ellis, she had to give him that. Only a true friend would intervene in order to bring about matrimonial happiness for another. Unless he was completely lying and was trying to ruin something for Mr. Ellis, but Jane did not think so. She had seen the devious streak in Simon, but he would not go so far as to wound Beatrice, of that she was certain.

Which meant he truly believed Beatrice could be a perfect fit for Mr. Ellis. For someone who disliked love and romance, he was growing rather keenly invested in securing such for his friend.

Perhaps in this scheme of theirs, she might come to know Simon a little better, if for no other reason than to understand the puzzle he presented.

That could be a private entertainment for herself during the musical presentations that evening. If the four of them were in a group together with his aunt, and likely hers, she could use the opportunity to learn stories of the men, either together or separate, from their youth. Under the guise of helping Beatrice learn about the man with whom she was so infatuated, she could discern if this man she was working with was as puzzling as he appeared.

Perhaps then her curiosity regarding him would be satiated.

Yawning, Jane stepped away from the door and shrugged out of her dressing down, draping the garment over the chair beside her. She looked at it for a moment, smiling slightly as she recalled Simon's description of it.

Shapeless, had he said? She had tied the sash rather tightly at her waist, but perhaps he could not see that with the way her arms had been folded.

She looked down at her nightgown, and all-out grinned. Now this *was* a shapeless garment, but she certainly knew better than to parade herself about for anyone's eyes in that alone. Yet he'd had a point when he'd commented there as well. It had been in her bed with her.

Why did that seem oddly intimate to suggest?

And why did it seem to tickle now as she recalled him saying it?

Surely, he hadn't meant anything by it but to shock her. Surely, he had been baiting her. The man could not have found anything improper about the picture she presented, albeit an unconventional one. He himself had been unshaven, which was hardly proper appearance, and he hadn't worn a cravat.

Which had provided an excellent view of his throat and neck, not that she had particularly noticed.

Ought she to have noticed that?

Had she seen a man without a cravat before? It could only have been her cousins, and she was not likely to have noticed much of a difference there, but there was something . . . appealing about the way Simon had appeared this morning.

Very appealing.

Oh, she needed sleep, she was absolutely certain of it. Finding the incorrigible man attractive first thing in the morning because he hadn't shaved or worn a cravat. What nonsense! He was a handsome man, anyone with eyes would have admitted the same freely. To be struck by such a thing after seeing him several times previously spoke of a want of sense and a need for respite.

Fatigue was the enemy of a woman's sensibilities and sanity, and that was exactly what she was experiencing. An excess of silliness because she was lacking in proper rest.

It would be an amusing story to tell Simon when all this was over. When their partnership was at an end, and they could be pleasant acquaintances who could be counted on for witty commentaries or an illustration in sarcasm.

He would find it hilarious and lord it over her for ages of time, if not forever.

Nodding to herself in satisfaction, Jane clambered back onto her bed and burrowed under the covers rather like a child. She nestled into the pillows, deepening her breathing in an attempt to force herself to relax quickly into sleep.

But sleep was not easily found.

Not when a certain corridor and unshaven, cravat-less man kept appearing in her mind's eye. Leaning close and smiling softly while eyes of ice kept her literally frozen in place.

And yet, how warm was the experience of such freezing.

CHAPTER TEN

Hazel eyes. That's what they were. A perfect blend of green and brown and gold, somehow, and varying between light shades and dark depending on the surroundings and the time of day.

They were lovely, there was no question. He'd never seen anything like them.

And he'd certainly never seen eyes made brighter by the color of a dressing gown.

He'd never seen any sort of dressing gown on a woman whose eyes he had noticed.

It had been the most . . . unexpected surprise.

And to find her furious with him while he had been parched in the throat had been the perfect excuse to be cantankerous while he found some semblance of balance between the floor and the wall.

Even removed from the experience as he was now, Simon could see it perfectly and feel the echoes of his multitude of emotions.

They were the most inconvenient companions on this hunt.

Well, perhaps not *the* most inconvenient.

"And then she said that she had never read anything of the sort in the Bible, which, she assured me, she had made a great study of. As though I have not dedicated my life to the study, interpretation, and application of religious texts. But no one takes clergymen seriously, gentlemen. We are seen as figures of fun rather than religious scholars." Mr. Burton, a short and unimpressive man serving in religious orders on the estate at Dewbury, had inexplicably been invited onto the hunt, but at this rate, the only thing that was going to be shot was him.

By Simon and at least five other men.

"Perhaps that is because a great many of them are," Ellis commented when the gnat of a man managed to take a breath from his extensive monologue.

That was not the reaction Mr. Burton had anticipated, and he looked at Ellis in abject horror. "Oh no, sir. No, they are not, I can assure you."

"I do not include you in my assertion," Ellis told him before he could say more. "But the curate we had in my village as a boy, and indeed, on my uncle's estate, which I visited frequently, were very much not the scholarly sort. Very awkward and bumbling with scripture, and begging for invitations from the fine families, all with the aim of trying to marry one of the daughters. They did not even extend charity to the poor, sir."

Mr. Burton's bug-like eyes went somehow wider, the simple knot of his even simpler cravat now resembling a noose. "I have . . . never in my life . . . I cannot begin to . . ."

Ellis nodded sympathetically as the man scrambled for words. "One of them even spent Sundays after services drinking excessive amounts of wine, sir. Until he was quite blatantly flushed. We would see him staggering along the street."

"No . . ." Mr. Burton looked as though he would fall to his knees and pray for their souls at this moment. Then he frowned darkly and shook his head. "This is what comes of limited opportunities for younger sons to gain employment, sirs! Disreputable men who have no business spreading the word of God are forced into orders because they possess neither military demeanor nor the judicial mind. And to even think about going into trade . . . I ask you, sirs . . ."

Simon glared at Ellis, who was now bearing a small smile of amusement as they walked. "What the devil did you start all that up for?"

Ellis chuckled and raised a brow. "I couldn't help it. And surely his ranting is better than his sermonizing."

"I'll give any man here a hundred pounds to silence him in whatever manner they see fit," Mr. Gideon grumbled from behind them.

Simon glanced at him, flashing a quick grin. "Would you prefer Cavernaugh's incessant commentary? I do believe the clergyman is quite devoted to the family."

Gideon met his eyes with complete unrepentance. "Yes." He cleared his throat and shouted, "Cavernaugh! How long has the hunt been a tradition at Dewbury?"

On cue, Burton clamped his mouth shut and gestured for Cavernaugh to take over speaking.

Why there was only one man permitted to speak at any time in a group of this size was entirely unclear.

Thankfully, Cavernaugh was relatively soft-spoken, and desperate to please, Burton hurried to be closer in order to participate in the conversation.

"At last," Simon murmured on a sigh. "Now we might actually have a hunt."

The three of them allowed their gaits to slow in order to put more distance between the tiresome and themselves, and the walk became much more pleasant because of it.

Gideon, perfectly agreeable with being solitary, ambled just ahead of Ellis and Simon, looking far more at ease than he had a moment before. And as for Ellis . . .

Well, the man was smiling for no good reason, looking at

the sky above them and the trees around them as though they had been placed there specifically for his enjoyment.

Madness. Absolute madness.

"You seem to be in a cheery mood this morning," Simon commented in as light a tone as he could manage while being torn between irritation and amusement. "What has tickled your fancy so?"

"Isn't it obvious?" Ellis asked him, laughing.

Simon allowed himself a much-needed snort of derision. "Obviously not, if it requires my asking."

Ellis gave him the look of blissful delirium he had anticipated. "I just might find myself in love, Appleby."

"Oh, devil take it, man, you are not," Simon retorted, rolling his eyes. "It has been two days."

"Perhaps that is all I need." Ellis shrugged, grinning shamelessly. "She is perfection, Appleby. Beautiful, lively, witty..."

"Is that what makes perfection?" Simon made an exaggerated sound of consideration. "I thought it required intellect, education, accomplishment, grace, dignity, charm, and manners as well as beauty and wit and energy. Have I truly been so wrong all these years?"

Ellis ignored him. "I've never met anyone like her. Never."

"I met five of her last week."

"Anything she says is fascinating."

"Doubtful."

"I could spend a lifetime in her presence and never be bored."

"That sounds like *your* issue."

"I want to marry her."

Simon gripped his arm and forcibly pulled him to a stop. "Now *that* is nonsense. What the hell is wrong with you?"

Ellis finally frowned, seeming bewildered by Simon's behavior. "I am entirely serious. Why shouldn't I marry her? People have married for less."

"People," he said firmly, "are imbeciles. You are not."

"Why would marrying her make me an imbecile?" Ellis demanded, folding his arms. "Why?"

Simon exhaled and started to walk once more. "I am not saying you would be if you married her, only that doing so now is . . . Dash it, Ellis, you have known her for two days. You cannot possibly know someone well enough in two days to claim love and marriage. If you were marrying for fortune or convenience or connection, that would be one thing, but you cannot claim anything more so suddenly. You are infatuated, nothing more."

"It feels rather intense for simple infatuation," Ellis remarked as he came back to Simon's side. "I'm all tied up in knots and feel like a complete clodpole when I'm around her."

"Because you *are* a clodpole," Simon muttered. "Look, I am not denying that Miss Wyant is beautiful and witty, and anything else. I simply beg of you to use caution. Use your head. More than one idiot has found himself leg shackled to a silly wife because he did not take a moment to think and to understand."

Ellis was silent for a moment, the only sounds that of his boots on the grass. "You think I'm being hasty?"

"I do," Simon confirmed, praying Jane would never know that he was encouraging reticence among their project couple. "You cannot possibly propose until you've known her a little longer. Be in love with her, if you must, but do not be overcome by the sensation of it."

"How should I come to know her better?" Ellis shook his head, his eyes focused ahead. "We cannot go for carriage rides or to the theater or anything we might do in London. We are hemmed in by the constraints of the house party."

Simon looked up at the trees above him, wishing he could rid himself of this entire situation. Why was he supposed to be the maestro for his friend's romantic opera? Surely the man could find his own ideas and methods of wooing a woman. What would Simon know about any of it?

"Well," he began, trudging into the treacherous stream of his friend's amorous plotting all the same, "there is always talking."

Simon felt himself blink in shock at his own statement. Talking? That was his brilliant solution to the problem? Talking? That was what had led every intervention they had staged yesterday. The complete lack of actual, truthful conversation between the fools.

Talking.

Good heavens, someone ought to shoot Simon on this hunt and set to rights whatever had gone askew.

"And walking," he added quickly. He nodded at this idea, and kept nodding as though in encouragement. "Walking and talking."

Oh gads, he was growing stupider by the sentence.

"We did that yesterday," Ellis pointed out, apparently missing the stupidity of Simon's words entirely.

"Do it again," he insisted. "Do it every day, if you can. Somewhere, somehow. Among the rest of the activities of the day. Gardens, the orangery, the gallery, anything."

Jane was going to kill him. But he was saying truth, so how much trouble could he be in?

"We'll split into groups here, gents!" the gamekeeper shouted from up ahead. "My lord, you and those accompanying you will come with me. The next three or four gents will go with Mr. Martin, and the rest will be divided among the other hands."

The group divided up according to the given direction, with Ellis and Simon headed along a new path with their designated guide. Simon paid no attention to who was in the smaller group with them, not particularly caring one way or the other whom they were shooting with.

None of it mattered anyway.

"I sound like a fool, don't I?" Ellis asked him as they walked through the brush.

"At this moment? Not really."

"No, about Miss Wyant."

Simon winced, knowing it wouldn't be seen by his friend, as he walked slightly ahead. "I don't know, Ellis. I am not an expert in love, women, or matches. I have no insight on any of those subjects. It just seems poor logic to suddenly claim love with a woman you've not even known for forty-eight hours."

"I can see that," Ellis murmured.

Fearful he might be discouraging, Simon glanced back to see his friend better. Ellis now bore a somber attitude and expression, eyes cast down, slight crease between his brows, shoulders slightly slumped. He didn't look quite like a defeated creature, but he certainly was not the almost-whistling figure he had presented moments before.

Blast. This was exactly what Jane had been afraid of. Discouragement from overthinking.

Or in this case, discouragement from Simon overtalking.

Idiot.

"Tell me why you think you love Miss Wyant," he asked suddenly, keeping his tone steady.

"Why?" Ellis repeated. "Because I cannot think of anything or anyone else. What else could that be?"

"Obsession," Simon quipped before he could stop himself.

Ellis threw a frown his way, which he only caught by looking over his shoulder in anticipation of it.

"What is it about her that you think you love?" he continued. "I am not trying to be cynical, only asking you to think."

"Her smile," Ellis said at once. "It . . . it brightens her entire face in a way I have never seen. And it makes me smile."

Simon nodded thoughtfully, hiding a smile of his own. "A good smile is an encouraging thing. What else?"

"Her energy. She is so full of life and spirit, even when she is silent. I watch for her in any room I enter, and everything changes when she is there." Ellis laughed once. "That doesn't even make sense, does it?"

"No, it does not," he agreed, doing his utmost to not make the answer sound derogatory. "You cannot explain yourself, am I correct?"

Ellis heaved an almost weary sigh. "Yes. I have no idea what is happening to me. How can one person be so utterly fascinating in every way?"

"I don't know. I've not met anyone who fascinates me to that degree." Simon would have shrugged had his mind not conjured up the form of Jane Richards in his mind.

Oddly enough, it was not the Jane he had talked with this morning, the one with a dark green dressing gown and a long plait of brown hair who was just as witty on little sleep as she was at any other time. It was the version of Jane that had walked away from him at the assembly ball the night before. The one who had scolded him for being cross and given him a dark, almost betrayed look.

That version of Jane couldn't possibly fascinate him. She was stuck up, unreasonable, and stubborn, furious with him for not perfectly understanding or agreeing with her, scheming in ways that were utterly ridiculous, and then claiming to be the one who had sense. And that *he* was the one who was over-thinking all of this.

No, she could not be fascinating to him. She would not be fascinating to him. She could be as beautiful, witty, and charming as she was, but he would not be utterly fascinated by her.

Only a little curious, and only while they were working together for their friends.

That was all.

And that would not count.

"You just need to plan a little better, my man," Simon told Ellis as he shook the image of an angry Jane from his mind. "Think through how you might court her while you're here. I am sure Cavernaugh would be happy to tell you what is scheduled in coming days if he thought a courtship would come of it. Or an engagement. I know his mother is anxious to have engagements come from this event."

"Don't you think this might all feel a little contrived?" Ellis asked him. "If everything I do at this house party circles around Miss Wyant, might it not feel as though I have set my sights on her without considering anyone else?"

Simon gave him a strange look. "Were you planning on considering anyone else here?"

"No . . ."

"Were you planning on considering anyone else in general before this?"

"No, of course not," Ellis retorted. "I never thought of marriage or courtship."

Simon flung one arm out in a gesture of something rather obvious. "Then how, pray tell, could you possibly be manipulative or hastily selective?"

"I don't know!" he replied, clearly exasperated now. "I've never been like this, felt like this, or met anyone like this! I don't know anything!"

Torn between laughter and impatience, Simon turned and patted his friend lamely on the arm. "There, there."

Ellis glared at him. "Your sympathy is very touching."

"I know." He offered a tight smile. "I told you, I am not an expert at any of this. If you want to pursue the lady, then do so! Just don't lose your head in the process."

"Who would be after my head?" Ellis demanded, his eyes twinkling all the same. "My head is exactly where I expect it to be."

Simon opened his mouth to give a perfectly inappropriate response to the statement, then thought better of it and shook his head.

"Restraint? From you?" Ellis whistled low. "I am impressed, Appleby."

"Caught that, did you?"

His friend nodded. "I did. It was the perfect opening, and you just let it pass."

"What can I say?" Simon played at unabashed humility, clasping one hand across his chest. "I am under a new and reformed influence."

"Must be due to your time with Miss Richards."

Simon tripped unexpectedly, his foot catching on a root or a hole or some inconvenient obstacle, he was sure. He was not the sort to trip. He was an excellent walker, his gait always steady and smooth, never clumsy or accident prone.

"Careful, sirs," their guide said, catching sight of him just as he avoided stumbling completely. "The ground is uneven in these parts."

"Indeed, it is," Simon remarked, ignoring the panicked skipping of his heart. He cleared his throat and looked at Ellis, who had no reaction to his near disaster. "What were you saying about Miss Richards?"

Ellis blinked once, then gave him a sheepish smile. "Well, as I have been spending so much time with Miss Wyant, you, of necessity, have been forced into company with Miss Richards. I have no doubt it makes Miss Wyant more comfortable to have her friend so nearby, and you are a good sport for humoring me in this. I can only presume that Miss Richards has some influence over your present restraint. Guarding your tongue around her must be a difficult enterprise."

Simon stared at his friend, amazed at the calmness that washed over him and the ease with which his heart began to steady. "Yes," he said slowly, unsure if he was answering Ellis or answering the incoherent questions that had begun flooding his mind. "Yes, it is difficult. But if it helps you woo her friend, I shall keep at it."

"I appreciate that," Ellis said with the most sincerity Simon had ever heard him use. "I am convinced this is love, Appleby. Or will be shortly, if it isn't now. I cannot give up on it."

Well, at least Jane would be delighted to hear that.

Simon offered him a smile that was not at all forced. "Then don't give up on it. I believe there is music tonight, and if nothing else, you might learn her taste for it. Perhaps you may share an interest."

Ellis's expression shuttered completely. "I know nothing about music, and you know it. I would not know a good song from a bad one, though I do believe my ears would know a poor singer, if they heard such a thing."

"The fact that you cannot admit that you have never heard such a thing proves just how hopeless you are in that regard," Simon told him easily, striding forward to reach their guide. "One must only hope that Miss Wyant does not fancy herself musical, or she may ask what you thought of her performance. What would you say then, hmm?"

"That it was perfection, of course."

"And if it was not perfection, and she knew that?" Simon raised a brow, grinning mischievously. "Are you a liar, Ellis? A flatterer? Is this the night your facade must finally fall?"

Ellis scowled. "That's not funny."

"Isn't it, though?"

Their guide turned, putting a finger to his lips and gesturing for them to take up positions.

Simon did so, taking his rifle from his shoulder and moving into position where the guide indicated.

Ellis was still frowning when he stood in his place just a few yards down from him.

Simon glanced over, still grinning.

"I hate you," Ellis mouthed, hefting his gun.

Simon restrained a laugh and propped the butt of his rifle neatly against his body. "Sorry," he mouthed in return before turning his attention to the sights of his gun and waiting for his prey to appear.

CHAPTER ELEVEN

"This is insufferably boring."

Jane could not have agreed more, but dared not make an audible response. For one thing, she was not supposed to be listening to the conversation in which this had been heard. For another, she was at least forty years too young to be so free with her opinions.

The fact that Simon's aunt had been the one to make the comment was utter perfection, but how in the world could she make use of the occasion?

To Lady Clarke's credit, the statement had been given in an undertone to her two companions rather than at the top of her voice, but an undertone to Lady Clarke was simply the typical softly spoken level for anyone else.

Jane glanced in that general direction, hoping to catch her aunt Anne-Marie's eye, but she was wholly focused on her embroidery.

Why, she could not possibly imagine. Anne-Marie despised embroidery; she complained about it often.

"Why would her ladyship not prepare activities for the ladies during this time?" Beatrice hissed beside Jane. "It seems frightfully shortsighted to only entertain the men."

"Notice that Lady Cavernaugh is not in the room with us," Jane murmured in response. "She can have whatever entertainment she chooses for herself while the rest of us suffer in silence. Perhaps it is a test of our endurance."

"Or our propriety," Beatrice added, scoffing very softly. "The most proper among us wins Lord Cavernaugh's hand?"

Jane raised a brow. "Then find me a scandalous activity and I will engage in it with all haste!"

Beatrice snickered into a hand, her eyes squinting shut with her mirth.

It had been like this ever since breakfast, and they were now on the other side of luncheon. The meals were the punctuation to their day, and everything in between was utter boredom.

Utter. Boredom.

There was no structure to the day. No ideas given. No invitations extended. All of the women were simply gathered in the same room doing absolutely nothing but reading, embroidering, drawing, and blankly staring at the four walls encasing them.

It was, in truth, all that ladies were expected to do to fill their days, but it seemed rather like purgatory this time. Was that because they knew the men were out engaging their minds and hands in a widely accepted hobby? Was it that there were several of them in this room doing various hues of the same thing? Was it that last night had been so filled with energy and activity and today was . . . not?

Jane found it difficult to describe the depths of her boredom and her growing intolerance for feeling that way, even in her own mind. Why wouldn't someone, anyone, go into the library to read? Why wouldn't someone decide they wished to sketch in the orangery instead of in this drawing room? Why hadn't someone asked to play in the music room, claiming preparation for the evening to come? Would it really be so impossible for anyone to ask if they could go into the village and visit the modiste or the milliner?

Why hadn't Jane asked to do any of these things?

Oh right, because she had decided that her particular aim for the day would be connecting Beatrice with Simon's aunt, Lady Clarke, in order to garner an invitation to sit beside her that evening to encourage an exhibition in humor among Mr. Ellis and Beatrice.

The things she sacrificed for her friend.

She ought to keep a list that she could provide Beatrice after the wedding, just so she would properly appreciate the lengths that had been taken up to make this match.

She would never believe it.

Again, Jane threw her gaze over to her aunt, who just so happened to raise her eyes at that moment and meet hers. She seemed surprised to be at the center of her attention and gave her niece a bewildered look.

"Help," Jane mouthed, widening her eyes.

The bewildered expression deepened, the lines on her face increasing with the change. "How?" she mouthed in return.

Jane shrugged, then gestured walking with her fingers.

Aunt Anne-Marie tilted her head, deep lines forming above her eyebrows. "Garden?"

Jane pressed her hands together in a praying motion.

Her aunt's face cleared, and her jaw tightened, something almost hard forming in her features.

Jane knew that expression well.

She was going to be in her aunt's debt for this.

Which was totally unfair, as her aunt had to be as bored as anyone else at the moment. But it would be far less uncomfortable for everyone if an older woman made a suggestion instead of a younger one.

And Jane was just enough of a coward to not wish to stand out in such a way.

Blessedly, Aunt Anne-Marie set aside her embroidery and

rose. "Lady Clarke, I feel the need for some fresh air. You may join me, if you wish."

"I think I shall, Mrs. Richards, thank you." Lady Clarke propped her walking stick in front of her and pressed herself into a standing position. "I may need a younger person to help steady me."

"My niece and her friend Miss Wyant will accompany us," Anne-Marie assured her. "My ankles are not as strong as they were when we were girls, I can assure you." She laughed to herself and gestured for Jane and Beatrice to join her.

In a flash, Beatrice was to Lady Clarke's side, offering her arm. "Here, Lady Clarke, lean on me, if you have a need to."

Lady Clarke laughed, the sound hoarse and cackling. "I am not in such a state as yet, Miss Wyant, as to require full leaning, but I thank you for the offer. Just a bit of steadying is all I require."

Jane looped her arm through her aunt's and smiled at Lady Clarke. "Beatrice is very steadying, my lady. She will be a great comfort to you."

"Sturdy girl like her? I should think so." Lady Clarke patted Beatrice's arm as though she had given her some great praise.

Beatrice smiled at her, no tension or resentment anywhere in her features.

Good girl, that would earn her some favor with the lady.

"Now get me out of this room, girl," Lady Clarke hissed, keeping a smile on her face. "The lack of intelligence is catching."

Beatrice clamped down on her lips hard and led her out of the room, Jane and Anne-Marie following behind.

Once out in the corridor, Lady Clarke heaved a sigh that seemed too large for her petite frame. "Thank you, dear Miss Wyant. I am not nearly as frail as I claimed, but there is something comforting about having someone younger and stronger beside me. You never know when age will strike and sink its unfortunate teeth into you."

"Very true, Louise," Anne-Marie commented. "We are hardly decrepit, but there is an inconvenience about the aches coming earlier than they once did."

Jane gave her aunt a bemused look. "You told me that only the inelegant have aches, Aunt."

Lady Clarke coughed a loud laugh as they moved towards the garden.

Anne-Marie met Jane's eyes without humor. "I lied."

"I knew it," she hissed, tugging her aunt closer with fondness.

They were out on the low terrace leading to the garden then, and all four seemed to take a moment to breathe in the fresh, clean country air. It was a fine day with a gentle breeze, though the clouds seemed to be gathering more and more as the day went on. Perhaps it would rain later and give them all a better reason to stay indoors than what had been offered so far today.

But for now, it was a perfect day and time for walking about the garden.

Dewbury's gardens were unique, in Jane's mind, from any other gardens she had seen on grand estates. They were tiered, in a way, creating several terraces of gardens or green, with stone stairs linking each terrace to the next. One terrace was all floral with small paths among the buds, one had a fountain with a statue in the center, one was a simple green that was probably used for lawn games or the like, and on and on they went. At least four tiers, and the gardens sometimes varied from one side of the stairs to the other.

Jane hadn't thought to ask how the terraced aspect of the garden had been created, whether the house had always had them or if something else had been there originally. It was such a memorable aspect of this castle, and probably her favorite piece of the place. She liked being able to alter the scenery about her with only a few steps and yet still feel that she was among the natural beauty of the estate.

Her aunt, on the other hand, thought the tiered aspect was a ridiculous thing and that having to climb stairs to enjoy the gardens was cruel to the aged. It was a poor excuse to bring unnecessary exercise into the lives of the people on the estate.

It did not stop her from walking them every morning with Jane, but she had to complain throughout them.

"What are you about, Janet?" Anne-Marie asked her very softly as they walked through the flowers.

Jane played at surprise, letting her eyes go wide. "Whatever can you mean?"

Anne-Marie's expression was sardonic, one painted brow rising. "Janet."

Why was it that Jane could hide her thoughts and feelings from practically everyone in the world, but her aunt could see right through her facade without any effort at all?

It was as unnerving as the ominous message she had given Jane in the carriage on the way here.

And she knew full well that going against her aunt would not end well for her.

The only recourse was to tell her the truth.

Jane looked ahead at Beatrice and Lady Clarke, who were far enough away that a low conversation would not be overheard. She leaned closer to her aunt, keeping her eyes on her friend.

"I'm matching Beatrice with Mr. Ellis," she whispered. "She found him attractive, and then when they met, they were both so unbearably awkward that I could not stand it. I am trying to give her the opportunity to get to know him better, and she cannot do that if she is not comfortable."

"Oh, I do like that pairing," Anne-Marie praised, almost purring in satisfaction. "Beautiful. Their children will be stunning."

Jane's mouth curved to one side. "Steady on, Aunt. There is no guarantee this will work. But this will certainly help; thank you for asking Lady Clarke to walk."

"Lady Clarke?"

Blast.

Jane could have kicked herself for being the greatest idiot known to man. She could have simply left well enough alone, but no. She had to let her mouth ramble on and say too much. Now she would have to explain the scheme in greater detail, if not let her aunt in on the entirety of it.

"Janet," she said slowly. "What does Lady Clarke have to do with anything?" Anne-Marie gestured towards them subtly.

Jane hesitated just a moment longer, desperate to keep Simon out of the story she told. Her aunt would think too much of it and would smell a scheme in the mix. Jane would have no freedom to talk with him alone again, as her aunt would be watching them closely. She could not sacrifice her association with Simon. It would ruin everything.

About the matchmaking. It would ruin the matchmaking.

And that could not be.

How could she explain this?

"I have noticed," Jane told her in careful, precise words, though she wasn't certain which ones would come tumbling out, "that Mr. Ellis is rather attentive to Lady Clarke. I believe she is a relation of his friend, Mr. Appleby. I thought if Lady Clarke liked Beatrice, she might invite her to sit beside her tonight, and if Mr. Ellis is about as well . . ."

"Janet Catherine Rose," her aunt breathed. "I have never been more proud of you in your entire life."

Jane covered her mouth to keep from laughing out loud at the statement. Truth be told, she had not been entirely certain in which direction her aunt's reaction would go, be it pride, disapproval, or mockery.

Pride was definitely the most pleasant of the reactions to receive.

"What a brilliant scheme," Anne-Marie went on. "You are quite right to have Lady Clarke be an unwitting assistant to your aims for this evening. She is good company for anyone, particularly if one can appreciate a touch of cynicism in their humor. And Beatrice, lovely girl that she is, would only benefit from association with her."

"Glad you approve," Jane murmured, unable to keep from smiling at her aunt's take on the situation.

"Oh, more than approve," Anne-Marie told her as her own lips curved into a mischievous smile, the lip paint not quite matching up on both sides. "I will do what I can to help you with matching dear Beatrice to her dashing beau."

Jane gave her a warning look. "Don't interfere too much, Aunt. I am working very hard to keep this appearing like her own work and only friendly insight for my part."

Anne-Marie, thankfully, did not take offense at her words. "That is the beauty of being my age, dear. I can always be interfering without anybody thinking anything of it."

That was, unfortunately, true.

Well, mostly true.

Jane could usually see when her aunt was interfering and infer something of the sort, but that was only because she knew Anne-Marie so well. She knew how quickly her mind turned to scheming and had learned in which direction those schemes would trend. In fact, Jane now considered her aunt scheming at any given time she was awake. If she was not actively involved in some scheme, she was plotting a future one, and if she was not plotting a future one, she was reveling in the success of a previous one. If, and it was an almighty if, she ever failed in a scheme, she would spend some time correcting what had gone wrong in the operation in her mind and run the scenario again and again through her thoughts until it could no longer fail.

She was not the sort to wallow in her tragedies. She picked herself up and plunged forward in spite of her obstacles and found ways to make things better. There were no failures to Anne-Marie Richards—only learning opportunities.

She really was an inspirational figure, this aunt of hers.

Jane could learn a thing or three from her, should she take the time to observe and apply. But as most of the time the scheming was directed at Jane's life and habits, she usually spent her time avoiding Anne-Marie's thoughts and processes, if not outright ignoring them.

The fact that Jane was, in fact, now scheming on behalf of her friend and earning her aunt's praise for her methods and aims . . .

Oh good heavens, was she turning into her aunt Anne-Marie?

That was enough to scare any person out of their wits, and Jane was now utterly terrified.

"Anne-Marie, come up here," Lady Clarke yelled over her shoulder towards them. "Miss Wyant has asked a question that requires both of us to speak."

Anne-Marie released Jane's arm and hastened ahead with the gait of a much younger woman, making Jane snicker softly as she tried to keep up with slightly less determination than her aunt.

"Yes, dear?" Anne-Marie asked Beatrice when she reached her, Jane just a few paces behind.

Beatrice glanced over at Anne-Marie as they all moved over to the stairs to descend to a new terrace. "I merely asked Lady Clarke how long the two of you have known each other. It seems to me that it extends beyond this house party, but I might be mistaken."

Anne-Marie and Lady Clarke exchanged fond smiles that Jane was curious about. If Anne-Marie had a close friendship with Lady Clarke, Jane had certainly never heard of it. Polite association was to be expected between them, as they were of an age and in the same circles, but surely it was nothing more than that. Surely Jane would have known . . .

"We came out the same Season many, many years ago," Anne-Marie told Beatrice, and by extension, Jane. "We were presented to Her Majesty, Queen Charlotte, on the same day at Court. Louise had a much better presentation than I did."

"But your gown was better," Lady Clarke assured her. "And Susanna King outshone all of us."

Anne-Marie nodded in near-reverence. "She was the Incomparable that Season, there was no question. And what a match she made that year!"

Lady Clarke released a startlingly girlish sigh. "Yes . . . Lord Belvedere, cousin to the Duke of Devonshire. The man was . . . divinity in human form. A delicacy for the eyes. And his fortune was especially attractive for the time. Any of us would have prostrated ourselves on the ground before him if it would have done any good."

"But it would not?" Jane asked, grinning in amusement.

"Alas, no, Jane," Anne-Marie said with her own whimsical sigh. "He only wanted the Incomparable, and no one else even existed.

Jane frowned at that. "Does not speak particularly well of the man, does it? To only seek what the Queen has deemed to be the best. What if she was a dreadful woman and would be a shrew of a wife for him?"

"By all accounts, she was both," Lady Clarke told her. "Couldn't stand her myself, but she made the match, and so to her went all victory and praise. We could not hold a candle to her, and she knew it well. We were all so envious about the match she made, silly creatures. I had a happier marriage, to be sure. And I have no complaints for the physical creature my husband was, goodness knows."

Beatrice started giggling, flicking her eyes to Jane quickly, her cheeks turning pink.

If she had wanted to be obvious about her present state of infatuation, she had certainly done the deed well.

"Oh now . . ." Lady Clarke chimed in with a note of teasing. "What does that blush reveal, Miss Wyant?"

The color in Beatrice's cheeks flamed brighter still, but her smile deepened as well.

"Beatrice!" Anne-Marie faux gasped. "Do you have a secret to share?"

Jane watched the joking with a mixture of horror and entertainment, with fear and with fun, wondering what she ought to stop and what she ought to allow. If she intervened too much, she might raise suspicions. But as her friend, she could hardly let Beatrice be thrown to such outspoken and interfering wolves.

What to do?

"Don't be bullied, Beatrice!" Jane called over with as much playfulness as she could manage. "If you want to keep your secrets, keep them!"

Anne-Marie gave her a half-bewildered, half-scolding look, clearly thinking Jane had lost her mind.

But she had not lost her mind. Quite the contrary, she was keeping it.

And solidifying her position.

"There may be," Beatrice began slowly, still smiling between her pinkening cheeks, "a gentleman that . . . well, he . . . I feel . . ." She huffed, shaking her head. "I like him. Is that too frank? I don't know how else to say it."

"I think that says it perfectly," Anne-Marie assured her.

Lady Clarke patted Beatrice's hand, smiling up at her. "Delightful. I always think a woman should be frank when she can get away with it. You like him. Is this a new romance?"

Beatrice bit her lip. "Very."

Jane winced to herself at the word choice. Would it have killed Beatrice to be vaguer in her admission of the romance? Or in its timing? Now these women would pounce upon her, and Jane would not be able to save her.

"Might he be here at this house party, then?" Lady Clarke asked with interest. She was the only woman in the group who could have asked it and not have had the benefit of insight to the truth of the situation.

Still biting her lip, Beatrice nodded with the eagerness of a child.

Lady Clarke thumped her walking stick against the pavement of their path. "Most excellent! I have paid little attention to anything, so you must tell me, if you can, who it is. Or I shall have to observe you most closely and make my own assumptions."

"Oh, do that, Louise, by all means!" Anne-Marie suggested with a laugh. "It would be far more agreeable for Miss Wyant to not confess *everything* at this moment and for us to discover it by degrees. We might even help our dear friend here, once we discover who is the subject of her fancy."

"Indeed, yes," Lady Clarke gushed. She chuckled and patted Beatrice's arm again. "Don't tell me, dear. I want to discover this for myself. I will help you where I can, Miss Wyant, if he is a worthy suitor. It will be a vastly agreeable amusement for myself during this drudgery."

Beatrice looked between the older women in shock, though still entertained either by her impending romance or by the antics of elderly ladies. Or perhaps by something else entirely —Jane wouldn't put her own impressions on her friend in this moment.

But she was not entirely certain she liked the way this afternoon walk had gone and was going. She didn't want additional intervention in the matchmaking scheme she and Simon were engaged in; it was complicated enough as it was. And more involvement meant it would grow more obvious, which would mean they could be found out.

Simon was going to kill her.

On the other hand, if Anne-Marie and Lady Clarke were going to be blatantly pushing Beatrice towards Ellis, once Lady Clarke figured out that he was the subject, then it would open doors for Jane and Simon to act independently. And be less likely to be discovered.

This might be the greatest opportunity they'd had yet. If the aunts were the distraction, she and Simon could truly act in the way they wanted and felt best for their friends. It could be the neatest, easiest solution to the conundrum possible.

From problem to possibilities in a matter of mere moments . . .

She could only hope that Simon would see it that way, too.

Either way, the evening ahead of them would be interesting.

CHAPTER TWELVE

There was something agonizing about musical evenings, no matter who was hosting or who was in attendance. The anxiety of not knowing who would perform or the quality of any performances taking place drove Simon utterly mad while he was forced to sit and endure the occasion. Always had and, he suspected, always would.

The problem lay with having to select participants from the guests. Why did the hostess not arrange to have acknowledged talent entertain them all? Why subject them to the unknown talents of whomever they had chosen to invite to their event? Unless they had only invited the musically talented, it was a great risk.

Simon knew full well that Lady Cavernaugh had not invited only the musically talented, as he was not musically talented, and according to Jane, neither were she nor Miss Wyant.

Why, then, had a musical evening been included in the events of the house party? Was there some unwritten rule that a musical evening *had* to happen at a house party? Or at least once a week when in London?

Had he been in control of his own schedule this week,

Simon would have avoided anything musical. He did not dislike music; he rather enjoyed it, when it was done well. But when it was not, there was nothing in this world that was worse.

Absolutely nothing.

The performing had yet to begin, and already Simon was wanting to retire to his bedchamber under whatever guise would get him there fastest.

"Stop scowling, man," Ellis scolded, the words hissing through his smiling but clenched teeth. "You'll scare anyone away from us."

Simon gave him a sidelong look. "Then go stand over there, away from me. This is my face, and this is the expression it will wear this evening."

Ellis rolled his eyes, shaking his head and looking around the room. Simon knew full well who the man was looking for, and why he was concerned with Simon looking agreeable.

He wanted Miss Wyant to come over, and he wanted her to *want* to come over. But really, if she was as interested in him as he was in her, or even close to it, wouldn't Ellis like for her to desire to come to his side regardless of the expressions of the company he kept? It could be a test for her earnestness, if not sincerity. Would not that help the situation a great deal? It might answer some questions and doubts, which would be much preferred, certainly.

Simon was *helping* his friend by looking this way. The sooner he saw that, the better.

But as Simon watched, Ellis seemed to grow more and more impatient. His hands were behind his back, and he clapped the back of one into the palm of the other. He rocked on his heels ever so slightly. He scanned the entire room over and over again, his head moving as though on a swivel. Just back and forth in the same motions, never pausing or hesitating.

What his eyes were doing wasn't evident from Simon's

position, but he had no doubt they were raking the room and the small gathering already mingling about in it.

"You seem to be searching for something, Ellis," he mused aloud. "Or someone?"

"Stop playing coy," Ellis barked. "You're worse than your aunt."

Simon coughed in surprise, laughing as much as he coughed. "That is the worst thing you have ever said to me. I am not entirely certain our friendship can recover."

Ellis grunted once. "You'll recover. And I hope that someday I get to see you in this same state of madness. I haven't seen Miss Wyant the entire day, and it feels like a lifetime. I'm afraid she's changed her mind, that the separation was too much, that she'll have decided to speak with someone else..."

"That is insanity," Simon breathed, no longer laughing in the least. "You have just described actual insane thoughts. It has been less than a day since you've seen her. You barely know the chit!"

"I did not say," Ellis ground out, "that it makes any sense, Appleby. I'm irritated by these thoughts myself. But it is the truth of the situation, and until I see her smile in my direction, I shall not be easy this evening."

Despite what Simon knew, and had seen, despite his involvement in helping throw Ellis and Miss Wyant together, despite actively contriving to force the very relationship Ellis himself was seeking, Simon was horrified by what he was hearing.

His friend had gone mad. Actual raving mad. All from the influence of one woman. What was worse was that Ellis was fully aware of it. He wasn't giddy about every aspect and throwing metaphorical flowers into the air about the situation.

He was angry.

Which, to be fair, was the sanest reaction Simon had ever heard of to such a predicament.

He was tempted to yank Ellis from the room, pack him off into a carriage, and send that carriage headlong for the hills, but he knew he would never get the man away from here. Ellis was bigger and stronger than Simon, and though he was presently mad, he was not made weaker from it. If the man had been drunk, that would be one thing, but he was in full possession of his mental faculties.

Faintly, Simon began wishing that Miss Wyant wouldn't appear this evening. That his friend would be disappointed so he could move on from this madness. That they would be done with this foolishness. But he also hoped that Miss Wyant *would* show, that she would smile, that she had spent her day thinking the very same thoughts as Ellis, just so his friend would not suffer disappointment and torment. So he might have what he presently most desired and would adapt to the madness therein.

Then he might return to sense, but with the woman he cared for by his side. She could very well be an improvement for him, and he might make fewer stupid decisions under her influence.

That alone would be worth it.

And if Miss Wyant came, so would Jane.

Which, ironically, made Simon smile.

What nonsense! *Of course* they would both come. Unless they were actually unwell and had begged off to stay in their rooms—which would irk Lady Cavernaugh—they would come to the events of the house party like any other good guest. And unless some disaster had occurred during the day that he was unaware of, Miss Wyant's feelings were not likely to have changed so suddenly.

All he had to do now was help encourage his aunt to invite Miss Wyant to sit by them.

Which ought to be simple enough, if she was well dressed and well behaved.

His aunt, that is. Not Miss Wyant.

Miss Wyant would be the better behaved of the two, he was quite certain of that.

A motion off to the right of the room drew Simon's attention, and he smiled to himself as he saw Jane and Miss Wyant entering the room arm in arm. They both wore shades of white or cream, as all of the ladies present seemed to be, though some had delicate designs on their gowns as well, and both looked remarkably pretty, he was honest enough to say. But it was Jane upon which his attention rested most, wondering if her expression would tell him anything about her mood or the state of her mind. If she would be forcing politeness for the evening or if she would truly enjoy it. If she would be pleased to see him or simply tolerate his presence for the sake of their friends.

That last one bothered him a little.

Why did that bother him?

Behind the young ladies were his aunt and Mrs. Richards, and the four of them seemed to be rather jolly with each other, which would make Simon's task this evening rather simple. Jane had mentioned she would work on associating his aunt with Miss Wyant during the day, and it would seem that she had been successful in some respect at least. He had never doubted that she would have some success, but he'd not expected to see his aunt actually laughing vocally at something Miss Wyant said.

What sort of brilliance had Jane Richards managed in his absence?

Miss Wyant began to scan the room in an eerily similar fashion to Ellis's antics, but was quick to spot him, if the brightening of her entire being was any indication.

Simon decided to do both of them a favor and nudged him, nodding his head in the ladies' direction.

Ellis wasted no time and strode over to them. He bowed before Miss Wyant and immediately began conversing with her, both of them speaking so rapidly that he wasn't certain how either heard a single word.

Making his way over to them at a more sedate pace, Simon gave Jane as bemused a look as he dared before their aunts.

She returned it, seeming to be restraining laughter. "Good evening, Mr. Appleby," she managed with a quick curtsey.

He bowed in a perfectly perfunctory manner. "Miss Richards. Mrs. Richards. Aunt."

"Simon, darling, you look better than I expected," Louise commented, tapping her cane against the ground. "The hunt did not exhaust you?"

He looked at her with rank impatience. "When has a hunt ever exhausted me, Aunt? I may not be the most physical of men, but I have yet to be driven to my bed because of one outing."

Louise smiled and laughed incredulously. "How am I supposed to recall how you feel after any given activity, my boy? I simply do not pay you that much attention."

"Believe me, Aunt," Simon told her, giving her a fond additional bow, "I am well aware that I barely warrant your notice most of the time."

Mrs. Richards chuckled a warm laugh and took the liberty of patting his hand. "Oh dear, Mr. Appleby. You must forgive a relation's humor from time to time. It is plain that your great-aunt is fond of you."

Simon offered her a smile that was as warm as it was polite. "Mrs. Richards, I thank you. I am well aware of my aunt's patronage, when she chooses to apply it, and that such patronage may also wear the guise of criticism, when she is of that mind. But above all else, I am cognizant of the truth that such patronage is due to the genuine care and concern Lady Clarke holds for me."

"Well stated, nephew," Louise praised, giving him a slight wink. "Now, do stop talking and stand aside. I believe I want to see what you are presently blocking." She raised her cane and pressed it against his side as though to move him forcibly.

Never one to ignore force, Simon moved, though not without offering his aunt a quizzical look that she ignored. Mrs. Richards seemed unperturbed by the action and leaned close to his aunt to begin talking in low voices. The only thing he could possibly have been obstructing from their view was that of Mr. Ellis and Miss Wyant still speaking over each other in rapid sentences, neither seeming to take a breath.

He looked at the ladies more closely, then at their quarry, and realization dawned.

They knew.

Simon looked at Jane, knowing his expression reflected just how startled he was. She moved around the aunts and came to him quickly, somehow still smiling.

"It's all right," she soothed as though he had made a protest. "They're only now identifying him as the object of her affections."

He immediately looked at the aunts again, desperate to check that they were not hearing their discussion.

Whether their age had finally affected their hearing, or their distance was indeed far enough from them, he could not say with certainty, but it was enough to keep them safe either way.

"How did they know she had an object of affection?" Simon asked in a low voice. "Have you told them?"

"I am not nearly that idiotic," Jane replied lightly. "I may have told my aunt, when pressed, that I was hoping to help Beatrice with her aims upon a gentleman here and, again when pressed, who that was, but I said nothing further."

Simon frowned, not liking that one bit. He did not blame Jane for relating the information, if she was indeed pressed by her aunt, as an elderly aunt of a certain demeanor pressing for information was a force not to be trifled with lightly. But he did not like having the aunts involved in their schemes. It would get out of hand rather quickly, of that he had no doubt.

"So she knew," Simon concluded, "and told my aunt."

Jane laughed very softly just for the two of them. "Wrong again, sir."

He glanced at her in surprise. "How?"

She indicated their friends, both of whom were gesticulating almost wildly as they continued to speak. "Beatrice told them herself. Not the man in question, specifically, but that she liked someone here. My aunt prevailed upon yours to allow them to discover his identity for themselves, freeing Beatrice of interrogation. And thanks to our exuberant friends, they have now discovered it."

Simon exhaled slowly, knowing precisely what the delighted and scheming expression of his aunt would mean for Ellis and Miss Wyant. "So we are in trouble, then."

"That is precisely what I thought as well," Jane admitted before folding her arms and leaning just a tad closer.

The subtle shift placed her in just the right position for the warmth of her presence to make itself known against Simon's side, though they did not touch. As though that side of him were being immersed in a bath of a perfectly heated temperature, it spread from the tips of his fingers on his right hand up his arm, and simultaneously down his leg, reaching deeply in between each rib and seizing hold upon that lung. Even the tips of his hair on that side of his head seemed to catch flame somehow.

He'd never felt anything like it before, and it rendered him quite incapable of adequate thought or breath.

"But," Jane went on, her voice lower and echoing the warm ripples taking place in his body with ones directly centered within his chest, "it occurs to me that this may actually help us. If those two are publicly scheming for Ellis and Beatrice, and they know that, it saves you and I the danger of detection in our aims. We may become a greater friend to each of them as they try to get away from the scheming aunts, and we will just steer them in the direction we wish them to go."

Simon stared at her, trying to ignore the unsettling heat in his body while listening intently, his ears on both sides of him absolutely burning at the sound of her voice.

It was utterly ridiculous, the whole lot of it.

But he would endure whatever strangeness was happening, and continue to be sane, rational, and fully aware of his situation.

"So they are a distraction for us," he summarized, his voice sounding faded to his ears.

Jane nodded, a smile spreading across her lips. "I think so. They have no need for discretion, do they? Everybody expects meddling elderly ladies in Society. It will come as no surprise. And you know full well that those two won't do anything to get in the way of a match they like."

Simon found himself chuckling at that, his mind belatedly catching up with his hearing. "That is absolutely true. Louise is still congratulating herself on orchestrating the match of my cousin Anne with her husband, and that was over ten years ago. They could not stand one another at first, but she persevered."

"As I suspected. They could prove quite useful to us." Jane hummed in satisfaction and shifted her stance a bit, her body now angled slightly away from him.

The right side of him went cold almost immediately, and he actually shivered from the sensation.

Bizarre.

"Except your own aunt knows your scheme," Simon pointed out, instinctively leaning closer to her warmth. "Won't that come back to haunt you?"

Jane pursed her lips, her brows lowering.

Why did that motion of her lips tighten something in his stomach?

He swallowed, forcing his attention on Ellis and Miss

Wyant and their bizarre mirroring of each other's toying with the gloves they wore.

It was slightly awkward, those motions, but not yet to the point of needing to intervene.

Not yet.

"I suppose it could," Jane murmured through her pursed lips. "Anne-Marie may try to take over my attempts with Beatrice. She may lie in wait, though, and see what I bring about. Or what she thinks I bring about. If she starts to get in the way, I will try to have words with her."

"And if that fails?" he asked, his eyes disobeying him and moving back to her.

Jane slid her glance to him, her mouth curving upward in almost the exact angle her eyes did. "Then I will send you a note and all the work will be yours, Simon."

He could not look away from her, somehow. Could not return her teasing. Could not laugh. Could not respond with any dramatics or angst, even pretended. He just stared at the hazel eyes that had struck him so early that morning and had somehow remained in his thoughts in spite of other topics weaving in and out of them. They had always been there, and much as he had inadvertently dwelt on them, he had not managed to remember them correctly at all.

They were hazel, that much he had secured in his mind, but the balance of them, the swirls within them, the beauty of them, the power in them . . . He had fallen far, far short in his memory and re-creation of them. The sheen of gold in them was practically ethereal and gave her a captivating edge that she certainly did not need, to his mind.

She was captivating enough.

Her looks were a perfect combination, he decided. The shade of her hair was not the same shade as the brown in her eyes and was not dark enough to compare to ebony or mahogany or the like, but was something that seemed far more natural and even forgettable. But as he examined it more closely, the chestnut locks had an almost reddish edge in this light, something shimmering and almost liquid in spite of the twisting, plaiting, and curling mass of it all.

The contrast of such ribbons of color against the white fabric ribbons and small white flowers was something out of nature itself, wildflowers in a dark wood or some such.

Except the green of her hazel eyes wasn't out of nature, of that he was certain. It was something out of an artist's palette, something blended and mixed over and over again until the perfect shade was created. Something agonized over until it was a masterpiece, a shade that could combine with the brown and gold and not be lost among them.

And somehow, her hair and her eyes were the perfect accessories to the shade of her skin, the shape of her face, the variety of her expressions . . .

If he thought the word perfect any more where she was concerned, he would lose the power of the idea altogether, but it was all he was capable of thinking.

And yet . . .

She was not the classic perfect beauty. One might objectively not look at her when she stood next to a woman like Miss Wyant, or even Miss Beacom.

Understated. That's what Jane Richards was. An understated, but no less perfect, beauty.

And that, it seemed, was exactly Simon's preferred type.

His eyes widened as the thought shrieked across his mind. His type?

What the devil was he thinking?

He couldn't be thinking. He was so much better than this, and he must have simply had too much sun in the hunt. Despite the tree cover and mostly cloudy skies.

Simon wrenched his gaze away from Jane, which felt positively herculean, though what she thought about his frank observation and lack of response would be a complete mystery. He stared across the room entirely, no longer interested in their friends or anything but recovering something resembling his stoic reputation again.

"What filled your day, then?" he asked in a very stiff tone. "After you went back to bed."

Oh, why had he mentioned that? His mouth had run away from him, and now he could only think of the Jane he had met that morning, wreathed in a freshly woken appearance, a thin linen nightgown, and a rich-green dressing gown. Gads, she had been lovely.

And he had been a cantankerous fool.

Probably cantankerous because she had been unexpectedly lovely, and he had not been awake enough to properly appreciate it.

But he could appreciate it now. And he dreaded how she would answer. Whatever she said would linger in his mind longer than was appropriate.

"I slept, ironically enough," Jane told him, her voice softer now than it had been moments before. "Not long, but some. Went down to breakfast, felt judged for taking a second piece of ham ..."

Simon's smile erupted across his lips at that, but he forced himself not to look at her.

There was no telling what he would do if he looked at her while in the throes of such an unrestrained smile.

"Once all the ladies were up and fed, we sat in the large drawing room. All of us."

"And did what?" Simon inquired when she did not go on.

Jane grunted just once. "Nothing. Well, not nothing. Just the things ladies are expected to do when there is nothing to entertain them."

The utter disdain in her voice was oddly charming.

"Which are?"

She huffed rather darkly. "Our options are usually one of the following: reading, embroidery, drawing or painting, writing letters, or staring out of windows longingly because your mind craves any sort of activity at all. And I will have you know, Lady Cavernaugh was not in the room with us aside from the first ten minutes after breakfast had been cleared away and the other ladies who'd had trays came down. Then she disappeared and we saw nothing more of her."

"She abandoned the ladies?" Simon scoffed, shaking his head. "I don't suppose she offered her guests any options of finding other entertainment?"

"Of course not," Jane retorted. "Why would she? We were not told how long we were to sit there, if we were welcome to go elsewhere in the house, if there was anything else scheduled for us . . . In fact, nothing changed until we were told there was a cold luncheon at our disposal, if we wished. And then we returned to the drawing room and continued in our boredom."

The guests in the room began to migrate towards the chairs and instruments that had been set up to one side, and Simon moved his attention to the aunts and the couple they were observing. He did not dare move until he knew their aims, and he felt Jane would think the same.

Their scheme was the reigning motivation for everything now, no matter what else crept into the mix.

"How did you escape the boredom?" Simon whispered while his eyes tracked their aunts, now heading gradually towards the chairs. "I can see my aunt's fondness for Miss Wyant plainly, and that was not crafted from hours of boredom."

"No," Jane admitted with a quiet laugh, "but the boredom provided the opportunity. My aunt suggested a walk for the two of them, and that Beatrice and I would accompany them. We went out to the gardens and walked, which as I am sure you can imagine, included talking as well. And there is nothing your aunt likes so much as a secret, and Beatrice had her favorite kind."

Simon chuckled easily, offering his arm absently so they

could follow their group. "Of course. And who gave your aunt the idea to go for a walk?"

"I did, of course," came the easy quip from the woman whose light touch seemed to set his toes on fire. "Well, not the specifics. Anne-Marie suggested the company all on her own."

"Very nicely done, Miss Richards," Simon praised as he ignored the conflagration of his feet.

Jane patted his arm, an action he could not imagine she'd done intentionally. "And you? What of your day? How was the hunt?"

Hunt? What hunt? Had he hunted?

Was he supposed to have hunted?

His mind graciously caught up with him and played his day back in a quick scanning of pages. "Ah, the hunt," he said slowly, giving himself time to recall the details and the words to describe it. "Given the nature of our host, it will not surprise you that it was near drudgery."

A series of snickers escaped Jane, and she covered her mouth with a pristine glove.

Why was that so deuced encouraging?

"He was outmatched, however," Simon went on, "by the local vicar, which means I will be dreadfully unwell, should we still be here for church on Sunday." He paused to allow Jane more restrained laughter, smiling at the limited sound he could hear. "We were all rather pleased to begin shooting at anything, but alas, Dewbury's animals avoided the conversation long before the guns came into play. They must have heard about the torment from others."

"Oh stop," Jane gasped, still giggling, and dropping her hand to her throat. "Simon, stop."

He didn't want to stop. He wanted to continue making her laugh until the end of time, until tears of mirth streamed from her eyes, until she was entirely breathless and rosy, until he was literally holding her up in lieu of her collapsing with the hilarity.

He wanted . . .

Heavens. He wanted Jane.

His throat went instantly parched and he ground his teeth together, moving them towards the chairs, only to realize that his aunt had arranged seats so Ellis and Miss Wyant sat between her and Mrs. Richards rather than the arrangement he and Jane had predicted.

Which meant he would likely need to sit by Jane. He didn't have any complaints about that, it was just . . .

Just . . .

How could he calmly sit by her when this realization had suddenly come to be?

"That's going to work out better than I'd hoped," Jane murmured, nudging her head towards the seating arrangement. "I'll sit beside my aunt and see what I can hear." She released his arm and moved away, taking up the seat beside Mrs. Richards without any further comment.

Leaving Simon standing alone behind them.

He glanced to one side of the room, where footmen were arranging a punch bowl and glasses.

Good. He was going to need a drink of something to get through this evening, one way or the other.

CHAPTER THIRTEEN

Another early morning, another round of pacing, and another few moments spent waiting for Simon to appear.

But Jane did not feel irritated this morning.

This was all nerves.

A night of almost no sleep, filled with anxiety, leading to this frantic nervousness while she waited for Simon, unsure what he would want, what he would say, and what any of it would mean.

Rationally, she knew it would probably be about their friends and something to do with their matchmaking, but receiving a late-night note of a particularly cryptic nature from a gentleman who she was finding increasingly . . . distracting . . .

Well, it was enough to turn any sane woman slightly mad.

There wasn't even a specific moment from the night before that had made Jane especially distracted, but she had been so perfectly at ease, so delightfully entertained, so remarkably warm . . .

And there was the fact that the smile on her face had been

impossible to remove for the entire length of time she was in Simon's presence.

None of this had come to her as unusual until she had received his note, at which time all of her internal organs had begun to buzz and flutter about like a hoard of perturbed butterflies.

All was still within her now, but not in a consoling way. It was more like a numbness. A frozen sensation. A complete inability to function in the usual manner in the face of impending doom.

At least she was fully clothed this time. She wasn't about to be relatively undressed in front of him again, particularly when he put her in such complete internal chaos. Her hair was still plaited over one shoulder, but at least she was in full structured garments, so to speak. A blue morning gown with a gray pelisse, which might have been excessive, but she felt the need to be exceptionally covered this morning.

Layered against the man with whom she would meet, as though the added garment of cotton was actually armor.

And they weren't meeting in the corridor this time.

They were meeting in the terraced green located just off the corridor. It was almost a garden, although there were no cultivated flowers or bushes there. Only ivy crawling the wall and a rich plot of green grass. It would have been a perfectly secluded pocket of space, a breath of nature on their floor of the castle, had it not been for the windows lining the corridors on two sides of the plot.

Which begged the question: Why were they meeting here at all? It was so easily observed by anyone, and yet they were going to meet unaccompanied and unchaperoned? The hour was early, but if they were up at this time, anyone else could be as well.

It was a risk, there was no question.

Yet she was here.

Waiting.

"You're here."

The soft statement sent her heart launching into her throat, and somehow, she managed to turn without whirling in a startled fashion.

Simon stood in the only entrance to the castle from the green, finely dressed and perfectly shaven, cravat firmly in place. Had he also felt the need to avoid the rumpled state in which they had met the morning before? Or was it just a coincidence?

Jane swallowed and forced herself to smile at him, the action feeling more frozen than her insides. "Of course I am here. You asked me to be, did you not?"

His smile was as soft as his words, and it tickled the back of her throat, prompting another swallow on her part.

"I did," he confirmed, stepping into the green. "But I wasn't certain if you'd show. I was afraid you'd already be asleep when I had the note sent."

The freezing ends of Jane's smile began to thaw, yet remained in place without much effort. "I was not. I was too busy entertaining myself by replaying the conversations I overheard from Ellis and Beatrice."

Simon raised a brow, his smile turning perfectly lopsided. "Indeed? I heard some, but not all, from my stance. They seemed to be enjoying themselves, in spite of the mediocre musical presentations. What did they speak of? Quills and apples again?"

Jane giggled and absently toyed with the end of her plait. "Not this time, no. At first, it was a conversation among them and the aunts about the music itself, but then they began to talk of the sort of dances that could be done to each song."

Now both of his brows rose, and he seemed impressed, if the leaning back and folding of his arms were any indication. "Did they, indeed? What an interesting idea. Some of those songs would be dreadful to dance to."

"Precisely their point," Jane said with a few quick nods.

"Which prompted some laughter between them. From my point of view, it was a perfect discussion that showed the sense of humor of both, and shared humor is a sure way to encourage closer ties, is it not?"

She thought of their own laughter the night before, and the newfound fondness it had engendered in her, which seemed to send some sort of metaphorical arrow shooting out of her heart directly towards Simon. A strange physical sensation that could only be described with the sound of a keening cry.

It was uncomfortable, unexpected, and unwise, to be sure.

But it was there, and she'd had no power to keep that arrow from flying.

"It is indeed," Simon murmured, his eyes fixed on her in an unreadable manner.

Jane did not dare look away, despite the slow burn in her cheeks. What if she missed something in his face? What if his smile shifted and made her swoon? What if she saw a hint of impatience that would end her madness and return her ease? What if . . .?

"What did you need?" she asked suddenly, startling herself with the outburst. "This early, I mean. It is beastly early, Simon."

"It is no earlier than your summons for yesterday, Jane," he retorted without heat. His smile spread and he chuckled to himself, the sound sending heat to the very ground beneath her feet. "You did warn me that crankiness was contagious, though I had not expected such a delay in your symptoms."

Why was he being playful? How could he be so amused when she was just standing here losing her very mind?

She probably looked as unhinged as she felt, and that would not do at all. Perhaps that was why he was so amused. Perhaps she was a perfectly comical sight at the moment.

"Very well," he went on, the teasing fading just a little, "I have concerns about today."

Ah, sensible conversation. That she could manage.

Probably.

"Today," Jane repeated, clearing her throat. "Right, today is lawn games and picnics, is it not?"

Simon nodded, remarkably unperturbed for someone in the presence of a babbling woman. "It is. Ellis already has plans to make Miss Wyant his partner where possible; he told me so last night."

"Good." Jane tucked a strand of hair behind her ear, absently nodding as she looked down at nothing. "That will take care of a great deal of difficulty that the day could present. What is the problem?"

She heard him exhale heavily and glanced up to see his frown. "He wants . . . He wants to do something for Miss Wyant. A gesture of some sort that will woo her in some way." Simon scratched at his head, his frown deepening. "He did not ask me for ideas last night, but if I know him, he will do so this morning when his night of thinking produced nothing worth pursuing. And I have nothing."

It would have been a hilarious conundrum had Jane been more in possession of herself or her mind. Two men trying to figure out how to woo one woman and having no ideas when provided with a specific opportunity to do so. Pure fodder for future laughing sessions, there was no doubt.

But at the moment, it was just a conundrum.

Jane looked around the green and then slowly began walking as she thought. "A gesture. It could not be very grand, or the others will notice and embarrass both. I don't recall seeing many wildflowers on the grounds, did you?"

"Honestly, I am not certain I would have noticed if I did," Simon admitted, falling into step beside her, though keeping enough distance that she could still think and breathe rather freely.

It allowed her to smile at his words, and she glanced over at him. "Not fond of wildflowers, Simon?"

He smiled back, shrugging. "Not particularly aware of

them, more like. There was no need to. My sister picked all her own flowers."

"I did not know you had a sister," Jane replied as her smile faded in lieu of her curiosity. "Is she older or younger?"

Simon's smile turned remarkably fond. "Older. Annabelle. She tried to mother me to death in our youth. She lives in Devon now. Has four children, and I think another on the way."

"You think?" Jane pretended to huff, looking away. "You don't even know for certain—what sort of brother are you?"

"The sort that does not get every explicit detail from his sister about the timing of her confinement!" he shot back, all defenses now. "I expect to receive a letter when the child is born, and then, when enough time has passed, I shall pay a respectful visit, I assure you."

Jane tossed a grin at him. "Good."

His returning grin flipped her stomach on its end and sent a strange distress call to her kneecaps. "You approve, then?"

How did he manage to speak while smiling in such a way? And did it have to be so perfectly handsome? Really, it was as if he were trying to distract her.

Devilish brute.

"I do," Jane heard herself say. Hearing the breathy quality of her voice, she wrenched her eyes away and cast around for anything else to stare at. "Provided you do not stay long and are no trouble to your sister or the babe."

"Why would I be trouble to either?"

"I am certain you would find a way," she replied in distraction, pulse pounding in her neck as well as her ears.

Her eyes fell on small white flowers scattered among the grass to one side of the green, and her mind immediately began to spin.

"Flowers," she murmured to herself, moving for them.

"Yes . . ." Simon answered hesitantly as he followed. "But you just said there aren't any on the estate."

Jane shook her head as she crouched before them. "These are different. These are . . . well, I think they are some species of daisy, but they are also wild. I am not a gardener, nor a scholar, but the name does not matter." She plucked the small flower from the grass, as well as the one beside it, and rose, turning to face Simon. "I am going to teach you something."

He looked at the flowers and then up at her uncertainly. "All right . . ."

"Oh, don't look so scared," Jane told him, stepping closer. "You want to give Ellis a gesture Beatrice will appreciate, yes?"

"Yes . . ." he said again, no less hesitantly.

Jane gave him a scolding look. "He can make her a flower crown. Or necklace. Or bracelet, even. A chain, if he must, but it will do the trick."

"Why in the world would Ellis know how to do this?" Simon demanded. "Playing with wildflowers? Honestly, Jane, leave him some dignity as a man."

"Have you always been this fragile in your perception of manhood?" she asked him impatiently, propping one hand on her hip. "Or do you just have an aversion to romantic gestures? I promise, you will not catch romantic feelings from participating."

Simon scowled at her. "Why am I participating?" he grumbled, notably not answering her questions.

Jane snorted. "Well, I cannot very well teach him how to do this, can I? That would spoil everything. Now, you asked why he would know. Does he have any sisters or female cousins at all?"

"He does. Two sisters."

"Good. Then he can claim they taught him as a boy and he hasn't forgotten, I do not care. And you can tell him the same thing. Say Annabelle taught you. Now, pay attention." She placed one flower in the pocket of her pelisse and showed him the stem of the other. "You need stems that are long. That is crucial. Make a loop out of the bottom and thread the stem through, just as if you were tying a string on a package." She slid the tip of her finger through the loop she had tied and reached for the small flower in her pocket. "Then the stem of this one goes through."

Simon stepped closer and folded his arms, looking intently at the flowers. "Then pull the ends of the first knot tight to secure?"

Jane nodded as she did the exact motion he described. "Mm-hmm. And you can do another knot, if you must, but the stems are delicate and may not sustain more." She showed him the link between the two flowers. "See?"

He took the linked flowers from her and moved to another clump of them in the grass, plucking one quickly before turning back to her. "So, make a loop in the stem of this new one . . ."

"Or in the stem of the linked one," Jane pointed out.

He nodded, but continued with the one he was twisting. He tucked the linked stem into the hole he'd created and tightened the knot as Jane had shown him.

His smile as he held out the extended chain was the most childlike smile she had ever seen a grown man wear, and if her heart hadn't already fired an arrow at him, it would have unleashed an entire quiver at that moment. He looked so delightfully pleased with himself, she could not help but laugh and applaud softly. She was positive there had never been a more adorable sight than this, and she had to commit it to memory somehow.

"So you would just keep going," Simon said, his smile fading as he examined the chain, "until it reaches the size you need, and then the loose end goes around the first bloom. Am I correct?"

Jane clasped her hands under her chin as she nodded. "You are correct. I would recommend a crown for Beatrice, given her affinity for the royals."

Simon scoffed very softly. "I'd forgotten about that. I'll do my best to recommend it." He raised his eyes to Jane's. "You really think this is the way to her heart? She won't think less of him for it?"

"I promise that she will find it utterly charming as a gesture," Jane told him with all sincerity. "And that the story behind it will also charm her."

"The story is a lie," Simon reminded her, wincing just a little.

Jane shrugged one shoulder. "She will probably also be charmed to know that you taught him because he was eager to perform a gesture. I don't believe she will be easily offended by our means, Simon. Not if the ends are what she desires."

"Fair enough." He looked at the flowers again. "One could make a ring out of a flower, too, I suppose."

Again, Jane's heart leapt, this time seeming to settle just below her tongue. "They could," she managed weakly, "but it would likely be taken as a symbol of something more."

Simon hummed very softly, then curled the flowers into his palm, something in Jane's stomach curling in precisely the same manner. "May I keep this?"

"Of course," she whispered. "You'll . . . need something to show Ellis, won't you?"

"Yes, I will. He is a very visual learner." He tucked the flower chain into his pocket, smiling at Jane a little. "Thank you."

There was something about gratitude that positively chafed at the moment, the uncomfortable abrasion taking place in at least four places in and along her body. She chafed at the inside of one knee, the connection between her right lung and three ribs, the space between her lips and her tongue, and the rim of her left ear. All of it from hearing his thanks, experiencing his gratitude for something he had asked of her.

She didn't want his thanks. She didn't want any thanks. She wasn't quite certain what she *did* want, but it was certainly not this.

Anything but this.

The sound of other conversation distracted her from her present irritation and sent her attention to the windows at once. Were the voices approaching them? Fading? Were they in danger here?

"You say the green is over here?" a voice asked clearly. "Why would you need a green on the same level as the bedchambers?"

Jane looked at Simon in horror, finding his own eyes wide and round. He closed the distance between them and took her hand, tugging her towards a near corner of the green. There was a slight rise and a patch of dirt leading to a large slit in the stone and, it seemed, that was where he was headed.

They reached it shortly, and Jane found herself pressed into a tiny alcove beside the slit, Simon joining her in the space and putting a finger to his lips.

She couldn't have spoken even if she'd wanted to.

He was so near . . . *so near* to her in this space. She could feel the fabric of his coat with every breath she took, catch the heat of him on his exhales, feel the spice of sandalwood and amber in her nose as the air swirled the scent of his body towards her . . . She nearly slumped against the aged stone behind her as the torrent of sensations threatened to overwhelm her, but her eyes somehow managed to remain fixed on the loose knot of Simon's cravat.

It was right there before her eyes, hovering over her and so reminiscent of what was happening within her. Knots forming and knots unravelling; where the knots were and how they came to be a complete mystery. But knots there were, and she felt the urge to coil up into a ball against those knots. To become such a knot.

Something changed then. Something stuttered, either in his breathing or hers, and suddenly the air was heavy and tight. Her ears rang with the pounding of her pulse, the rushing of air from her lungs and her lips, the breeze from his own lips rustling the hair at her brow. Her throat burned and buzzed with new fire that reached down, down, down until her heart and stomach were sheathed in flame she did not understand.

"Jane . . ." Simon's voice rasped, the sound rolling over and through her in delicious waves of new friction that arched her spine towards him.

"Wha . . ." she began, less of a word and more of a rush of feeling. She tried for a swallow and failed. "What . . . is that w-window?"

Simon did not move, did not turn, frozen and yet not at all frozen as his presence scorched the air about them. "Arrowslit," he told her, his voice clipped. "Balistraria. Arrowloop."

The words were nonsense to her ears, and it took all of her energy to focus on maintaining any sort of steady breathing. "Which one is it?" she whispered, her lips positively trembling.

"All of them," came the barely audible reply. "Take your pick."

Sensing they were not talking about windows in the least, Jane felt a shudder slowly ripple through her body, her pulse skipping as some part of Simon's clothing brushed against her achingly sensitive being. Her eyes fluttered shut, the stone at her back cold and damp, yet doing nothing at all to soothe or steady her frame.

Gads, she was going mad. Deliriously, hopelessly, deliciously mad here. Surrounded by heat and amber and sandalwood and grass and *him* . . .

Something so very powerfully, presently him.

Death would be a release, would it not?

Soft lips dusted against her brow, and she broke like a wave upon the sea. All other feeling stopped, and only that contact upon her skin existed. Somehow, her fingers remained alive and crept upwards, finding his coat and gripping its fabric hard. Clawing into it to secure him exactly where he was.

No closer. No farther.

Exactly right there.

"What a lovely little green," a voice chirped as though at a very great distance. "One could forget there is any other part of the castle when in here."

"Indeed, madam. I believe her ladyship has kept it unencumbered by other plants to secure its natural state."

"I won't say that a bit of flowers or some wisteria wouldn't go amiss, but the ivy and grass alone does provide the space an ancient sort of feeling. This might have been here from the beginning of the castle itself."

"I don't know, madam, but I can ask her ladyship's staff, if you would like."

Jane had no idea who was speaking, nor did she care. Simon's lips moved slowly across her skin, staying perfectly at her hairline and wandering no farther. Her fingers throbbed with the pain of gripping his coat so tightly, but she dared not slacken her hold. She would collapse to the floor if she did, there was no question of that. His coat and his mouth were the only things keeping her upright.

Where his hands were, she couldn't say. She was only aware of those lips and the pulsing in her fingers.

And very faintly, the words of their intruders in the space just beyond their hiding place.

"I shall ask Lady Cavernaugh if I may take tea out here this afternoon. It will be a blessed respite from the chaos of youth she has invited here. Now come, Mary. I am chilled."

"Yes, madam."

Their steps retreated, the distinct crunching of soft grass deadening the sound until they reached the castle again, where the clipped tread against stone echoed faintly.

When there were no more sounds, Jane released a whimper of sorts, biting her lip hard to restrain it.

"Shh, shh, shh," Simon soothed, his lips still at her brow. "It's all right. It's all right."

Jane's fingers spasmed open, releasing her hold on his coat, but did not move anywhere else as her breathing suddenly quickened. What was happening to her? What *had* happened? Was she afraid of discovery? Was she distraught that the moment would now end? Was she raw from so much feeling in so short a time?

Yes. Yes, she was all of those things, and more besides.

But what was he? How was he? Why was he not moving away?

Why were his lips still touching her?

As though in direct answer, his lips pressed against her skin more pointedly, and somehow more leisurely as well. Tender. Gentle.

Hypnotizing.

Jane's hands began to move along his coat, wrapping around his waist and sliding along his back until her fingers linked. A hug without truly hugging, holding without intentionally holding, securing herself without securing . . . anything.

She wasn't securing anything. She just wanted him to keep his lips on her as long as humanly possible.

Come what may afterwards.

"Jane," Simon murmured against her, no question in his tone, no statement in the word, just her name on a single breath of his.

Never had anything sounded more lovely.

"Simon," she heard herself whisper, the feeling of his name on her buzzing lips something out of a dream.

He exhaled slowly, his hands suddenly at her shoulders, rubbing up and down her arms. Had they always been there? Where had they come from?

"We have to go," he murmured. "We'll be missed."

How was he in any way sensible at the moment? Had he not been completely turned inside out in this alcove?

Oh good heavens, was she alone in this?

His hands suddenly moved to cup her face, and he leaned into one more kiss against her brow—one more kiss which contained somewhere between three and a thousand kisses within it.

She was not alone.

"I'll see you soon," he breathed, the faintest sort of nuzzle taking place between his hands.

Then he was gone, and the cool morning air swept across Jane's front, shocking her body and eliciting cascades of shivers.

She folded her arms and took several moments to breathe and to give Simon time to return to his rooms without anyone else looking. Every breath cleared her mind a bit more, every blink restored her sense, and every beat of her heart sent more and more calming influence on her frame.

"Oh . . . my . . . days . . ." Jane whispered when she was able to do so, shaking her head. Then she straightened and left the alcove, arms tight against her, and returned to her rooms.

CHAPTER FOURTEEN

Water was a delightful feat of creation and nature and life. It reflected any single particle of light it encountered, it bore secrets within its depths, it could carry enormous weight, it destroyed with a strange silence and finality . . . And it was one of the single most relaxing things the world could ever boast.

Simon liked water. He liked sitting on a shore and staring at water.

There was a pond on his estate in Derbyshire, a stream through his woods, and a lake that bordered his estate and two others. He spent as much time as he could sitting and staring at those bodies of water when he was home.

He was sitting and staring at this water now at Dewbury, his coat off and lying on the ground beside him, when he should have been helping Ellis practice his flower creations.

But he was not.

He could not.

He was sitting here on the shore, thinking about Jane.

Or more specifically, thinking of his experience hiding in an alcove with Jane.

Hell and the devil, that had been something.

What exactly, he wasn't sure. It was invigorating, exasperating, encouraging, exhilarating, confounding, defining, incendiary, revolutionary, extraordinary, involuntary . . .

He was running out of words, and somehow had not managed to accurately capture all that it had been.

And it had also been fun.

That was the most shocking word he had found as he considered it. He'd enjoyed it immensely, and, despite his present state of befuddlement, had no notion of regret. Not an iota. On the contrary, he'd been occasionally struck by moments of laughter in the hours since he'd left the alcove. He'd found himself smiling at nothing in particular. Thoughtful in moments of silence. Lighter in his manner and being.

And eager.

Eager to see Jane again, eager to examine these feelings within him, eager to discover if he would feel them again when he saw her, eager to kiss her . . .

He was definitely eager to kiss her again. And kiss her properly this time.

He was a sensible man, and he would never have considered himself particularly passionate, but the idea of properly kissing Jane and taking quite a deal of time to do so thoroughly was a primary aim of his thoughts and was in danger of becoming an obsession.

That was something he actually feared. He'd met people who were obsessed by one thing or another in their lives, and he was in no haste to allow himself to be subjected to such captivity. Resignation wasn't often encouraged when one was faced with obsession, as it would only lower that person and reduce the reserves of their strength. Resistance against obsession was preferred and would show endurance and character.

Resistance. Not due to regret, but due to safety and the retention of one's sense of self.

It did not mean he could not admire Jane and enjoy

spending time with her. She was a good influence and a friend, and their aims for their friends were coming from a truly wholesome place. It was up to Simon to make certain that his own aims did not supersede those and turn this enterprise into something wholly self-serving.

If he happened to benefit himself while engaging in something for the good of his friend, so be it.

Sitting on the shore here and allowing his thoughts to proceed without fear of detection or expression analysis by onlookers was the best way to process all of this. There were a few more days of this house party to endure, and he was only in the middle. He could not afford to falter now.

And if these changes in him were telling him what he thought they were telling him, he just might have a surprise for his aunt in a few weeks' time.

Not before then, of course. As he had told Ellis, one week was not enough time to be certain of anything.

But upon their return to London, he just might surprise everyone with what he would take up. So long as he did not take Jane by surprise.

Surely, she would already know.

Surely, she would have some idea now.

Surely . . .

Well, it had been so confusing an experience in close quarters, he supposed it was entirely possible that she did not know or suspect anything at this moment.

Was this something they ought to talk about? Or was it something that was best left alone and kept in memory?

Dash it, now *he* needed to talk to someone about romance and courtship and affection.

And it bloody well could not be Ellis.

That would be an explanation he could not give. No one would understand how he and Jane had become so close so quickly unless they revealed the matchmaking scheme, and if they did that, it would undermine everything they were trying to do and possibly undo it. And if the matchmaking scheme was undone, it would taint the connection they were beginning to form and possibly foment resentment between them.

And Simon could not allow the possibility of resenting Jane.

That was unthinkable.

Anything without Jane was unthinkable.

Which, if he followed that line of thought, meant anything *with* Jane *was* thinkable.

Not necessarily possible, but thinkable.

And that opened a great many mental doors.

Simon felt his chest expand with a great, heavy inhale, and sighed as the exhale followed, wondering about the strange floating feeling he was experiencing while he was quite clearly sitting on solid ground. There was no weight to his chest, no cloud of thought in his head, no boulder in the pit of his stomach. It was astonishing he was even capable of being confined to the earth, given the utter nothingness he felt at the present.

And yet . . . he was hardly giddy. There was no madness. He did not suddenly see hearts and flowers before his face, nor did the sun continue to shine when it was behind clouds. He was fully cognizant of where he was and when, of the items pressing upon his schedule for the day, and his present tasks and goals. He did not believe he would die if he did not see Jane in any certain amount of time. Did not want to run to her side and never leave it. Did not believe that associating with anyone else would be a waste of his time.

He even had other thoughts in his head besides Jane while he sat here at the water's edge.

Not many, granted, but that was to be expected as he attempted to understand his own mind and his feelings. As any natural man or woman with potentially romantic thoughts and experiences at hand ought to do. This, then, was the solution to the frantic nature so often described by those who thought themselves in love. To take quiet moments of reflection and fully examine the truth at the center of such feelings.

If he could do it, so could anyone else.

It was all a matter of being determined to find sense, truth, and logic in the midst of newfound impressions and awareness.

Simon's truths were these: He liked Jane Richards as a person, he was attracted to her as a woman, and he found himself wanting to spend more time with her in close proximity. Admitting and acknowledging these things would help to guide him amidst whatever else might cloud his judgment. Such as the near-strangling breathlessness that had consumed him earlier as she'd clung to him in silence.

He'd never struggled to exist so much in his entire life as he did then, and somehow, he had never felt more vibrantly alive at the same time.

It was an intriguing combination of contradictions, and he wondered how long such an experience would last, should the situation ever be repeated.

Faintly, the sound of footsteps on grass reached him, and Simon glanced over his shoulder to see who approached. "Got confused again, have you?"

"No," Ellis protested defiantly, his steps slowing. "No, I've quite figured it out, thank you very much."

Simon grunted. "Good. Miss Wyant will be well pleased, then."

"You're certain it will work?"

Rolling his eyes, Simon turned back to focus on the surface of the water. "Quite. She may know how to do it for herself, as I am sure your sisters do, but having you create the thing for her will be quite charming. If I am wrong, I will help you stage an adequate apology at the ball tonight."

"If you are wrong," Ellis replied as he came to stand beside him, "I'm not likely to trust your opinion on what sort of apology would suit later on."

"Fair enough." Simon closed his eyes as the sun peeked out from behind a cloud, sending warmth down on him.

There was silence between the friends for a long moment, the only sound that of the gentle lapping of the lake against its shore.

"Is there a reason you are sitting out here alone at the lake?" Ellis asked eventually. "You look rather pensive."

"Perhaps I am pensive," Simon answered. He took a pause to inhale and exhale slowly. "Perhaps I seek a moment of solitude amidst the melee of the house party. Perhaps it is simply a fine day and I wish to enjoy it."

Ellis snorted once. "It's barely past breakfast, Appleby, and it is still cold."

"It is not. The sun is quite warm, as the day will be." Simon smiled, still keeping his eyes closed. "And we finished breakfast nearly two hours ago."

"Did we really?" There were a few quick sounds of fumbling with fabric and a clink of metal. "Dash me, so we did. How did you know that?"

Simon's smile turned rather smug and satisfied. "I can estimate time, man. I've been sitting here long enough."

"To what end?" Ellis demanded, seeming to put his pocket watch back, if the sounds of metal and fabric were any indication. "It will soon be time for the lawn games, and you cannot miss that."

"I have no intention of missing it." Simon sniffed and opened his eyes, taking in the surface of the water and its glow of reflected sunlight with some intensity. "I am debating the wisdom of a quick swim in the lake."

"You what?" Ellis crouched down beside him, his face all bewilderment. "Are you mad?"

Simon looked at him, grinning now. "Probably, but why should you think so? It is a summer's day, and we are in the country."

Ellis was already shaking his head. "Because it is *morning*. And because we will shortly be in the company of the ladies."

"I am hardly going to strip myself naked," Simon laughed, clambering to his feet and undoing the buttons of his waistcoat. "We are far too close to the castle for that."

His friend put a hand to his eyes, dropping his head. "You have lost your mind. You have honestly and truly lost your mind. I don't know what has come over you, and I cannot explain it."

Simon tossed his waistcoat down upon his coat and began working on the process of removing his boots. "Who has asked you to? It is really quite simple: I feel like a swim. No one has said that we cannot, and now is the time for me to do so." He grunted as he struggled against his boot, but managed to wrench one off before focusing on the other.

"What if the ladies see you?" Ellis hissed, a note of desperation eking in. "They could very well be on their way here!"

With a gust of effort, Simon freed his foot from the second boot and set both aside. "Then keep a sharp eye open, and I'll return to the house by a less direct route." He untied his cravat with quick tugs and undid the button at his throat. "It is already a warm day, and a cool dip in the water is just what I need if I am expected to engage in politeness and sport shortly."

He stepped closer to the water's edge, and dove in easily, submerging himself in the cool water and reveling in the welcome change. It also had the additional effect of soothing the more confusing thoughts and memories of Jane, returning him to blessed clarity that was free of any heated edges.

Water was an incredible thing.

His head broke the surface, and he took in a clear breath of air, brushing his hair back with his hands. "Marvelous. Absolutely marvelous." He opened his eyes and looked at Ellis on the shore. "Not coming in?"

Ellis could not have looked more irritated as he shook his

head very firmly. "Absolutely not. You've had your swim, now get out."

"I've not swam at all," Simon corrected. "I've only dived in. Give me a moment." He leaned his head back in the water and allowed his body to float to the surface before reaching his arms behind him to press the water in a smooth, even stroke. "Oh, this feels refreshing, indeed. It is wondrous what a swim can do for the soul."

"What, wash it?" Ellis called. "What have you done that your soul needs refreshing? Wondrous, indeed." He scoffed and turned to look at the castle, no doubt watching for any possible witnesses.

Simon allowed his expression to turn less playful now his friend's back was turned. What had he done? Trapped a woman in an alcove at a castle to save them both from detection, only to find himself neatly in the throes of the very same situation and sensations that might have been suspected, had he simply allowed the two of them to be caught. Something one ought to apologize for, and yet he was not at all sorry for. Something Jane had encouraged, likely without intending to, and yet nothing that would actually cause a scandal for anyone, if the truth were known.

And yet, in this day and age, it would be more than enough to force them to wed.

That was what he had risked that morning. He hadn't intended to, he had been trying to save them from such a thing, but instead . . .

How could he have known that being so close to her in such a space would set his world on fire? How could he have foreseen that he would be filled with the most intense desire to kiss her senseless when he had never done anything of the sort? How could he have dreamed that Jane Richards . . . Jane . . . would drive him so bloody mad that he had been talking about arrowslits without actually caring about arrowslits?

Apples and quills.

It might as well have been apples and quills.

Bloody hell . . .

No, he would not allow his mind to say the word. He would not even consider the word.

It was the surprise, that was all. Which was why he was in this cool water now.

Sense, sanity, and clarity.

He rolled over on the surface of the water and took a few more strokes, expelling air from his mouth in the water before drawing his face to one side for more air and repeating the motions. He'd learned to swim well as a boy in the lake at Geigle Park, and to this day, he enjoyed doing so when he was at home.

But he'd never had to swim to recover from being in close quarters with a woman. From layering her brow in kisses.

His stomach clenched as his lips burned in memory of the feeling of her skin beneath them. He ducked his head into the water and expelled air forcefully, trying anything to change what he felt. The water buoyed him up, literally, and reminded him what was real. He could feel the water around him, seeping into his clothing, bobbing around his fingers and toes, reaching deep within his ears . . .

He focused on those feelings, concentrating hard on the water itself and its physical effects on him. He paused his swimming and raised his head, treading water a moment. A breeze moved across the water and his dampened skin, raising shivers and gooseflesh.

That was real.

And that was enough.

"I see people," Ellis called over his shoulder.

Simon nodded, though Ellis would not see it, and swam over to the shore. "Very good. I will make my exit."

"How are you going to get to the castle without being

seen?" his friend demanded as he emerged. "The line of trees is not that thick."

"I will have to rely on quick motions, the distraction of guests towards activities set to take place away from me, and the distance between myself and them to confuse my identity." Simon shrugged, shaking his head hard to rid his hair of some moisture.

An irritated bark of a cry came from his friend. "What are you, a dog? Honestly, Appleby, I have no desire to match you in appearance."

Simon chuckled and ran a hand through his hair, ruffling it wildly. "Sorry. Habit, I suppose."

Ellis turned and glared at him. "You are a sight. Your aunt would positively expire to see you like this."

"Not likely," he countered, scooping up his clothing and boots from the shore. "She has seen me like this many, many times."

"In company?"

Simon paused, considering that. "No, I'll grant you that one. And she would be a trifle irritated if I were seen by Lady Cavernaugh or any young lady she was trying to push towards me. On the other hand, she might just scheme to have me spotted in such a state if she thought it would help the situation."

Ellis groaned and covered his face with both hands. "Don't tell me that. I know she's trying to help with Beatrice and me, and I'm terrified by what she'll attempt."

There was an odd delight in hearing that, and Simon tsked as he started towards his friend, giving him an encouraging nudge to his arm as he passed. "Chin up, old boy. I'm sure she'll not be so forward with you. You're not a relation, after all. And we are in company."

"That doesn't help," came the muffled reply.

Simon chuckled and moved away, staying on their side of the trees and veering towards the farthest corner of the castle that he could see from here. It might not help much, but he'd attempt it to try and avoid being seen.

He could be a tenant on the estate, after all. A local farmer on his way to the castle to discuss business with his lordship. An interloper from the village, even. There was no reason for anyone to suspect that Simon was actually a guest at the house party.

And besides, he was not that concerned about it if he were discovered, so long as the entire house party did not see him at once. He was not prone to embarrassment for himself, as he never acted in an untoward manner, and he did not really care what anyone thought of him, so long as it was not improper.

Jane would find it amusing, of that he was sure.

He smiled to himself as he walked through the tall grass towards the castle. He could see her reaction clearly in his mind's eye. The way her smile would bunch up her cheeks, even if she tried *not* to smile. The light that would enter her hazel eyes moments before laughter was audible. The shade of pink that would dust into her cheeks the more she tried not to laugh or attempted to restrain it. The manner in which she would quirk one brow, though it never rose all that much higher than the other.

And the way she would eventually give up and grin outright.

They might never talk about it afterwards, but he would know, and she would know, and when they next saw each other, they would be tempted to burst out laughing regardless of what was happening around them.

Yes, that would be the way it would all play out, if Jane caught him like this. It was almost worth letting her catch him, though how he would manage to only be seen by her and no one else . . .

It simply wasn't possible, but he might have to tell her about this later on just to garner some shadow of the reaction he'd imagined.

But then, they'd likely be partners for the lawn games so as to allow Ellis and Miss Wyant to be partners. It was the natural progression of matters if they were going to continue as a small group. If others were involved in the particular activity, there were no guarantees, but he or Jane could do their best to promote Ellis and Miss Wyant partnering up. They'd not likely have such power over their own partnering, if they exerted efforts for their friends, but that would be well enough.

They had to remember their aims, regardless of how it impacted themselves.

It wasn't as selfless as it sounded, when he thought about it. They wanted their friends to be partners in life, as they were so well suited to each other, and they were ensuring neither of them ruined such a prospect. It was helping them, yes. But it was also...

Well, what was it? He wanted Ellis to be happy, and he thought Miss Wyant was the way to enable that. He wanted his friend to be his best self, and he needed help to be that while he adjusted to the influence Miss Wyant had on him. He did not want his friend to feel he had ruined a situation that could have ended well, and he did not want to see him make a match that was unequal.

Was that because he cared about his friend or because was not sure how to be friends with a man who had to cope with such disappointment?

And now that Simon acknowledged his attraction for and interest in Jane, he was far more interested in opportunities to spend time with her than sparing any thought for their friends. In fact, Ellis and Miss Wyant were fast becoming the excuse he needed in order to be familiar with and close to Jane.

He could not manage any semblance of guilt about that.

Only enthusiasm.

The telltale laughter of females drew his attention through the trees to his left even as he continued on his path towards the house. Ellis had been correct—the trees were not all that thick along the route to the house, and it would have been easy for someone to spot him, had any of the guests been paying attention. He'd have to put even more distance between him and the trees, just to ensure he wasn't easily identified.

One of the ladies turned, and Simon felt something resembling a gasp rise up in his chest, though it never quite made it to his mouth.

Jane.

She saw him one heartbeat later, and stilled as their gazes collided. He slowed his step, wondering if he should stop as well, or continue going on his way. He could not stand and stare, not with the risk of others spotting him, or seeing this connection they were feeling, or . . .

He saw her eyes flick to the rest of him, and he couldn't tell if he was hot or cold as she did so. Was both an option? He seemed to be both, particularly in his cheeks and ears.

He should smile. She was looking at him, for heaven's sake, why wasn't he smiling? That was part of the joke, that it was hilarious to have her see him completely drenched from a swim in the lake. Shirt clinging to him, no hint of finery, hair in disarray . . .

Wait, she was seeing him like this?

It suddenly felt as though he were wearing nothing at all, and that was terrifying.

He needed her to laugh. Not at him, but at the situation. To do exactly as he had imagined and turn the whole encounter into something hilarious.

But Jane wasn't laughing. Her eyes were wide, her cheeks were rosy, and one hand . . .

It rested at her throat.

He suddenly had to swallow, though there was nothing physically provoking him to do so.

He could not see her eyes as well as he might have liked, but there was no light of laughter, as he'd expected.

No, her eyes were dark as they stared at him. Shamelessly

stared. No horror, no turning away, no crooked smile of amusement, no anger or disgust.

Just attention. Frank and raw, and wholly on him.

How was a man to breathe when a beautiful woman looked at him like that?

Jane finally blinked, and Simon felt a rough breath escape from his chest. Belatedly, he realized he had stopped. He should not stop. Could not stop.

Yet he was stopped.

He could not leave her without saying or doing something. Needed her to know that . . .

To know that . . .

Swallowing again, Simon inclined his head, keeping his eyes solidly on her.

He watched her throat bob and her chin dip in response.

His mouth flicked in a hint of a smile, and he turned for the castle, forcing his steps to be as long and fast as his aunt once claimed they were.

All the while, he tried to remember to breathe.

CHAPTER FIFTEEN

Jane hated lawn bowls.

She hated them with a passion.

But after she and Simon had ensured that Ellis and Miss Wyant were partnered for archery together, other guests had taken up all other lawn games that had been arranged, leaving only bowls for them. Battledore and shuttle-cock was full, archery was full, lawn tennis was full, pall-mall was full, ring toss was full . . .

The game she hated most was the only option, and she had to play it beside the man she could not bring herself to look at.

Not that she did not want to. She wanted nothing more than to look at him. She had enjoyed looking at him far too much that day, and now it was all she could think about. All her mind seemed capable of considering.

All her eyes could actually see.

Which was one of the reasons why her score at bowls was as abysmal as it was.

He, on the other hand, seemed to be perfectly capable of concise thought, speech, and maddeningly enough, accurate tosses of his bowl.

Jane was doing her best to force herself to be cold. Not in

manners, but in actual physical being. If she was cold, she would be less inclined to be close to him. She would curl into herself, so to speak, and not focus on every sleek motion he made as he tossed his bowls, nor his stride as he moved to right both sets of pins, nor the utter silence they were passing as they played.

Played. What a strange word. Playing gave the impression that fun was being had, that laughter was present, that there was a lightness of energy and spirit, and that those present were experiencing enjoyment.

Participating was far more formal, and that was all they were doing here. Participating. Mindlessly going through the motions of an activity they were all but forced to engage in. But there was no playing.

This was endurance.

Again, Jane rolled the bowl and had no reaction when she struck three of the pins at once, the most she'd managed yet.

"Any notion of what the score is?" Simon inquired in a low, innocent voice.

She shook her head. "None."

He bowled on his set, taking out five pins.

"I daresay you are winning," Jane mumbled, feeling as though she ought to say something.

"Does that upset you?"

Startled, she looked at him. "Why would that upset me?"

Simon's bright blue eyes searched hers, his expression rather tight for some reason. "You seem . . . bothered by something."

She managed a laugh that was halfway genuine. "Not by the score of bowls, I can assure you. By playing bowls, perhaps, as I hate it."

His head cocked to one side. "Why do you hate it?"

"Because I am dreadful at it," Jane said with a faint gesture towards her pins. "Haven't you been watching?"

"Not really, to be honest." He chuckled a little and brushed at something at his knee. "It's just something to do, isn't it?"

Jane wrinkled up her nose in agreement. "It really is." She heaved a sigh and looked over at the archery, where Mr. Ellis and Beatrice were shooting with others, and both their aunts were observing there. "I hope someday they appreciate the sacrifice we've made for them."

"We'll tell them at the wedding," Simon assured her. "While they are exceptionally grateful to be joined together."

"Excellent plan." Jane looked back at the partially fallen pins and scowled. "Do you think we might be close enough to luncheon to give up on this?"

Simon laughed again, and she did her best to ignore the warmth that lit up at the base of her spine. "Probably. But I have to know: Do you hate the game because you are bad at it? Or are you bad at it because you hate the game?"

The question had been unexpected, and Jane laughed before she could think twice about it. She could not help but laugh; it was completely instinctive when she was with him, and, heaven help her, it felt so good to do so. Her chest felt light and free, and the frozen nature of her body positively melted away.

What did she need to be so careful about anyway?

Simon was her friend, whatever had occurred between them that morning. And she wanted to laugh with her friend.

"Probably both," she admitted as they wandered away from the incomplete bowl set. "I have never been able to manage playing it well, and because of that, it has never been enjoyable. And I have tried." She looked up at him with a playfully serious expression. "I have tried, and I have tried, and my father and my uncle and any number of my cousins have worked most arduously to help me to improve my skills at lawn bowls. We all fail, each and every one of us."

"So you are in no way interested in further attempts to

improve there," Simon suggested with a wry smile, clasping his hands behind his back as he walked beside her.

Jane shook her head. "Not at all. I would rather do anything else."

He tsked and looked around them. "Well, there does not seem to be anything else to do. But I suppose we might be able to manage a walk either now or after luncheon is over. Any sign of our host and hostess?"

She scanned the entire expansive lawn before them, and found another laugh at hand when she spotted Lady Cavernaugh. "Her ladyship is sitting just there observing the pallmall, where her son is playing. Do you see who is beside him? They're just there between the fourth and fifth wicket."

Simon's eyes narrowed as he peered over, then his mouth curved in a small bemused smile. "Miss Dawes. Interesting choice."

"Not particularly," Jane said bluntly. "She has no personality of her own. She is perfectly adaptable to any person or situation, which might be what Lady Cavernaugh is looking for."

Simon seemed to choke for a moment, and Jane gave him another look. To her surprise, he was snickering almost uncontrollably, covering his mouth with one hand.

"What?" she demanded impatiently. "What is so funny?"

He exhaled slowly, holding up a finger. Then he swallowed and shook his head. "When we arrived at Dewbury, Louise asked me to tell her who else I saw and to tell her the blunt, unvarnished truth about those I knew. I said almost exactly the same thing about Miss Dawes to her then as you have just done now."

Jane smirked up him. "Well, we cannot help that, since it is true, bless her. It may mean she will be perfectly happy with a bore like Cavernaugh. We may have found the perfect match there."

"I beg your pardon, that is not perfection." He took another breath, his laughter fading, but not his good humor. "That is simply sad. Now, over there . . ." He gestured towards the archery, where Beatrice had just loosed an arrow that had apparently struck well, based on her grin and the applause of others, none more so than Mr. Ellis.

"Hmm," Jane murmured in satisfaction. "Yes, I believe they are. I think we've done well, don't you?"

Simon made a face of consideration, a higher-pitched sound indicating he was less certain. "I think we *are* doing well, but I do not think we are done yet. There are two more days here, and with all the time spent together, much can happen."

Jane bit her lip to try and hide a smile as they neared the archery. "How did he do with the flowers?"

"Seemed to catch on well," Simon replied, lowering his voice. "He was more concerned about giving her a reason he'd create such a thing than actually accomplishing it."

"Oh good heavens." Jane rolled her eyes, heaving an exasperated sigh. "Did you tell him not to overthink it?"

"I did." Simon cleared his throat. "Don't cheat, Ellis! I see you altering your step!"

Ellis glanced down, then glared at him rather darkly while the aunts tittered with their shared laughter.

"Don't be cruel, Simon!" Jane hissed, though she was laughing at the color rising in Mr. Ellis's cheeks. "He was not doing anything!"

"You don't want him growing arrogant, do you?" He paused his step, watching his friend loose the arrow. "He's an excellent marksman," Simon told Jane, dropping his voice to a near whisper. "And I do not want him to have that unfair advantage while I can help it. He may be trying to impress Miss Wyant, but it should not be done via archery. What would that impress her for anyway?"

Jane looked away with a startled laugh, fighting the urge to slap Simon's arm as she might have done with Taft or one of her cousins, had they said such a thing. "I think you will find that a young lady who fancies a man will be impressed by almost anything he succeeds in. It does not matter that he will never have to shoot an arrow to win her favor or hunt their supper or protect the keep. She could be impressed by his penmanship, or his Latin, or the way he holds his knife and fork. Anything he does well will reinforce the rightness of her fancy of him."

Simon whistled low. "Now you make me grateful my sister did not confide in me when she was being courted by her husband."

"It is utterly ridiculous," Jane agreed as she slid a finger between her palm and the fabric of her glove to scratch an itch. "Any love match has it, though. I've never met a woman who married for affection who did not get impressed by something truly trivial in her man."

"What would impress you?"

Jane almost stumbled a step, but turned it into a skip before Simon could see the faltering. Before he would need to help her. Before she would appear to be an idiot damsel who could not answer a simple question.

A deuced uncomfortable question, but an altogether simple one.

"Who can say?" she answered with a hopefully airy manner. "I would need to fancy someone first before I would have any idea what he does that impresses me."

"You don't have a set trait or skill or quality that you generally look for?" Simon pressed, apparently genuine in his curiosity, or his concern, or his . . . interest.

Was he interested? Was he asking for more than pure discussion on the topic? Could he be seeking something particular from her answers?

If so, what did he want her to say? Not that she would say it. She was only curious.

"Swimming," she said without thinking. "Beneficial exercise and a safety concern."

Simon coughed, and Jane felt her cheeks burst into flame. She closed her eyes, clamped down hard on her lips, and shook her head.

"What?" His voice was somehow lower still, gentle yet urgent, and it reached for her very soul.

"I'm sorry," she whispered. "I shouldn't have . . . I should have . . ."

He plucked her hand from where it was still fiddling with her other glove and held it tightly, the pressure ricocheting up her arm and directly to the center of her chest. Gripping and releasing there with every aching beat.

How had they gotten back here so quickly?

"Jane . . ."

Unable to ignore him, and unwilling to, she turned and looked at him, searching his face.

They had stopped walking and were only spared being in sight of the others by trees and archery targets. But even so . . .

Simon offered a soft smile, squeezing her hand in his. "Don't be sorry," he murmured. "Ever. I should never have asked. And . . . well, quite honestly, Jane, I should be sorry that you saw me after I had decided to go for a swim, but I'm really not."

Her eyes widened. "You're not?"

He seemed to be restraining laughter now as he shook his head. "I am not. I thought it would make you laugh."

"Normally, it would have," Jane admitted with a small giggle, which turned into a near-snort. She covered her mouth and nose with her free hand, then shook her head. "It would have."

"But . . . ?"

Was he really going to make her say it? What's more, was she really going to?

She attempted a swallow, wanted to exhale, but could

seem to do neither at the moment. "After this morning," she managed, her voice hoarse, "laughter wasn't possible. Not seeing you like that so soon after the alcove."

Simon stepped closer, and Jane felt her throat tighten and her heart skip. "I hoped that was it. I hoped it wasn't offensive or embarrassing or . . . I wanted you to laugh, and when you didn't . . ." He looked down at the hand he held, then reached for the other one. "I cannot properly explain this morning, nor what was changed between us, but I'm not sorry for it."

Relief had never tasted so sweet, and Jane thought, for a moment, that she might cry with it. But instead, oddly enough, she found laughter.

Deep, rolling, breathless laughter.

Gripping Simon's hands, she laughed, and she laughed hard.

"This is not the best time for you to be laughing, Jane," he told her with pretended firmness, though she could see a bit of tension and uncertainty in his face. "I might begin to think you are laughing at me, or that this entire day has been comical to you."

"No," she managed between laughs, trying to squeeze his hands in reassurance. "No, it's not you. I just . . . I have been so knotted up and so tense, and now you tell me . . . And I am just so relieved, Simon, I cannot help . . ." She dissolved into further giggles, nearly hunching forward with them.

Now he began to laugh as well, and turned her gently to the tree nearest them so she could lean against it in her hilarity. She did so, bracing her brow against her folded arms, and Simon rubbed his hand in soothing circles on her back.

"I don't know whether I should say 'there, there' at this moment," he mused aloud, "or beg you to pull yourself together."

Jane shook her head, fighting for control and knowing she looked as ridiculous as she felt, leaning against a tree and laughing her blasted bonnet off right as the man she fancied had told her he was not sorry for setting her entire life aflame. He was saying everything she wanted to hear.

And she was laughing.

"I'm so sorry, Simon . . ." she gasped, giggling and trying to look back at him. "I'm so sorry."

His smile was brilliant, glorious, and devastatingly handsome. "I've already told you, don't be sorry. Especially don't be sorry for laughing, if it's for a good cause." He chuckled softly and shook his head. "Bloody hell, Jane. Do you have any idea how beautiful you are when you laugh?"

The last hint of laughter dissolved in Jane's chest, and she stared at him over her shoulder in silence. Waiting for him to laugh or to joke somehow. To backtrack or turn away in embarrassment.

But no, he stood there, hand still on her back, his expression perfectly open and breathtakingly direct.

Jane straightened and turned, placing her back against the tree, trying at least three times to find any power of speech. After a painful swallow, she managed to squeak, "No . . .?"

Simon's shoulders moved on an exhale, and he, blessedly, kept his position where it was. "You're a beautiful woman, Jane, at any given moment. Surely this is not a new idea to you."

"There is no fair way for me to respond to that," she whispered with a slight shake of her head.

"Fair enough, though you have to understand that you are," Simon went on, unconcerned by her discomfiture. "But when you laugh . . . your entire countenance outdoes a sunrise."

Jane's throat tightened, along with, it seemed, all the rest of her. "Tell me."

What in the world had prompted her to say that? She did not need him to tell her more, or tell her in greater detail, or tell her anything at all. She needed him to *stop* telling her things so she could find a way to think! How could she possibly be staging a mutiny against herself at this moment?

Simon's brilliantly blue eyes darkened, reminding her of a stormy sea, which made her the hapless ship upon such torrential waves.

"You want to know what I think of you?" he murmured softly. "You want me to tell you that I think and dream of your eyes almost constantly and still cannot capture their beauty in its fullness? You want me to compare your complexion to roses and cream like a poet, but also to say that it reminds me of home because that is how I feel when I see your face? You want me to struggle to find the words to describe your hair when I have never seen anything like it? You want me to explain how I've been driven mad all morning because I cannot get the scent of your skin out of my mind?"

Jane was going to die where she stood, that much was quite clear. She was going to burn to death slowly and surely, and the heat was already unbearable. "Please," she rasped, trying to shake her head, to beg him to stop, to have mercy, but unable to move.

Simon did shake his head, very slowly. "I won't say any of those things, Jane, though they are all very true. I don't know what to say to you anymore, or how to behave with you, because what I want and what I am seem in complete contrast now." Just as slowly, his shoulders rose and fell in a shrug that mirrored her own breath. "I don't know who I am anymore."

"Do I say sorry for that?" Jane asked him, the words feeling strange in the blatantly parched state of her mouth and throat. "Or are you going to tell me not to apologize again?"

"Never be sorry for that," Simon told her, taking one step forward. "As disconcerting as all this is becoming, I don't mind feeling it. I'm quite at my leisure. But I do not wish to make you uncomfortable in any way. You were relieved by knowing I was not sorry for the lake, but that does not mean . . ."

Jane reached for his hand so quickly, she wasn't aware she

had done so until the heat of it began to warm her fingers and spread up her arm. "I'm not," she began, her voice shaky even as her grip was strong, "uncomfortable. At all. I mean, of course I am, but it is not . . . it's not . . ." She felt a growl of impatience and irritation coil in her throat. "I cannot quite describe it, which is utterly infuriating, but it is not a bad discomfort. It is more . . . ticklish."

Simon's hand clenched against hers, curling around her fingers. "Good. That is . . . very good to hear." His smile was almost hesitant, and he raised her hand to his lips, pressing his mouth to the suddenly thin fabric of her glove.

"What is happening, Simon?" Jane let herself ask as a shiver of appreciation raced through her. "How did we get here?"

"I haven't the faintest idea," he quipped, laughing once as he ran his thumb over the back of her hand. "I've mocked men for acting a fool when growing particularly fond of a woman, and here I am, driven to distraction by you."

Jane's lips parted as a smile dawned of its own accord. "You aren't acting a fool."

"Perhaps not," he allowed, "but I gave myself a very long and thorough talking to on the shore of the lake this morning and thought through how and what I felt."

"And you've made sense of it?"

He barked a loud laugh and kissed her hand again. "No, not at all. I only managed to identify what I was feeling and that I was feeling it. I've never been a fool, nor acted like one, but that does not mean that I always have the sense I was born with. And for some reason, of late, you drive that sense from me."

"Well, that only seems fair," Jane said softly, wondering if a smile could break someone's cheeks. "Since you do the same for me."

Simon raised an impish brow and his smile turned crooked. "Do I, now? And will you now wax poetic on my virtues?"

"No, I will not." Jane shook her head firmly, gripping his hand. "You have no need of your ego being inflated by my flattery, however sincere. And if you could not garner some idea of my appreciation from the way I gawked earlier, that is your own stupidity coming into play."

"Ooh, that is cruel," he groaned. He clasped a hand to his chest and acted the wounded soldier a moment. "Raising my hopes and insulting me in the same breath. How am I ever to gauge my status in your eyes if you are constantly matching good with ill?"

Jane sighed in exasperation and moved away from the tree, keeping her hand locked in his. "I have never been the sort to let a person become unbalanced. You must take it as a mark of affection that I am willing to offer the bad with the good. If I did not care, I would never be honest enough to say anything negative."

"Thank you, I think," Simon said as he followed her. "So I ought to worry when you aren't as honest?"

"Probably."

"Right, noted." He exhaled, his thumb still grazing over the back of her hand. "Where are we going?"

"Luncheon. You'll have to let go of my hand soon." She looked back at him, then at their hands pointedly.

He did not let go. "I will. When I must. And after I've let go, just know I am still holding your hand in my mind."

Jane's heart fluttered and turned on its back like a small dog begging for attention. Thankfully, her face kept its composure and she only smiled. "Well, then, I shall have to remember not to blush in front of our aunts, shan't I?"

CHAPTER SIXTEEN

F lirting was deuced good fun, and Simon would never have thought that possible. Honestly, five days ago, he would have said he did not know the first thing about flirting or how it ought to be accomplished or what the point of it was. He laughed at the very idea and scoffed at those who attempted to employ it.

Yet here he was, lying on a blanket on the ground beside a hamper of food, surrounded by other people.

And he was flirting.

Well, sort of.

He was staring at Jane whenever he could manage it and giving her very slight smiles. If she stared back for a length of time, as she did occasionally, he would alternate between splaying his fingers and slowly curling them one by one.

Her cheeks turned a remarkable shade of pink that even her bonnet did not adequately hide.

The joy of such a complexion shift under these circumstances was that any of the ladies could have a heightened color due to their being out of doors, and no one would blink at it. So Simon was free to make Jane blush as much as he wanted, and nobody would suspect a thing.

Given the number of people around them, he could also stare wherever he liked without moving and no one would accuse him of singling anybody out.

It was utterly perfect.

And Jane was growing so cross with him, which was even more perfect.

It would appear that she did not care for his flirting under these circumstances, and yet she was smiling in return, even when her eyes widened, and her jaw became tight.

Most of the time, from what he could tell, she was trying not to laugh.

Flirting, then, was finding occasion to make the young lady of his affection smile, blush, or stare back at him, all quite innocent, when there were others around them. A secret sort of romance that only the two of them would understand and, even if observed, would not be as plain to those who might see. Simon could simply be smiling with due politeness for the benefit of their company, and no one could say that he was not.

What a day this was turning out to be! From a simple conversation about flowers and forming them into a crown to admitting just how attracted they were to each other . . .

It was remarkably freeing, in Simon's mind. He did not have to hide how he felt or that he felt anything at all, and she was comfortable enough to not hide her feelings as well. They could share their thoughts and their feelings, their impressions and their attraction . . .

They could not, perhaps, be completely frank, but neither of them was the sort to be secretive. It was not in their nature to be less than they appeared.

And together, they seemed more of themselves.

Well, Simon did, at least. He could not speak to Jane's mind, not yet. He believed she felt the same. He believed she was growing fonder of him and believed she was as keen to spend time with him alone as he was with her. He believed she was comfortable in his presence, and knew, as she had said, that she was the ticklish sort of uncomfortable as well.

Ticklish. What a playful word. Uncomfortable in a ticklish way might be his new favorite description of the feelings she aroused in him.

Although he could likely never tell her that. Imagine admitting that he felt ticklish when he was around her; the very idea. What would she think of that?

Have you always been this fragile in your perception of manhood?

He laughed to himself as her scolding barb to him that morning replayed in his mind. She had a way with words, he would never argue that, and she had a way of delivering them that was impeccable. She did not shy away from the less delicate words and feelings she had, unlike other ladies he knew. She actually reminded him of his aunt, and hers, in that way.

Which was also something he could never tell her, as he was not entirely certain it was a compliment.

But there was a reason why he adored his great-aunt Louise, and it was partially because she said what she liked without fear or shame. Part of that was due to her age, of course, but most of that was due to her nature. And Jane's nature was built of similar stuff.

She would never outright ask a young lady about her fortune or discuss her complexion or the sort, but she would be direct with a person and measure her politeness with honesty.

Simon loved that about her. He hated artifice in all its forms, even under the guises of modesty and affability. He found being with Jane refreshing and each moment somehow rewarding regardless of what it contained. Each conversation was entertaining. Each walk was energizing. Each glance between them was fulfilling.

Perhaps this was the madness that everyone talked about when they discussed romance. Everything was beginning to become wrapped in and tangled about his moments with Jane.

And he was feeling ticklish.

It was utterly absurd.

"When do you think I can slip away with Beatrice?"

Simon sighed a long-suffering sigh and glanced over at Ellis, who was mirroring his pose on the other side of the basket. "You are still eating, man."

Ellis gestured helplessly with the half-eaten sandwich in question. "I continue to eat because we continue to lounge about here among the food. No one is getting up," he went on in the same undertone as before.

"Because we have not been told to get up," Simon explained as though to a child. "We are not in charge here, Ellis. We do as we are told, and until our host and hostess see fit to release us from the constraints of our meal, we remain here."

Shoving the rest of the sandwich into his mouth, Ellis glowered and looked around them. "Wha's ootop ush fwom . . ."

"Georgie, chew your food first, there's a good boy," Simon interrupted, holding up a hand.

Ellis rolled his eyes, then pointedly chewed his food, swallowing. "What is to stop us from getting up and walking away ourselves?"

Simon nodded sagely, choosing to ignore the fact that he'd had no idea what his friend had been trying to say through his food. "Nothing, I suppose. Except for the direct attention of the entire party."

"What do you mean?" Ellis demanded. His eyes narrowed in speculation. "What direct attention?"

"Everyone always stares at the first person to rise," Simon told him. "Always."

His friend's brows snapped together. "Do they?"

Simon gave him a flat look. "You know they do. For heaven's sake, Ellis, it is like you've never been in a public gathering before."

"I am distracted," he said, all but slapping the blanket beneath them in his insistence. "Someday, I hope you will understand that, but I highly doubt you will ever subject yourself to such a mortal affliction."

Simon bit down softly on the inside of his cheek to keep from laughing. If his friend only knew just how distracted he was...

But that was going to remain secret just a bit longer.

"You are more than welcome to get up now, if you do not mind direct attention," Simon invited. He gestured towards the green behind them. "There are any number of walks to take on the estate, and I am sure your Miss Wyant will enjoy many of them. But if you do wish to find some time alone to show her your new skill . . ."

"You know I do," Ellis grumbled, leaning back on both elbows moodily.

Simon nodded. "Then I suggest you wait until we are invited to do something else or follow the lead of others rising."

Ellis sputtered on a long, slow breath and glanced at him in irritation. "Do you know how much of a dark cloud you are?"

He shrugged as much as he could from his position. "I am a purveyor of truth, nothing more."

"You could purvey the truth with a touch more optimism," Ellis suggested. "Give me some hope that I might be able to slip away with my beloved."

Simon jerked in surprise and stared at his friend in shock. "Your *what?*"

Ellis began laughing, dropping his head back with the humor. "Your face! Oh, devil, you look like a mother who has just heard her son utter his first curse."

"You just said . . ." Simon shook his head, words failing him. "You said . . ."

"Beloved," Ellis repeated, the word slow and drawn out

even as his expression remained filled with laughter. "Yes, I did. And she is."

"What is so funny over there?" Simon's aunt demanded, clacking her stick against the leg of the chair she sat upon. "I require some humor."

Ellis continued to chuckle and turned his attention to Louise. "I was reminding Appleby of the time we were playing on the Geigle estate, and his sister and I decided to tie him to a tree on the sheepwalk."

On cue, Louise burst out laughing, her stick thumping against the ground. "Oh yes! He was nibbled on by so many of the sheep!"

Simon shook his head, more for the benefit of those who could hear the story than for genuine irritation. "I've never seen anyone so keen to torment his friend in my life. You did not hesitate to take up Annabelle's charge, did you?"

"Well, I was in love with her at the time," Ellis scoffed, crossing his ankles. "I was ten, she was twelve, and the only girl of my acquaintance. Don't tell me you are still offended. She punched me three days later for giving her a poem."

Louise cackled at that, one hand going to the beads around her neck and slapping them gently against her skin in time with her laughter. "Oh, that darling girl! She never told me whom she'd struck, but I remember her cradling her hand and admitting she'd hit a person."

"It was me." Ellis waved his hand in acknowledgement. "And quite a good strike it was, as well. I never looked at her again until the day she married."

"You missed the best parts," Simon told him, grinning at him. "Her courting years were the most entertaining. Every time I was in London with the family, there was a line out the drawing room door. I had to wait my turn to bid her or my mother good day."

"Oh, surely you did not," Miss Wyant exclaimed, laughing and setting aside her luncheon plate.

Simon offered her a fond smile. "I assure you, I did. At least on one occasion. No one believed I was related to her, and all thought I was trying to gain some advantage in courting her."

"Where is Geigle, Mr. Appleby?" Jane asked him, sitting forward from her position on the blanket not far from him.

"Derbyshire, Miss Richards," he replied, his smile turning to the same one he'd been using with her all meal long. "A very pretty corner of the Peak District, if I do say so myself."

"Have you been to Derbyshire, Miss Richards?" Ellis inquired as he took a pair of grapes from the bowl nearest him.

Simon was of half a mind to crown him for interrupting a potential conversation between him and Jane that they could have in front of people, but also pleased to let him say what he would if it might improve her opinion of him.

That would all depend on what Ellis would say, of course, but Simon trusted Jane to be a fair enough judge of his character, just as she was on her own.

Jane smiled at Ellis as though she knew Simon's thoughts. "I have not, Mr. Ellis, though I have been to Yorkshire and the Lake District before."

"Ahh, you have missed the best district." Ellis heaved a rather dreamy sigh, given his usual temperament. "Derbyshire is rich and green, rolling hills and flowered dells, and spotted with lakes and streams . . . I have never seen any county to rival it in all my travels. And Geigle, I must say, is the loveliest estate there is within its boundaries."

Simon inclined his head in thanks. "You must take some credit for your estate, Ellis. Bradseth is delightful."

He shrugged. "I have no complaints about the place. The grounds are improving every year, and when the reconstruction of the garden is complete, it will be improved further still."

"Have you dug the eyesore up, then, Ellis?" Louise asked, leaning on her walking stick from her seat. "It is about time: the were so overgrown and out of date. Your father had no taste. I am delighted to hear you're not of the same ilk."

"I do hope, Lady Clarke, that you will come to Bradseth when it is done and give me your opinion," Ellis said with a dip of his chin. "It would be an honor to host you."

Louise nodded at him. "I would be happy to, my dear boy. Now, will you take me on a walk to the gardens so I might instruct you on finer points?" She leaned over and rapped Miss Wyant hard on the shoulder. "Come with me, dear Beatrice. I cannot possibly instruct him while he has my arm, and you are a steadying influence."

Ellis leapt to his feet with all the youth and vigor of a puppy and offered his arm to Louise as she struggled to rise from the chair. "My pleasure, Lady Clarke."

"Yes, of course, my lady," Miss Wyant answered, rising delicately and adjusting her bonnet.

Simon did not rise, though it certainly would have been polite to do so. Yet he could not let his aunt go without providing her with the usual sort of insolence she had come to expect from him. She would suspect something if he remained silent, and he could not have Louise sniffing around.

"What are you going to instruct him on, Aunt?" he asked with a laugh. "He just said his gardens are in reconstruction, and if anyone ought to be instructed, it is his gardener on what to plant where in the new layout."

Louise speared him a dark look. "The gardener's plans must be approved by Mr. Ellis, Simon, as you must know. He would do well to start considering his tastes now."

Simon would give her that, but threw an incredulous laugh into his response all the same. "And in what manner are you going to instruct him? You have not had your own hands in the dirt for this past decade."

His aunt went out of her way to thump the base of her walking stick onto his hand. "Impertinent boy, I don't know what I shall do with you. Come along, Beatrice. Mr. Ellis." She strode away from the picnic on Beatrice's arm, Ellis on her other side, and whatever further conversation went on between them was impossible for the gathering to hear.

Simon let his attention slide back to Jane, feeling rather smug that his aunt had managed to put their friends together in a perfect situation that would not attract any particular attention from any guests at all. And, subsequently, had allowed the other guests to disperse from the picnic at their leisure.

He could not tell if Jane was biting the inside of her lip or merely clamping down on them, but there was a tension to her mouth and lips that spoke of restrained laughter. And he loved to see that as much as he loved to see her full-bodied laughter.

Just as lovely, just as entertaining.

Her eyes lifted to his and, he flattered himself, appeared to wink with some intention.

The soles of both his feet caught fire, and he had to stretch them out just to be sure it was only a figment of his imagination.

Or a metaphorical burning rather than an actual one.

Or . . . whatever it was.

Others began to rise from the picnic without instruction or order, wandering away from the blankets and food to resume new activities out of doors. Lady Cavernaugh removed herself indoors and Lord Cavernaugh took Miss Dawes by the hand very politely and began walking with her towards the archery targets, accompanied by her chaperone.

Simon sat up and brushed off his hands, looking around them to see who was left in their area. There were a few ladies and only two gentlemen, but they were all engaged in active conversation, and seemed to show no intention of leaving anytime soon.

Without some direction, how would he and Jane be able to leave without arousing suspicion?

Then an idea occurred to him.

"Anyone fancy a game of pall-mall?" he asked, looking over at that group again.

Each of them looked at Appleby and shook their heads.

He'd anticipated that and looked at Jane. "Miss Richards?"

Shrugging, she rose from the blanket. "Why not? I can always improve my game." She looked to her aunt in the chair nearest her. "Aunt? Will you join us?"

Simon hid a grin as he pushed himself from the ground and adjusted his coat. "Yes, Mrs. Richards, do play with us. Three players are far better than two."

Mrs. Richards chortled a high-pitched laugh. "Oh, you are so droll, Mr. Appleby. Imagine playing pall-mall at my age."

"You could watch, Aunt," Jane pointed out. "You do enjoy healthy competition."

"Yes, but I have been out of doors quite enough for one day." She smiled up at Jane with real affection and fondness. "I shall go indoors and read before having my rest. I am quite well, dear, do not fret. I have never enjoyed too much sunshine at once. And you know how vexed I become when I have not had afternoon rest."

Jane nodded, returning her smile. "Yes, Aunt. Then you will not mind if Mr. Appleby and I go to begin our game?"

Mrs. Richards shook her head. "No, dear. Play well and do not draw blood in your determination to win."

"Is that a risk?" Simon asked, looking between the two women. "I see I am duly warned." He gestured the way to the pall-mall set. "Miss Richards, please."

With a very small smile, Jane walked past him in that direction, her pace serene and dignified, in complete contrast to the competitive spirit her aunt had just described.

"Pall-mall?" she complained when Simon was near enough to hear her. "Really?"

He chuckled easily. "That group I asked had already played pall-mall this morning, so I knew they would not wish to play again unless they were passionate admirers of the game."

Jane snickered and slid her gaze to him. "Clever man."

He inclined his head in thanks. "And it was a stroke of genius for you to ask your aunt if she wished to play."

"Thank you, I thought so." Jane hummed, rather pleased with herself. "I knew she would refuse, though she has surprised me before, and playing with her would not be as dreadful as an entire group, so whatever her answer, it would be worth it."

"I should let you know," Simon murmured as he stepped just a touch closer to her side, "that I have no intention of playing pall-mall."

Jane gasped very softly and looked at him. "What? Then why would you—?"

"Oh dear, Miss Richards," Simon said in a louder voice as they reached the set. "There appear to be missing balls. Did you happen to see where the others were playing this morning? We must ensure the entire set is in place for the Cavernaughs."

Rolling her eyes and biting back giggles, Jane nodded once. "I believe the wickets are this way, Mr. Appleby. Come, let us go and find them."

"Now you understand," he said in a low voice, guiding her away from the completely full set of pall-mall balls and mallets.

"As I said," she replied with a deep sigh, "you are a clever man."

Simon clapped a hand to his heart and bowed. "Thank you, Miss Richards."

"Call me Jane," she whispered, taking his hand and inter-twining their fingers. "I don't want any formality with you."

Unable to find teasing or even words at his disposal, Simon drew her hand to his mouth and kissed it twice, praying the fervency would be felt, as he could not utter it.

They walked in silence for a while, content to simply be without others around, and eventually happened upon a walking path through trees and brush. It was not a wide path of dirt, but it did allow them to be side by side, which was all that really mattered.

"Tell me more about Geigle," Jane said as they reached a bend in the path, tugging her bonnet off and hanging it from her elbow by its ribbons. "It sounds lovely."

"Do you even like the country, Jane?" Simon asked instead of answering directly. "All I hear and see of you is London."

She leaned into him, laying her head on his upper arm, which stole the very breath from his lungs. "I do. Why do you think I go to so many house parties? I could refuse any one of them, if I wanted to. But the country is so delightful, so refreshing. One can breathe and relax. When I am in Society and in London, I always feel this pressure to be a personage rather than a person. I am not a woman with opinions or a mind, but a female who must stand somewhere and look pretty and smile a great deal. I may be amusing and amiable, but nothing more."

"That is a great shame," Simon replied. "You are capable of so much more than that. Society brings out nothing good in me, but it quite literally stifles you. I wonder that you enjoy it as much as you do with that in mind."

"Well, there is entertainment in London that is not always found in the country." Jane sighed and placed her other hand on his arm. "But if I could always take walks like this, I would never need London again."

Simon looked above him at the tips of the trees and to the heavens beyond, wondering if it was possible for a heart to take wing and reach for those same heights. Logically, he knew it was not, but at this moment, he was utterly convinced that was where the organ was headed. That his earthly form would not be able to contain the feelings and sensations Jane stirred in him, and he would somehow end and begin anew at the same time one of these days.

"There are plenty of paths at Geigle, love," Simon told her, turning his head to kiss her hair. "Some better marked than others, but all perfect for wandering."

"And when would I have the chance to wander paths at your country home, Simon?" Jane asked him in a small voice, her fingers tracing an absent pattern on his upper arm.

Ah, he'd forgotten that she was not . . . that he was not . . . that they . . .

There was no courtship. No relationship. No understanding.

Why would she even be at Geigle?

Did he dare pose the question? Or one of the questions, at any rate. There seemed to be so many at the moment, and none of them easy.

"Geigle is on the very top of a small hill," Simon told her in a soft, low tone, keeping his mouth near her hair. "Just enough of a rise to provide the upper rooms with a perfect view of the surrounding areas. Some of the trees in the vicinity are large enough to obscure a few of the windows. There is a pond that can be seen from the south wing, a stream from the east wing, and a lake in the distance from the west. The lake does not belong solely to Geigle—it borders two other estates—but we have an agreeable arrangement that allows all three estates to share in its wealth equally."

Jane turned into him further still, allowing his lips to brush her brow as they walked slowly.

Encouraged, Simon went on. "Hills roll out across the estate and beyond, almost like waves upon a stunning green sea. And in the late summer or early autumn, when the farms are ready for harvest, the green is speckled with blocks of yellow and gold, and the wind ripples across their surfaces. It is like a dance of nature itself."

"For all your stoicism, Simon, you are a poet." Jane looked up ahead and suddenly pulled away from him, though her hand was still secure in his. "Look at that tree!"

He followed her gaze and smiled easily at the sight of an old tree with a rather thick portion of trunk that grew out at such an angle, and low enough to the ground, that it might have been a bench. It was long enough to allow at least three people to sit upon it, and certainly sturdy enough to support them as well. The whole thing was nearly parallel with the ground, and was certainly one of the more unusual branches of trees he had ever seen.

And oddly romantic.

He strode forward, pulling Jane gently along behind him.

"What are you doing?" she asked with a laugh. "What's the hurry?"

"No hurry," Simon quipped. "Just an idea." They reached the branch and he turned, grinning at her. "Ready?"

She laughed, searching his eyes. "Ready? For what?"

He put his hands at her waist and, without warning, hoisted her up to sit on the branch. Her hands flew to his shoulders in surprise, and she squealed with the motion, but once she was settled on the branch, she began to laugh.

And laugh and laugh and laugh . . .

Simon grinned up at her, stepping close. "How is the view from up there, Jane?"

"Positively delightful, thank you." She put a hand to her throat as she laughed again. "How did you know I imagined sitting here?"

He shrugged easily, covering the hand that still sat upon his shoulder. "What else would you imagine from this branch? It was the second thought that occurred to me when I saw it."

"What was the first?" she asked, tilting her head to one side.

Simon stepped closer still, so that her knees touched his chest, and his smile grew at the stutter in his heart at the sensation. "That I wanted a branch like this at Geigle so I might sit there and watch the sunset over the hills and green. With you."

Jane's hand moved from his shoulder to his cheek, the

contact stirring even with the fabric of gloves between them. Her brilliant eyes of indescribable color searched his, her lips full and smiling, and her thumb slowly brushed across his cheek.

"Simon," she whispered, quite possibly sealing his heart to hers in that very moment.

He could not respond, not even with her name, and barely with a breath. He was captivated, utterly so, and had no desire to ever leave this moment or this spot.

As if she needed to end Simon's life at that precise moment, Jane leaned down and pressed just the tips of her fingers against his jaw, leaning closer until her mouth was a hairsbreadth from his.

He needed no encouragement and wanted nothing more.

With the smallest tilting upwards of his face, his lips connected with hers, slowly and softly, without hesitation, but with every cautious and careful attention he might have wished to bestow on such a woman. Jane cradled his face with both hands now, sweetly fusing her lips against his with an untutored fervor and natural passion that made his knees tremble beneath him.

Simon reached for her, finding the base of her neck with eager, aching fingers, and held her close. As close as he dared and as tenderly as he had ever dreamed. Again and again, their mouths met, without haste or frenzy, fueled by pure feeling and raw need. The tension that had been building all day, and in the days before, finally crested on this delicious, divine wave, carrying them farther and farther away from land and into a glorious unknown.

Jane broke off gently, pressing her brow to his as she shuddered and shook, her breathing unsteady. "Simon . . ."

"Shh," he murmured, stroking the back of her neck with gentle fingers and kissing her brow. "You don't have to say anything."

"I feel . . ." She exhaled and nuzzled against him. "I feel ticklish. All over. What do you do to me?"

Simon laughed and cradled her head against his shoulder, pressing his lips to her ear. "No more than you do to me, love. Why should only one of us feel like this?"

"So this is all about fairness?" She laughed into him, leaning up and touching his face again. "Equals in all things, even this?"

"Seems appropriate, really." He made a playful face and moved his hand to her arm, rubbing gently as he looked into the distance.

What he saw made him chuckle.

"I think this branch is even more fortunately situated than we imagined," he said to Jane. "Look just over there."

She turned, bracing herself on him, then laughed aloud. "She is wearing a flower crown!"

Simon nodded, unable to keep from smiling. "She is, indeed. And my aunt is nowhere in sight."

"I don't care about that," Jane murmured, her fingers wandering from his shoulder into his hair, nearly making him purr like some strange overgrown cat. "They're perfectly fine. Just talking and smiling and sitting rather close."

"Like someone else we know," he mused.

Jane's attention returned to him, her smile soft. "Is that what we're doing?"

Simon let his fingers move to hers, gently tugging the glove from her hand. "Talking," he said as he raised her bare hand to his mouth. "Smiling." He kissed the base of her thumb. "And sitting rather close." He turned her hand and kissed her palm with the utmost gentleness.

He heard Jane sigh as though the wind had stolen it from her. "Why, so we are. So we are."

CHAPTER SEVENTEEN

How, exactly, was a body supposed to be capable of dancing when all the bones had been removed from their person?

That was the primary question Jane was struggling against now, and unlike most questions she had, she could not pose it to her aunt.

Not if she wanted to actually see the evening and survive the night.

What would Anne-Marie say if she found out? How would she react? What would she do?

Jane stared at herself in the looking glass as the back of her ball gown was done up, barely seeing herself in the reflection. She looked the same, as far as she could tell. Looked as healthy and as proper, as refined and as open, and yet . . .

And yet . . .

Her cheeks bore some new color that had not been there before. Her hair seemed a trifle more unkempt than it usually did. Her eyes held a new light amidst their color. Her lips were brighter and fuller, even if her smile was slower.

And all she had done was kiss Simon.

A few times.

It wasn't enough to ruin her, since they had not been witnessed, and where all decorum was considered, it was fairly innocent.

However not innocent it felt.

She felt . . . branded, in a way. Raw and singed from head to foot, every brush of wind or fabric heightened to an almost painful degree. Alight and conspicuous in every space she entered.

But, oh, how warm and safe she felt at the same time! Protected and shielded as though she had been encased in armor that radiated the warmth of the sun. Nothing could touch her and nothing could injure her. She was impervious now, and light as a feather. She floated when she walked and could dance on a breeze.

Everything was new and everything was bright.

But somehow, she could not smile.

She had not smiled since she'd left Simon.

Was it because she had left him that her smiles had seemed to vanish? Or was it the time to reflect upon her day that had rid her of them? Could she have regrets about what had transpired? Did she fear the future now that she also felt vulnerable? Now that she had opened her heart, was there a chance it would never close again?

Would she want to close it?

Had it been closed before?

Gads, it was maddening. She had never had to examine her heart to such a degree, and she simply failed to understand it now that she tried to.

"Are you displeased with the green silk, miss?" her maid asked as she shook out the ruffled skirts. "It suits your coloring marvelously, but if you do not approve . . ."

Jane shook herself and looked at her reflection more closely. "No . . . no, it is lovely. I like it very much, thank you."

Her maid smiled as though she had selected the gown personally. "Of course, miss. The rosettes offset the ruffles so well, and the ruched bowing on the bust does enhance your figure so."

Fire raced into Jane's cheeks. "Steady on."

"And the parting of the outer skirts from the waistline will billow beautifully when you dance," the maid went on, ignoring her. "With the floral edging, you will look like a woodland nymph."

"Well, that would be something," Jane muttered, letting her eyes move to her hair. She turned her head to examine the back of it as much as possible. "The plaiting is exquisite. I can barely feel the pins. And the gold is a lovely touch."

"Again, thank you, miss." Rising, the maid moved to the dressing table and picked up a necklace and earrings. "Here are some jewels your aunt sent over to match. Gold with diamond, and the set is quite delicate. It will complement all perfectly."

Jane took the earrings and fixed them to her ears, loving the dangling aspect of them, and finding a smile possible as the maid latched the necklace for her, the design a perfect match to that of the earrings. It felt cool against the skin of her throat and chest and rested perfectly upon her.

She felt rather lovely as she looked at herself now. She felt . . . alive.

Wonderfully and beautifully alive.

"Janie? Janie, are you ready?" Beatrice called from the other side of the door, knocking quickly.

"Yes," she replied, matching her tone and nodding at the maid to let her in.

Beatrice strode in, wreathed in bright blue, her gloves so white and pristine that they might have glowed in candlelight. She was utterly stunning, and perfectly arrayed for the evening ahead. As though a bit of the daytime sky had been snatched and brought down to earth to be wreathed about her very form.

She, unfortunately, did not seem to notice her beauty as

she moved directly to Jane, her eyes wide with panic. "Janie, help."

Jane smiled at her and took her by the arms. "Help with what, Bea? You look absolutely beautiful."

Beatrice shook her head, tossing the dark ringlets and dangling pearl earrings she wore. "I'm not here about that. I think . . . I think George might propose."

"George?" Jane repeated, searching her friend's face. "George . . . oh! Mr. Ellis?"

Beatrice nodded hastily. "We . . . we were out alone today. Lady Clarke went back to the house after five minutes in the garden, so we were unaccompanied and . . . He made me a crown of flowers, Janie. And we talked and talked . . . and he said he's never felt this way about anyone, and he did not say love, but I think . . . I think it is, Janie. And I'm terrified."

"Why?" She rubbed Beatrice's arms gently. "Do you love him?"

"Yes," Beatrice admitted with a catch to her voice. "Yes, I do."

Jane laughed and hugged her friend. "Then what is there to fear?" She pulled back and smiled as broadly as she dared. "Is this not what you want?"

"It is. And that is what I am most afraid of." Beatrice inhaled sharply and gripped Jane's forearms. "I have never wanted anything so fiercely in my entire life, and I am afraid that I shall die if I do not get it."

"Now, now," Jane scolded playfully, "you must not resort to dramatics. Mr. Ellis is clearly taken with you, and if you are not engaged by the end of the house party, I shall demand he rectify the situation and propose within three days."

Beatrice giggled and covered her face, squealing softly, making Jane laugh more. Then she stepped back and spun around in delight. "Come on, then, Janie! Get your gloves and let us go down!"

She sighed as though reluctant and reached for her cream

gloves. "All right, if we must. But I will not dance more than twice."

"You will so!" Beatrice insisted, taking her arm and all but pulling her from the room. "You will dance, and you will laugh, and you will be merry. And if I have any power over George, you will have a minimum of one dance with him, if not two."

"Do not force the poor man, Bea!" Jane pulled on her gloves as they moved towards the stairs. "I will feel like a spinsterly older sister dragged out against her will."

Beatrice did not seem to hear her as they made their way down. The other guests were milling about and beginning to enter the ballroom as well, so it was easy enough to join the flock of them without much fuss.

The ballroom was aglow with candles as far as the eye could see, the chandeliers brilliantly showered the entire room with additional light. The music had already begun and gave the space an energy that could have matched that of the assembly rooms, though the guests within were so finely dressed on this occasion, it could not have been more different. And despite the energy of the music, the expressions of the guests were all rather sedate.

What a bore.

Jane kept her smile fixed upon her face, but dreaded what the night would bring. If she could not be free of the constraints of this group, would she be able to enjoy her time with Simon? Would her London facade return to her, all politeness and affability? Or would her mind and heart remain her own regardless of her company?

And what of Simon? Would he be more aloof than usual because of the stiffness of those around them? Would they match their surroundings, or would they be themselves in spite of it?

With a full day of being so open with one another, were they even capable of being anything else?

How long would her secrets remain secrets? How long did they need to be?

With Beatrice being so close to her goal, the same goal that Jane wished for her, what occasion would she and Simon have to see each other, if the secrets remained?

"You may need to adjust the company you keep, Miss Richards. People will begin to think that you are taking after them."

Jane exhaled a delighted sigh and turned to face Simon as well as Mr. Ellis, to her surprise. "Are you telling me that I need to smile more, Mr. Appleby?"

Simon snorted, shaking his head. "No, I am not, Miss Richards. I find the very suggestion from any person to be unnecessary, inconsiderate, and patronizing. I am simply saying that, unfortunately, I may be blamed for the lack of your smile, as we did play pall-mall together today."

"That is true," Jane replied, though it very much was not true, and no such game had ever taken place. "But I do not feel like smiling at this moment. Can you not tell from the expressions all the guests wear?"

The gentlemen looked around, and Ellis, for one, began to laugh. "You are quite right, Miss Richards. A more unpleasant gathering, I have never yet seen. I think they may be waiting for someone to begin the dancing."

"You've always wanted to be an instigator, Ellis," Simon said lightly. "And I see that Miss Wyant is looking very pretty by the statue, and also very unaccompanied."

Ellis was gone with the final syllable, making both Simon and Jane laugh unintentionally. He moved to stand beside Jane, keeping enough space between them for sanity and clarity. "It would seem he has made up his mind about something."

Jane would have rapped his hand, had the man been standing closer. "Wretch. You knew he would react like that."

"I knew it was not without possibility," Simon hedged,

making a face of consideration, "but I certainly could not have anticipated such haste. But see, he is starting the dancing, which should lighten the mood considerably. And Miss Wyant does not seem upset with being so directly asked for a dance this early in the evening."

"No, I think she would dance with him all night, if she could." Jane smiled and nodded at her friend when their eyes met. "Have you spoken with him about the day he's had?"

Simon took a glass of punch from a passing footman and sipped before answering. "I have not spoken at all, but he has done a great deal of speaking in my company, if that helps. While the ladies were having their afternoon tea and respite, he and I played a game of billiards. At least, I think it was billiards. We did not keep score, and he took his turn more often than he ought to have done, but the principles were that of billiards."

Jane snorted a soft laugh and snapped open her fan to hide her amusement. "And what did he have to say?"

"Much," Simon grunted. "He loves her. Can't tell her, since it's not been long enough for him to be certain of her feelings."

"I hope you told him that was nonsense," she murmured.

Simon glanced in her direction. "What part of my not speaking did you miss earlier?"

Jane lifted her eyes heavenward and tried not to give any indication she was doing so. "Save me from the stupidity of men."

"What was that?" he asked, leaning closer, his tone so innocent that he could not have heard her.

She cleared her throat. "The ceiling depicts the clouds of heaven, look."

He glanced up, emitting an unimpressed sound. "I've seen better. At any rate . . ." He returned his attention to the dancing. "He plans to propose eventually, if that is what you are seeking."

"Beatrice is hoping for that," Jane told him with a smile.

"Quite desperately. She is madly in love, though she is not going to say such a thing without encouragement. Or his saying so first, I think."

"Hmm," Simon hummed slowly, watching the motions of the dance carefully. "How do we encourage them to say what they feel when they are both apparently reluctant to be the first to say it?"

That was indeed the question.

How did Jane say what she wanted to say when she wasn't entirely certain what it was that she wanted to say? Or if she actually wanted to say it?

Why did such confusion have to come from what was considered to be a very natural and human emotion?

"Ellis did say," Simon continued, unaware of her internal chaos, "that the flower crown went over splendidly. Miss Wyant was perfectly charmed and delighted by it. The gift led to a discussion about childhood, it seems, and was rewarding. For Ellis, at least."

"I don't know how Beatrice felt about any of it," Jane admitted. "Our conversation was very short and limited. But if her countenance was anything to go by, I think you can count it a success. And look at her now, Simon. She adores him."

He said nothing, and Jane could only assume he was watching Ellis and Beatrice dance together, as she was. They looked utterly delighted to merely exist in the same space, their smiles wide and bright and just for each other. Even if they switched partners as part of the dance, they looked for the other and they smiled. It was all smiles and adoring looks, and people were beginning to notice.

Jane frowned as she noted that. Several people were beginning to notice, whispering to each other behind hands and fans.

"Simon . . ." she murmured, looking around.

"I see it," he replied tersely. "It is to be expected, given their marked attention and notable affection. And as Cavernaugh and Miss Dawes are not about to show them up . . ." He snorted once, indicating the couple in question standing side by side against a wall. "The mood of this ball in general does not help much either."

Jane muttered incoherently, glaring at as many of the guests as she could, though none of them were looking at her. "It is as though none of them has ever enjoyed a ball in their life. Miss Beacom in the dance there is lively and enjoying herself, but as for much else . . ."

"We are going to have to intervene somehow, Jane," Simon told her. "Some of these people enjoyed the assembly ball in spite of themselves, and without their enjoyment, there can be little hope for our friends not to become the topic of speculation and gossip."

"That will destroy Beatrice, Simon," Jane hissed. "She might even shy away from Ellis if she thinks people are talking about them. She is far more sensitive than she appears, and if she overthinks all of this while she is sensitive, she could do something she may regret."

Simon looked around quickly, then moved to stand in front of Jane, facing her. He took her hand, hiding it between them, and kissed her wrist, though it was covered by her glove. "Don't worry," he murmured, rubbing her hand gently. "We'll fix this." He shook his head and held her hand to his lips for a long moment. "I had hoped to spend the entire evening with you, love. You look exquisite and I cannot breathe for the sight of you."

"I feel on fire," Jane whispered, letting her fingers stroke against his chin. "So on fire. But we have to . . ."

He nodded, lowering her hand. "We do. If we can stop the whispers and glances, we might be able to have a few moments just for ourselves. But if not, know that I want them more than I can say."

Jane smiled and squeezed the hand he still held. "So do I. Now go and do something noble and interfering."

Simon released her hand and stepped back several paces, giving her a very firm nod of the head. "Noble and interfering. Louise will be so proud."

"Of that I have no doubt." Jane shooed him away and began to walk about the room, blatantly ignoring him for the time being. It would not be easy to do so, as she was wild to see what he was planning on doing, but she would need to do some interfering herself if she wanted to help Beatrice and Mr. Ellis.

There would be much talking about them when their engagement was official and the house party was over, but there was no need to start the conversation before the commitment had been made, and before their feelings were declared.

The dance ended and the guests applauded for the dancers and musicians. Jane applauded as well and listened for the next song, hoping she could do something with whatever it was.

A jaunty country tune started, and Jane grinned and turned to the nearest group. "Who will form a square with me? Miss Cole? Mr. Fitch?"

To her relief, a few of the group came with her and they lined up in squares, along with other couples and groups ahead of and around them. Jane skipped forward to join hands with Mr. Fitch and rotated with him around Miss Cole and Mr. Palmer, their steps lively and light. They then joined hands as a set and circled to the right, then to the left, before forming into lines with other gentlemen and ladies.

Jane glanced down the line of couples as the ladies skipped and turned alone, and noted Simon dancing with Miss Dawes several couples off.

He was beaming as though nothing pleased him more, and Miss Dawes was laughing merrily, which seemed quite unlike her.

When it came time for the ladies to turn again, Jane cast her attention towards the wall where Miss Dawes had evidently been plucked from and saw Lord Cavernaugh watching, his expression surprisingly bereft and confused.

Jane looked up towards Simon as the gentlemen moved in their particular motions, watching as he danced with enthusiasm and energy, looking absolutely nothing like himself. It was both hilarious and envy-inducing, if she were to be perfectly honest with herself. She wanted nothing more than to dance with Simon herself, and yet Miss Dawes was having the pleasure. And enjoying a splendid time.

The lead couple progressed by the line off them. It turned out to be Beatrice giggling and bright on the arm of Mr. Gideon, less lively on a typical occasion, but laughing well enough at the moment. They were followed by Mr. Ellis and Miss Beacom, looking equally delighted to be dancing and quite the striking couple.

That alone would get people speculating.

Two more couples, and then there was Simon and Miss Dawes, making Jane stiffen.

As though he knew exactly where her thoughts and feelings lay, Simon looked directly at her and winked, of all things.

An arrow seemed to strike directly into the pit of her stomach with that wink, and it ignited something of a glow that spread through the rest of her. However boneless she had felt before, she could certainly feel every single one of them now.

There was nothing to do but sigh and attempt to remember what to do when it was her turn to move to the center and take Mr. Fitch's hands before promenading with him after the other couples.

The entire group was soon laughing and near delirious with enthusiasm, some even whooping and whistling in their enjoyment of the lively dance. An observer might never know that the ball was not taking place at the assembly rooms at Dewbury or in any other village, based solely on this dance. If one ignored the finery of the ladies and the refinement of the room, of course.

And this was precisely what they had needed.

Simon knew that. And now Beatrice and Mr. Ellis could do as they pleased, for the most part, and not shock anyone.

Of course, Jane was not so naive as to believe that one country dance was enough to solve all of their problems, but it had certainly changed the mood of the evening so far.

When it was finally over, she and the others applauded and gasped for breath and laughed, some mixture of all three rippling around them.

Mr. Ellis came towards Jane then, his smile hesitant. "Miss Richards? I wonder if I might tempt you for a dance."

Jane returned his smile rather fondly. "I would be delighted, Mr. Ellis, if you will not mind a brief delay."

"Oh?" His brow creased very faintly. "How so?"

"That last dance rather tired me out," Jane admitted, laughing and putting a hand to her chest. "I have not been that enthusiastic for that long in such an age, I am quite out of practice. Will you take me to get a glass of lemonade first? I think this dance will be short, and then we might catch the next one."

Mr. Ellis nodded and offered his arm, his smile growing. "Thank goodness you suggested that, Miss Richards. I am exhausted, but Appleby told me to keep dancing as long as I could bear to, though I have no idea why. But I am not nearly so young as I used to be, and the energetic dancing really ought to be left for the young."

Jane took the liberty of whacking Mr. Ellis's arm with her fan. "Oh, for shame, Mr. Ellis, you are not decrepit! If you say such a thing again, I will be forced to get you a chair and set you beside my aunt."

He chuckled at that. "I rather like your aunt, Miss Richards, and would be happy for the company. Speaking of, do you think she would dance with me?"

"Are you in earnest?" Jane leaned back to get a better look at him. "I do not know you well enough to tell when you jest."

"I am not wholly in jest," he said with a wrinkle of his nose. "If she is able to dance, I would be happy to do so. I'd much prefer partners that are good company to partners that are young and pretty."

Jane looked over to the wall along which most of the companions and elderly ladies sat, smiling as she caught sight of her aunt, who blew her a kiss. "I think, if a quadrille arises before too much time has passed, she would love it. She grows fatigued after supper, so she may refuse you then."

"Duly noted," Mr. Ellis told her as they arrived at the table. He poured a glass of lemonade for her, then took one for himself. "And if I can persuade Appleby, I'll see if he might dance with Louise."

"Lady Clarke?" Jane giggled at the idea before drinking deeply of her glass. "Would she even bother? She seems much more determined to be frail than my aunt."

Mr. Ellis grinned. "Determined to be frail is an excellent way of putting it. She is capable of more than she lets on, so it entirely depends on her mood." He sipped his lemonade and watched the dancing a moment. "I will be frank, Miss Richards. I would dance every dance with Miss Wyant if I did not think it would scandalize everyone."

"I think I got that general idea, sir," Jane admitted. "What's more, I believe she would do the same."

He looked at her closely, seeming to follow the motion of her glass as she drank from it again. "Do you really?"

Jane smiled and put a hand on his arm. "Mr. Ellis, Beatrice is exactly as you find her. She has little guile and no artifice. She has frank opinions and an open manner, but she is also incapable of hiding how she truly feels. I can safely say, without betraying any confidences, that she would dance every dance with you. Anything less would simply not do, if it would not tempt scandal."

Mr. Ellis grinned so broadly, she had to blink at the sight of it. "You have illuminated my entire evening into one of incandescence, Miss Richards. I am in your debt."

Raising a brow, Jane downed the rest of her lemonade and set the glass aside. "Let us leave incandescent things for Beatrice, shall we? She bears them so much better than I do. But if I can give you hope, that will be enough for me."

"Hope has never been so bright, Miss Richards." He finished his drink and set it on the table as well. "I am feeling quite refreshed. Shall we join in this dance before it ends? I promise to dance with you again later to make up for the shortness."

"Oh, why not?" Jane laughed and put her hand in his, letting him rush her to the floor to take up positions in the cotillion.

Mr. Ellis was an excellent dance partner, that was for certain. But this time, he was not dancing with Jane in order to dance with Beatrice in truth, as he had been at the assembly rooms. He had a way of engaging his companion during the dance in a manner that singled her out rather pleasantly. There were obviously others dancing among them, and occasionally with them, for a few motions, but she never felt as though they were truly there.

She'd never met anyone who danced like that before, and it was rather revealing about the man.

It was no wonder Beatrice felt so captivated by him; his attention was perfectly focused when it was on a person, and genuine intention was bestowed therein.

Beatrice would never want for affection when she was married to him, Jane felt she could safely say that.

Once their dance was completed, she took the opportunity to get some air on the terrace, the cool breeze of evening a perfect delight after expending so much energy. The music of a waltz struck up, and Jane smiled at hearing it. Waltzes were generally her favorite, but she would not be sorry for a respite this time. Without Taft to act a part along with her in a waltz, it became an experience in disappointment and longing.

She'd always thought of a waltz as a conversation between a couple, and one could feel and learn so much about the other while engaging in it. Which was probably why it had taken so long for the dance to be considered acceptable in England. It was entirely too familiar for the sort of reserve and propriety that English Society so prided themselves on.

She had always wanted to have that sort of familiar conversation through dance alone, and she had never as yet found it. The waltz she sought was a dream yet to be realized.

Sighing into the night air, Jane turned and watched what she could see of the dancing from the terrace. It was a livelier waltz than usual, which made her less forlorn about the prospect, even in passing, and she found herself laughing a little when she caught sight of Simon dancing with Lady Cavernaugh herself.

That would be an interesting story later.

A footman suddenly came out onto the terrace, bowing before her. "Forgive me, Miss Richards," he said simply. "I was asked to give you this if you were without a partner during the waltz."

He held out a small silver platter, upon which sat a flower and a note.

Frowning and curious, Jane picked up the note first.

With you.

The hand was Simon's, and it made her throat tighten as though she would cry. Sniffling, she picked up the flower, laughing as soon as she did so.

The tiny white flower had been fashioned into a ring.

As carefully as she could, she slid the delicate bloom onto her finger and folded the note, tucking it into her gown. She nodded at the footman and reentered the ballroom, her eyes seeking out one man and one man only.

He was watching her, even as he danced, his smile shifting

just enough to tell her that it was no longer for the benefit of onlookers, but for her alone.

In response, Jane held up her gloved hand and waggled her fingers, displaying the flower for his view.

His smile spread and he inclined his head, slowly returning his focus to his partner.

Jane, on the other hand, watched him dance the entire time.

CHAPTER EIGHTEEN

There had been no note that morning, and Simon paced his room at the selfsame hour they had met thus far, wondering why there was not a note waiting for him. Or one being delivered at this moment. Or one he was writing at this moment.

Why was he not writing a note to Jane at the moment?

He turned on his heel, strode to the desk in the corner of the room, and pulled a sheet of paper onto the surface, dipping a pen into the ink and holding the nib to the page.

And nothing else happened.

He waited for the words to come to mind, but all he could think were the words, *Dear Jane.*

Not precisely an eloquent start.

What did he need to say to her?

He blinked as a strange breeze of mental nothingness wafted over the contents of his head, overturning nothing and producing nothing.

Nothing.

He had nothing to say to Jane. He did not need to say anything to Jane. There was nothing *to* say to Jane, really.

Which meant he could say anything he wanted.

That did not help.

He wanted to tell her that he had missed her during the night, which was ridiculous, as they had never been together during the night. He wanted to tell her that he wished they could go for an early morning walk, which was nonsense, as it was far too cold at this time of day in this part of the country-side. He wanted to talk to her, which seemed an odd thing to put into a note, as she might not even be awake, and no one wanted to talk first thing in the morning. And he clearly had nothing to talk about.

He wanted to see her. That was all. He wanted to see her face before she was entirely awake. He wanted to see if her hair had maintained its plait as she'd slept or if it would be more rumpled. He wanted to see her long, slender fingers as they toyed with the stems of flowers, as she had done the morning before. He wanted to watch the morning light as it entered her eyes and brightened their richness.

How did he send a note so early in the morning simply asking to see her?

Granted, he had sent her a note during the ball that had only said, *With you*, which meant nothing out of context, but he had hoped she would take it to mean he wished he were dancing with her.

It had been a stroke of strange impulse.

He'd made the flower ring after their extraordinary kisses at the tree, after she had returned to the castle. And he had intended to send it during the ball in the hopes that it would send her rushing to his side so they might share an exquisite dance that neither would forget.

Alas for changing plans and acting for the benefit of others.

Still, she had worn it, and taken the time to show him, in spite of the more conspicuous nature of it, and he had felt, even as he had waltzed with Lady Cavernaugh, that they had shared a moment of connection that was significant.

But not sharing a meaningful moment with her other than their parting at the beginning of the dance . . .

That had caused him physical pain in a very non-physical way.

He still did not quite understand that particular sensation, but it was the only way to describe it.

And the fact that he now had nothing to say to Jane other than a rambling jumble of wanting to see her and talk to her and be with her without any set reason or aim made him feel practically unhinged.

Simon threw his pen down and huffed, turning away and beginning to pace again.

There was no plan for the day that he was aware of, and they had not had time the evening before to discuss anything of the sort. They'd managed to dance together once, but it had been a reel, so not exactly the best opportunity to converse.

He had hoped to secure her for the supper set, but it had been necessary for him to ask Beatrice Wyant instead so he could orchestrate her sitting across from Ellis.

As far as their friends were concerned, the night had been an unrivaled success. They had stopped the gossip, for the most part, and lightened the mood of the evening, which allowed Ellis and Miss Wyant to talk and dance as they wished. Simon had danced more in that ballroom than he had done in the last three balls combined and was feeling the soreness in his feet and legs at the moment, but he would be satisfied if Ellis and Miss Wyant could hold their heads up high during the activities today.

He'd even danced with Louise last night for a quick quadrille, and she had been so delighted by the offer that he was certain she would be quite sentimental around him for a time. If not outright affectionate.

She would also likely sleep until noon, as she had surprised him by not retiring early.

That brought Simon up short in his pacing.

It had been an extraordinarily late night filled with dancing and energy. Why in the world would Jane intentionally be awake so early after a night such as that? All of the ladies would likely sleep later than usual, and most of the gentlemen as well.

So it was entirely possible that there was nothing to do at this moment, even if Jane was awake.

Perhaps that was why there was no note.

And why it would not help if he sent a note.

He laughed to himself and at himself. This was exactly the sort of madness he mocked when it came to love and romance, and here he was . . .

In love. And trying to understand romance.

Simon sank onto the mattress behind him, eyes going wide as he replayed the statement in his mind.

In love and trying to understand romance.

He was in love. He was in the midst of a romance.

Of course he was. Why else would he be so confounded by what he was feeling? Why else were his thoughts lost on him? Why else would his entire nature and manner be so completely changed and yet feel as though he were entirely himself?

He was not mad or nonsensical. He was simply in love, and struggling to understand the adjustment of the thing.

Suddenly breathless, and still laughing, he rested his hands on his knees and dropped his head. What did he even do with this realization? How was it even possible to be in love with a woman he had barely known a number of days? What was it that Miss Austen had said—time alone does not determine intimacy? He'd mocked that, too. While for some people, it could take at least five years to be certain of themselves, no one in the world could fall in love within five days.

It was simply not possible.

Yet he did love Jane. He craved Jane. All that was true.

But it did not mean that it would last beyond this house party.

He could, quite simply, be deluded.

Still, he was willing to take advantage of what time he did have here, if for no other reason than to continue to enjoy the moments he had with her. It might allow him to determine, some weeks hence, if a future with Jane was logical.

He already knew it was wanted.

But wanting was not enough. Not in this. He refused to trap both of them for life by indulging in a potentially temporary wanting,

They deserved better than that.

Nodding, Simon pushed himself from the bed and moved to get his coat, great coat, and cravat, loosely tying the thing about his throat before leaving the room. If he was going to continue to torment himself with thoughts of Jane in his room, he would find something else to do to occupy his time and his thoughts.

He'd barely reached the bottom of the stairs when he crossed paths with the host himself, dressed rather simply in country clothes.

"Appleby," Cavernaugh said in some surprise. "You're up early."

Simon forced a tight smile. "Cavernaugh. You as well."

Cavernaugh shrugged his narrow shoulders. "I don't sleep late. I'm off to do some fishing in the lake before the sun gets too high. Would you like to join me?"

On a typical morning, Simon would have thought of any excuse to avoid spending time with the man, especially without others to act as buffer. But something about the informal appearance of the man gave him pause.

"I promise, I am not going to talk much," Cavernaugh added with a self-deprecating smile. "The fish can't abide early conversation."

Simon chuckled in spite of himself and nodded. "I'd be happy to join you, Cavernaugh. If you can spare the rods and tackle."

He nodded once. "I can. Come with me; we'll get us both sorted."

Simon followed the lanky man out to the gamekeeper's station, and once furnished with the necessary equipment, they continued out to the lake, exactly where he had taken a swim the day before.

True to his word, Cavernaugh said nothing as they fished, which suited Simon just as well. He had much to think about, and there was something rather simple about the act of fishing. He did not have to concentrate on his actions nor on maintaining some sort of conversation with his companions. He could let his thoughts wander freely and openly as he went through the motions of fishing.

Not surprisingly, his thoughts centered around Jane. But not necessarily on her person. He seemed to be reviewing each and every moment they had spent in each other's company as well as those where he could observe her. There was no order to these memories, just a randomly circulating arrangement of what his mind had captured. It was an extraordinary collage of moments, each making him want to smile or laugh in varying degrees, taking himself by surprise with the intensity of his reactions.

There was some deep truth to the feelings these memories inspired. He could not deny that after hours of standing on this shore and finding no change or alteration to those thoughts and feelings. All was the same.

He was simply more awake to appreciate the matter.

"Thank you," Cavernaugh said unexpectedly as they walked back to the castle when they had finished, "for dancing with Miss Dawes last night."

Simon looked at the man in surprise. "I thought you were rather irked with me for doing that."

"Initially, perhaps," he admitted, his smile very slight, "but not for long. I saw how she looks when she is enjoying a dance, and it made me determined to give her such enjoyment. I was not certain if I could bring it about, but you challenged me, and I am pleased to say I rose to that challenge."

"I didn't intend it to be a challenge, you know," Simon told him, setting his fishing rod and tackle against the side of the gamekeeper's station. "I merely thought she would be an agreeable dance partner."

Cavernaugh clapped him on the shoulder. "I know that. But it made me step up and step out of myself and proved a very rewarding enterprise."

This was the strangest morning conversation Simon had ever had, and he'd endured some rather strange ones. Still, he managed to smile and nod. "So will you marry her, then?"

"Probably," Cavernaugh said without shame. "After last night, I felt a more genuine liking from her, which gives me encouragement that she will not just adapt to whatever my mother thinks."

Well, now, that was a statement to make. Simon suddenly saw the man in a new light, though not necessarily an exciting one, and shook his hand. "Good luck with that, Cavernaugh. The lady would be most fortunate."

"Don't go that far, Appleby," he replied with a small laugh. "I'm still me."

Simon allowed himself to laugh as well and nodded, turning back for the house. It was high time he shared some of his morning's thoughts with the woman who was at the center of them. Perhaps not all of the thoughts, nor the complete depth of them, but he did have it in mind to be forthright with Jane about everything. It was surely the best way to go about things if he wanted to have any sort of future with her.

He might as well begin as he meant to go on.

He entered the castle almost whistling in his contentment and was surprised to find some of the ladies dining in the breakfast room. He checked his pocket watch quickly, confirming that it was an earlier hour than he anticipated for seeing so many of them the morning after a ball.

"Good morning, Mr. Appleby!" Miss Beacom called cheerily from the table. "Have you been fishing?"

Simon bowed in greeting. "Good morning, Miss Beacom. Yes, I have. Or rather, attempting to fish. Lord Cavernaugh had a better catch than I did."

"What a pity," Miss Beacom said in reply before taking a sip of tea. "Are you going riding with us?"

"Riding?" Simon repeated, noting for the first time that the ladies present were indeed wearing riding habits. "I did not know there had been a ride scheduled."

Miss Beacom nodded as she dabbed her mouth with her linen square. "We are the first group to head out. The second will follow in perhaps another half hour. Not all are going, but we are promised a fine day for a ride. You really ought to come with one of the groups."

Simon would rather enjoy a good ride on a fine horse, and it could provide him the perfect opportunity to talk more with Jane and to measure how she rode. It did not matter if she was a good rider or a bad one, he simply wanted to know which one she was. Or some blend of the two.

But he also did not know if she actually liked to ride.

If Miss Wyant was riding, Jane would certainly ride as well. Ellis loved to ride, so it would be a good opportunity for them both.

He'd need to see about arranging such, if it was not already set in motion.

"Thank you for the recommendation, Miss Beacom," Simon told her with another quick bow. "If you ladies will excuse me, I will change for the ride forthwith." He departed the room and did his best to make haste without looking as though he were making haste.

After all, it would not do to raise questions.

Ellis happened to be coming down the corridor just as Simon was reaching his room. "Ah, Appleby. Going to ride?"

"Shortly, yes," Simon said in a rush. "In which group will you be?"

"Likely the second," Ellis said with a wave of his hand. "I cannot imagine Beatrice and Miss Richards being fully prepared in the next few minutes."

Simon nodded and tried very hard not to smile. "Well, take yourself downstairs and enjoy a coffee, then. I will see you at the stables."

Ellis saluted jauntily and continued on, actually whistling as he went.

It was a strange thing, to suddenly understand why his mad friend was behaving as he was. It was as though the simple dawning of the new day was enough to fill him with joy.

As a man who was not prone to optimism, it was indeed a mighty change.

After a change of clothes and a shave from his valet, Simon descended to join the others as they moved out to the stables. He scanned each of the ladies as surreptitiously as possible, seeking either the ebony hair of Miss Wyant or the lighter chestnut shade of Jane's.

Simon saw neither, but some of the hats adorning the ladies hid the true shade of their hair almost completely. He had not yet seen Jane in a riding habit, so could not attest to her taste in the matter. He might not know until they were all mounted and off.

He paid little attention to which horse he was given, not caring one way or the other, as this was not a hunt, nor a solo ride across the terrain of the estate, as he might have done at Geigle. This was a more sedate ride in a group where a gallop might be permitted, but certainly not for a lengthy period of time. Not all ladies were as reckless at riding as Simon's sister, and some were only the politest of riders and never tried more than a trot with their animal.

It would be all too easy to become caught in a rather plodding sort of group, and that would be torture.

Unless he could plod along beside Jane without haste.

That would work rather well.

Once the entire group was mounted and settled, they were off, led by Cavernaugh with Miss Dawes at his side. Simon situated himself somewhere in the middle of the group to give himself a better chance of finding his friends. They were certainly proving hard to find, and not acting with their usual openness. He was barely hearing conversation of any sort, let alone any sort of good-natured laughter.

Heavens, was he actually hunting for laughter? That was not the sort of behavior anyone would expect of Simon Appleby, and no mistake. But hunting he was, and there was no hint of it anywhere.

Come to think of it, he was not seeing Ellis either. Frowning, Simon looked around the group again, this time only looking for the man in question. Deuce it, what had he been wearing when he had seen him in the corridor?

Had he been wearing brown? Green? Perhaps a deep red or blue?

He could not recall anything about what Ellis had been wearing, and the more he thought about it, the more the color of his coat shifted in his mind.

Growling to himself, Simon rode ahead to Cavernaugh and Miss Dawes, forcing his expression into one of utmost politeness. "Have you seen Mr. Ellis, Cavernaugh? I thought he was to join this group."

Cavernaugh frowned a little and looked at Miss Dawes. "Did he not go with the first group?"

Miss Dawes nodded at once and offered Simon a small smile. "I believe he did, along with Miss Wyant, Miss Richards, Mr. Gideon, Miss Beacom . . . It was quite a large group, and he did offer to wait for the second, but was persuaded to go along."

It was all Simon could do not to curse outright.

"Ah," was all he could reply. He forced himself to swallow as he continued to smile. "I suppose we will catch up with that group at some point."

"Likely not," Cavernaugh countered, shaking his head. "I believe they are also going into Dewbury. We are staying on the estate for a shorter ride, but certainly more scenic. It will be quite lovely; you will not be disappointed."

That was not bloody likely.

Simon tapped the rim of his hat and let his horse fall back slightly, eventually letting his expression fall as well. What exactly it would show for those looking, he did not know, nor did he care. A ride with a group of people that he had no fondness for nor connection with simply for the sake of letting time pass...

What a waste.

Of course, the estate was a pretty one, and he might find some ideas for the lands at Geigle, but all in all, he would simply be enduring the experience.

Did Jane regret that he was not on the ride with them? Had she even noticed his absence?

Oh hell, what if she hadn't even noticed?

That would be the absolute worst outcome.

But perhaps it would be because her focus was on Ellis and Miss Wyant. She likely had not thought it feasible to wait for him when she could help the other two on the ride. Her influence would aid the continuing relationship between their friends and would further the aims of their scheme. Begging off to wait for Simon would have drawn attention to some connection between them, and they could not have that.

She might have had no option but to go with the first group. And if they left as rapidly as they had seemed to, based on when Simon had seen Ellis before, there had likely been no time to send him a note.

He could only hope, and perhaps even pray, that the excursion onto Dewbury lands would be of short duration, and that the first group would return to the castle first, so he might rejoin his friends as soon as possible.

And if not his friends, then just Jane.

Just Jane would be more than enough.

CHAPTER NINETEEN

"It is as though someone does not want me to enjoy myself today."

"What was that, Janie?"

"Nothing, Beatrice, nothing," she said a trifle louder, forcing a smile for her friend as they sat in the drawing room after supper waiting for the gentlemen to come through.

Beatrice smiled at her and returned her attention to her cards.

Cards after supper just between ladies. It was almost more boring than sitting in a room and staring off into space.

To be fair, cards in general were not something to which Jane objected. She rather liked cards, in the right company. She had arranged card parties and had done enough innocent gambling among friends and family to be quite a worthy card player when it came down to it. But tonight, here, with these people, Jane did not want to be playing cards.

She wanted to spend time with Simon.

The entire day had been a waste in that regard. She had been coerced by Beatrice to rise early to join the first group for a ride on the estate and had not even considered the idea that Simon would not be among them. As Beatrice had been so determined to be in the first group, Jane had assumed, wrongly so, that she and Mr. Ellis had arranged things ahead of time for their foursome.

Mr. Ellis had been surprised to see them down so early, but not displeased. He'd mentioned something about Simon and fishing, but there had been no time to argue the point, as the first group was leaving imminently. And then that group had gone into the village after their ride, and Jane had been trapped into shopping with Beatrice, which was not necessarily a bad thing. Indeed, it was a pleasant experience, and Jane had settled herself with finding a new gown that required only a very little alteration. It was just a yellow muslin, but there was something about it that reminded her of the center of the small daisies she and Simon had turned into a chain for Ellis to learn from. And the ring that he had given her the night before.

She had pressed that daisy ring between the pages of her diary before going to bed last night, as well as the note that had come with it.

Having a gown that could have matched the color would be a sign of affection that only the two of them would know about.

She could not wait to wear it and see Simon's reaction. If he would notice the same thing. She suspected he would. They seemed to be of a mind more often than not. And Jane was not a sentimental or whimsical woman, so if she were to engage in such an action, he would surely know it had a reason.

When she would wear it was less certain. If she had known she would not even be able to talk with Simon at supper, she would have worn it tonight to have hope of some communication of her feelings.

After shopping in the village, they had returned to the castle and been told that the second group was indeed back, but that it was time for the ladies to have their respite.

Jane had had every intention of ignoring the opportunity of a respite to seek out Simon, but her aunt had asked her to find a book in the library and read to her for a time. And try as she might, Jane had not been able to find Simon on her way to or back from the library. Reading to Anne-Marie had been well enough, but her throat and eyes had been so tired that she had actually needed to take her own respite.

Then there had been preparing for supper, which had not taken long, as Jane did not care, and she had descended as quickly as she could to the drawing room, hoping to see him before supper and share a word.

He had not come down until almost immediately before the meal began, holding the arm of his aunt, who was moving slower than usual despite seeming in good spirits.

They had met eyes then, and she had not missed the abject relief in his expression at seeing her.

Jane had never worked so hard in her entire life to express so much in her face at once. She tried to tell him that she had missed him, that she was delighted to see him, that he was the handsomest man she'd ever seen, that she was wild to talk to him, that the enjoyment of her entire day had hinged upon this very moment...

She was quite certain he was going to be seeing a face full of consternation as she tried to say so much, but whatever he did see made him smile.

Then his aunt had prodded his foot with her walking stick, and he'd led her into the dining room. There had been no attempting to manage a seat near him, as those seats had already been taken, so Jane had been forced to sit between Miss Beacom and a rather arrogant man who seemed only capable of talking about himself.

She had been situated so far from Simon at the table that she had not been able to even hear his voice.

The ladies had been excused from supper rather sooner than expected, though certainly when all had finished their meal, and now they sat here waiting for the gentlemen to arrive before the evening's entertainment could begin.

No one knew what it was to be, and Lady Cavernaugh was remarkably tight-lipped about the whole thing.

"It is your turn, Miss Richards," Miss Cole quipped rather smugly from beside her.

Jane blinked and looked back at her cards. "Yes, so it is. Pardon me." She laid down a card and worked on composing her face into an expression of complete neutrality. She was tired of a smiling appearance when she had no desire to smile. What did she have to smile about on this day? She had encouraged a healthy conversation between her friend and her soon-to-be intended on the ride, and then had been in almost complete silence for the rest of the time. The man she loved was in another room, and here she sat looking at cards.

A lump suddenly lurched in her throat and Jane froze, her eyes fixed on her cards.

Loved. She loved Simon. How could she love Simon? She had barely known him a few days, and almost all of that time had been spent scheming for their friends. How could she have fallen in love while so intensely occupied?

But what else could this soul-deep yearning for the barest sight of him be? Why else would she be pressing a silly flower ring between pages of her diary? Why did the words of his note scorch themselves behind her eyelids?

Why did she dream of meeting him in the corridor or on the green when they had both risen from bed and neither was technically decent for company?

"Miss Richards, are you too warm? We are very close to the fire, if you should like to move."

Jane cleared her throat and fanned her face with the cards she held, smiling even as tears began to burn at her eyes. "I am quite well, thank you. I trust we shall not be sat here much longer, so my complexion shall soon recover. My skin is ever-so-sensitive to the heat, but I feel quite well."

The ladies all nodded sympathetically, then looked at their cards again.

Except for Beatrice. She was staring at Jane in abject confusion and suspicion.

Jane refused to meet her eyes. To explain her feelings for Simon would require her to explain her scheme with him, which would mean Beatrice and Ellis would know of the attempt to make their match, which would quite possibly ruin everything.

Absolutely everything.

And the aunts . . .

Oh heavens, what would the aunts have to say? They were of a mind, it seemed, when it came to matchmaking and schemes and the like, so they might be quite pleased with the result . . .

Or they could be miffed that they were not included in its inception.

Or the aunts could be less keen on each other than polite interactions appeared and . . .

Why was Jane even worrying about this matter? Simon had not offered her anything, nor had he declared anything. Although she had told him that creating a flower ring might suggest something more and he had done so anyway. Was he trying to say something without actually saying something? Or was he trying to be sweet although it might mean something to others, but not mean anything himself? Did he expect Jane to think it meant something? Was he thinking about something specific, but she was not supposed to think something specific?

Was anybody thinking about anything or were they not supposed to think anything and just do something that might not mean anything? Unless it meant something?

Good gracious, she was losing her mind.

She had already lost her heart.

The door to the drawing room opened, and the gentlemen began to trickle in from the dining room. It was all Jane could do to remain in her seat and attempt to finish their card game, assuming the others wished to.

Beatrice, on the other hand, put her cards down and blatantly looked for Mr. Ellis.

And so, the gossip would rise again.

But with the house party to end the day after tomorrow, that might not be so bad.

Mr. Ellis came directly to the card table, then took Beatrice's hand and brought it to his lips, making the other ladies at the table sigh. Jane smiled at it, but kept her eyes darting back to the entering gentlemen.

Where was Simon?

"Everyone!" Lady Cavernaugh intoned, clapping her hands. "Do not get comfortable. We have a very special presentation for you this evening. If you will follow me."

Mr. Ellis looped Beatrice's hand through his arm and led her out with the rest, the pair of them already deep in conversation. Jane slowly rose from her chair, seeking Simon somewhere in the stream of guests now moving in the same direction.

"Give me your arm, Jane," Aunt Anne-Marie instructed, seeming to appear out of nowhere. "My knees are very bad today."

"Of course, Aunt," Jane responded with the sort of instinctive obedience that was born of family relationships. If Anne-Marie's knees were truly bad, they could take a slow pace getting to their destination, which ought to allow Simon to catch up to them.

Anne-Marie, however, was like an eager pup straining on a lead. "Come along, dear, I said my knees were bad, not dead. Honestly, it is like being attached to a corpse."

As Anne-Marie was not kind enough to lower her voice, there was no alternative but to go at the pace she dictated. It was not particularly hasty, but it certainly would not allow for

Jane to find Simon, let alone for him to join them as they walked.

Lady Cavernaugh led them all into a different part of the castle that the group had not seen collectively as yet, and gestured grandly as they entered a large open space with tall ceilings and large dark beams lining it from edge to the central crease. Among those dark beams were rounded wooden arches and curved support beams, lending an air of majesty and ancient nobility to the space. On the floor, rows of chairs had been set up, each facing them, oddly enough.

"Behold," Lady Cavernaugh announced, "the great hall. Those beams are from the fourteenth century, and the windows there, you see, are original Norman arches. The tapestries are sixteenth century, and each piece of art has been hand selected by me from our gallery. We have three Gainsboroughs, you know."

"And, no doubt, some original Rembrandts from when her ladyship entertained his affections," Anne-Marie muttered. "What nonsense."

Jane stifled a laugh and did her best not to nudge her aunt.

"If you will all turn," Lady Cavernaugh instructed, "you will see our fifteenth-century screen we recently had installed, and upon which, for this occasion, we have built a stage. Tonight, we will be entertained by Dewbury's very own acting troupe!"

Applause scattered around the room and the actors began to appear on the stage built behind the screen, bowing in greeting.

"Come, let us take a seat by the window," Anne-Marie suggested, tugging Jane along. "I want something nice to look at in case this entire presentation is bunk."

"Aunt," Jane hissed. She tried not to dig in her heels as she followed. "It will probably be delightful."

Anne-Marie sputtered and scoffed noisily. "I highly doubt a

local acting troupe will be worth anything. If they pass around a bowl for donations, I will spit into it."

Jane sighed and shook her head. So, this was the sort of mood she would have to contend with this evening? It was all too perfect for the dreadful day she'd had thus far, and exactly what she did not want for the night. If Simon could sit on her other side, she might be able to find some joy in the experience, in spite of her aunt, but if he did not . . .

"Ah, there, sit beside Miss Cable." Anne-Marie pointed towards a stately young woman with a perfectly blank expression. "She does not speak and has no opinions. I sat beside her at tea, and it was silence and bliss."

There were only two seats beside Miss Cable, which would mean no space for Simon.

What had they ever done to earn this clear spurning from Fate?

Jane sat beside Miss Cable without a word, Anne-Marie taking the seat on the aisle, clearing her throat loudly as she fixed her attention to the stage.

The rest of the guests seemed to be taking their seats as well, and Jane took the opportunity to glance around, fixing the politest smile upon her face. Her eyes moved twice as fast as her head, desperate for any sign of Simon. It was a though he had left the house party, and no one had said anything.

Her heart screeched to a slamming halt against her ribs, her breath catching.

Oh heavens, what if he'd left? It was entirely possible for a guest to leave without any ado and have it not be announced to the others, and it was not entirely out of the realm of possibility for Simon's established reputation and personality. What if last night had ruined his mood and his favor? What if she had not made herself available enough to dance with him so they might talk, and he assumed that she was spurning him?

Then she saw him, and her heart, her lungs, and her smile all returned to their natural state.

He was across the room, a vast aisle separating them, and seated beside his own aunt.

Looking at Jane.

Her stomach clenched as she gazed at him, seeing the hungry, pained rawness of his features. His eyes seemed to glow in their transcendent blueness, calming her as much as they were freezing her in place. Filling her with hope and light while they also slowly robbed her of breath, drowning her in the glorious sea of all that he was and all he made her feel.

His lips moved into the most perfect smile she had ever seen, and her toes curled in her slippers. She swallowed hard and opened her fan, her cheeks giving off a telltale burning sensation that she desperately needed to cool.

Simon's smile deepened and he discreetly tugged at his collar as though it was too tight.

Was he truly saying . . . was he indicating that . . .?

Jane tilted her head in question.

He nodded once.

An exhale was ripped from her throat and lungs, teasing her lips into a sensitivity that only Simon would be able to soothe. Only Simon would know what to do with it. Only Simon could satiate her.

Only Simon.

Always Simon.

How could she continue to simply sit across from him in this space when her heart was quite clearly sitting in the palm of his hand? It felt unnatural to be separated in this way.

But what could she do?

Jane bit her lip and turned to her aunt. "Aunt, I see some space over there by Lady Clarke. There are exquisite windows there as well, would you like to move over and sit beside her?"

"I would not!" Anne-Marie chirped in a cold, clipped tone. "The woman is tactless, tasteless, and one of the most offensive creatures I have ever encountered on this earth."

Jane stared at her in horror, the sudden shift as unexpected as it was startling. "I beg your pardon?"

Anne-Marie glared at her. "You heard me."

"What happened?" she hissed, leaning close. "I thought the two of you were friends!"

"Well, I thought so too until yesterday!" Anne-Marie shook her head, muttering darkly under her breath. "That woman told me that your dowry is absurd and your father ought to be ashamed of himself for not providing better for his daughters. She wanted to know all the details of his entail, only to proclaim that an estate with an entail is no better than working in trade."

Jane blinked at the statement, knowing Lady Clarke to be eccentric and outspoken, but never outright cruel. "I thought . . . I thought she liked me."

Anne-Marie snorted once. "She pities you, Janet. She said it is no wonder you are not married at your age, as your dowry is not anything to entice proper suitors, and that your simple beauty—simple beauty, indeed—is not to be celebrated. You don't play, so she presumes you are not accomplished. And while I thought you were lovely dancing last night, she said you were positively savage and not out of place among the lower class."

It was like a series of knives had been thrown into Jane's chest one after the other, taking root at once and blooming into poisonous barbs.

Lady Clarke . . . Simon's aunt . . . thought *this* of her?

"I have no doubt," Anne-Marie snapped, "that she is spreading this tosh to her spoiled nephew. I don't care if he is friends with dear Mr. Ellis, you are not to see him again."

Jane's throat went dry. "We . . . we are at the same party, Aunt. How can we avoid each other?"

Anne-Marie looked at her as though she had lost her mind. "By avoiding him, Janet! I have written to your father to tell him all, and we will not be allowing association with that family in future. You will not see him, dance with him, speak with him, or be in a group with him while we are here, do I make myself quite clear?"

Not only was she clear, but she was also adamantly so.

Jane could not respond as she wished here, and certainly not in this company. Her aunt was exactly the sort to make a scene, and Jane would never recover from that embarrassment. Beatrice and Mr. Ellis might be forced to take sides, if this rift was as dramatic as her aunt seemed to think it was, and that would help no one. Lady Cavernaugh would have to ask Jane and her aunt to leave quietly, and they would almost certainly do so.

There was nothing to do.

No way out.

And she could feel Simon's eyes on her as she struggled not to cry, forcing her attention to the stage, where the performers were waiting.

"Janet," her aunt growled. "Am I clear?"

Left with no choice and no power to speak, Jane merely dipped her chin in a nod as she felt a pair of tears leak from her eyes and slowly roll down her face.

CHAPTER TWENTY

D awn. The green. Alone.
That was all the note said, and it terrified
Simon to the core.

It had come in the middle of the night, and he might have missed it entirely had he not tossed and turned for hours prior to hearing it slide under his door.

His sleep had been very fretful after he'd seen it. Torn between launching himself out into the corridor to catch her and returning to bed, he'd hovered somewhere between the two, marching to the door and back to the bed again and again. Shoving his fingers into his hair and scrambling in his thoughts.

Ultimately, he had tried to sleep, but imagined every wretched scenario known to man from those words. It could not have been about Miss Wyant and Ellis, not this time. Not after the perfect couple they had made watching the performance of the actors the night before.

There was no more help to be given them. The match was very nearly made, and the engagement was certainly due to follow.

If it was not about helping them, then what would require such terseness in the middle of the night?

Something had happened during the performance, any fool could have seen that had they been watching her. They'd been filling themselves with the sight of each other, even across the room, and, he thought, forging a connection, until she had talked to her aunt.

He had felt the temperature in the room drop markedly in perfect time with the color fading from Jane's face. He had never seen any person go so pale so fast. For a moment, he had thought she would swoon, and he was ready to spring to his feet to assist her. But then she had straightened and forced her attention to the stage.

He might have imagined it, but he was fairly certain he saw a tear, and that had ripped his heart in two from top to bottom.

She did not look at him for the rest of the night. Her features never regained their color throughout the evening, and she did not smile even for politeness.

Jane always smiled for politeness.

Something was wrong, and he was in hell imagining it.

So he had found himself walking the perimeter of the green far before dawn, clad only in his nightshirt, trousers, boots, and greatcoat, letting the predawn breeze ripple the fabric against his skin and tousle his hair as it would.

He would not be easy until he had seen Jane and spoken with her. Really spoken with her. They'd not exchanged words in over twenty-four hours, and it felt like an entire week of his life had been lost because of it. He was less irritated and more bereft, but there was certainly anger and irritation within its depths.

Anything that would keep him from Jane would cause anger and irritation along with loss.

But soon, all that would be rectified.

Unless it got worse.

He would not know until she told him what the matter

was, and until then, he would not know if there was anything he could do. If there was anything to do.

God help him, but he needed there to be something he could do.

Waiting and doing nothing was bloody agony.

"You are early."

Simon's lungs heaved of their own accord, and he turned to face the doorway into the green.

Jane stood there, lovely hair perfectly plaited and hanging over her right shoulder, nightgown visible beneath her cinched green dressing gown, her feet encased in slippers, her face drawn and haggard. A few strands of long hair hung loose by her left ear, and her eyes were red and puffy.

He had never seen anything or anyone look more beautiful.

He struggled for even a half-swallow. "So are you."

Jane started to nod, then her throat bobbed with evident tears.

Simon was moving before he knew it, and Jane stepped into the green, reaching for him. Their mouths collided in frenzied, passionate motions, his hands gripping at her waist and her hair, her fingers practically clawing at his face. It was wholly desperate, this luscious attack on each other, barely breathing, let alone thinking, as they reached for something within one another over and over. Jane arched into him, going up on tiptoe as her lips seared his skin and stripped his sanity bare. It was all he could do to remain upright in this torrent, clinging to her as though for life itself.

Then, of all things, Jane whimpered and began to cry, her tears rushing to their touching lips and bringing a sweet saltiness to his tongue.

Simon was suddenly holding her in his arms as she nearly buckled, supporting her as she sobbed into his chest. "What is it, love?" he whispered, his lips at her ear as he ran his hand over her hair. "What can I do?"

"My aunt . . ." Jane gasped, linking her hands around his neck and trying to straighten. "She . . . she said . . ."

Simon kissed her ear and pulled back just enough to cradle her cheek in one hand, smoothing her tears away. "Shh," he said softly, stroking her skin tenderly. "Take a breath, my darling. We have time. Take a breath."

Jane inhaled shakily, her entire frame trembling, and let it out without any sort of steadiness.

"Again, love," Simon urged. He smoothed away another tear. "Another breath."

She nodded and did so, only having slightly more success.

But it was enough.

"My aunt," she told him, her voice weak, "fought with yours. Their friendship is over, and she has . . . Simon, she has forbidden me to see you. Or speak to you. I am not even permitted to be in your presence with our friends around. She has written to my father and is hellbent on starting a feud between our families."

"What?" He pulled her waist closer, shaking her head. "What could Louise have said to set all this off? I know she's outspoken and frank, but even she is not . . ."

Jane's face crumpled and she took his face in her hands, touching their brows. "It doesn't even matter now, my aunt will not be appeased. But I cannot stay away from you, Simon. I do not *want* to be away from you. And I will not, unless you tell me it is best that we do so. I know we have not said anything with words, but . . ."

Simon silenced her with a kiss, fierce and intent, determined to leave no doubt in her mind on where he stood on the matter of the two of them. That she should know how he had ached for her. How he craved her. How he was lost without her.

How she was everything and anything in his life.

"I love you," he whispered, his thumb brushing her cheek, his mouth hovering just above hers. "Mad as it is, unlikely as it seems, impossible as I've claimed, I love you. From parts of my heart and soul I did not know existed and from the beginning of time to the end of it. None of it makes sense, and nothing has made more perfect sense. I love you, Jane Richards."

Jane touched his jaw and wrapped her arms around his neck, burying her face into him as she cried once more. "I love you, Simon," she said against his skin, her lips raking fire in their path. "I love you so much I will defy my aunt and anyone else to be with you."

Simon encircled her in his arms as completely as humanly possible. "There is nothing that heaven, earth, or either of our aunts could do that would keep me from you, my love," he told her. "Nothing. Do you understand?"

She nodded and raised her head, touching their brows and noses together. "With you," she breathed, sighing deeply. "That is all I need. Just you."

He kissed her again, very gently. "With you, my love." He chuckled and gave her another quick kiss. "How did we get here, Jane?"

She laughed in return and gripped the back of his neck. "I haven't the faintest idea. But suddenly, here we are." She pulled back, smiling amid her tears. "What do we tell our aunts, Simon? Anne-Marie will be livid no matter what."

He exhaled and shook his head, taking one of her hands and kissing the palm before lacing their fingers and starting to walk the perimeter of the green with her. "I don't know, to be honest. Louise says whatever she likes, you know that, and if she is losing her faculties . . . I may be able to coerce her to apologize, if she has had a recent sleep."

"I don't know if Anne-Marie will accept an apology," Jane murmured, covering their clasped hands with her free one. "She can be so stubborn. There may be no settling this matter with her."

"Does she have authority over your future?" Simon asked, thinking quickly. "Financial or legal?"

Jane made a face. "I don't think so. She does have remarkable influence over my father, but even he would not cut me off. I don't think."

"It's fine if he does," Simon told her, kissing her hand. "I don't care about a dowry, I really don't. And once we marry, I can arrange matters in such a complicated, thorough way that no one can touch you. There's a solicitor in London, a Mr. Tuttle-Kirk, my friend Larkin Roth told me of him . . ."

"You know Larkin Roth?" Jane asked in surprise, laughing a little. "So do I!"

Simon grinned at the revelation. "There, now. We'll have at least one set of friends, should all else collapse."

"I don't care if it does." Jane bit her lip, though it did nothing to restrain her smile. "I love you, and I have not slept all night trying to think of how to tell you and what to do."

"Good," Simon murmured, further words seeming entirely unnecessary in the wake of such a stirring admission.

Jane's eyes suddenly narrowed. "Did you just say, 'once we marry,' Simon?"

His stomach dropped to his knees, and he cleared his throat. "I might have done."

"Is that something we ought to discuss, perhaps?" she asked him, pulling him to a stop and raising a brow.

"Why? Do you object?" He gave her a searching look, his heart skipping a beat in spite of himself.

But Jane was not a woman to be trifled with and she matched his stubbornness. "I do not know. I have not been asked, and therefore, can have no thoughts on the matter."

Simon pressed his tongue against his teeth, fighting more laughter at the marvelous creature that was this woman. She would never let their life become dull and would never let him have his way just for the sake of it. She would fight with him, when need be, and make him laugh in the very next breath. She would keep him company as well as give him space. She would make her own way in whatever world they created together and give him a reason to live and breathe every single day. She would be the very life of him, and he would give his very life for her.

That, he decided, was love.

Even in its madness.

"I'm not asking you to marry me after four days at a house party, my love," he told her with a teasing smile, rubbing his thumb over her knuckles. "It is far too scandalous, considering our friends we have matched are not even engaged yet. But one day after one week of our meeting, I will come to you, wherever you are, and beg you to be my wife. It is entirely up to you what response you give, of course, but if your sentiments then are half of what my sentiments are now, I have every reason to trust that you will give a moderately enthusiastic yes."

Jane threw back her head on a laugh, the sound throaty and rich and very likely the cause of the dawn breaking over the horizon with its sheer joy.

There was nothing for Simon to do but kiss that woman rather thoroughly in response, and she enthusiastically returned it.

"Will you say yes?" he asked her, his lips brushing against hers with the question. "When I ask you?"

"Probably," she whispered back, letting her mouth slide to the stubble at his jaw. "And probably a right sight more enthusiastically than moderately."

Simon grinned before dipping his chin in a nod. "I was hoping you would say that, but it is ungentlemanly to presume."

"Very," she agreed. With a soft sigh, she stepped closer and leaned against him, her eyes fluttering shut. "We need to do something. We cannot stay here like this forever."

"Unfortunately, I agree." Simon rubbed his hands up and down her back, twisting his lips in thought. "Let us go to your aunt, love. If we can get her on our side, we need not be completely estranged from everyone. I'll do my best to show her I am sincere in my love for you and my support for you, and perhaps that will be enough."

Jane nodded against him, the warmth of her seeping through the linen of his shirt. "And if it is not?"

Simon shrugged, making Jane giggle softly. "Then we will go to my aunt and tell her yours said no and trust the feud to give you support. We can offer her the name of our first child, if she likes."

"We will not!" she protested, still laughing. "You are dreadful."

He kissed her hair and exhaled, starting for the door to the green, her hand tight in his. "Let's get this over with, darling. The sooner the better."

Jane said nothing, but kept pace with him.

"This way," she told him gently when they entered the corridor, tugging him to the right.

They moved a few doors down, and then Jane stopped, knocking softly.

"Enter!" a surprisingly brisk voice chirped.

Jane looked at Simon, her face full of anxiety.

He nodded in encouragement, squeezing her hand.

With a quick exhale, she opened the door to the room and entered, Simon on her heels.

Mrs. Richards was sitting up in her bed, clear-eyed and free of emotion. "Well, well," she said in a low voice as she looked pointedly at the joined hands of the two of them. "I don't know which to comment on first, Janet. The state of your apparel in the presence of this man, or the fact that you are intimately holding his hand despite the fact that last night I was quite clear in my feelings regarding him."

"I am in love with Simon, Aunt," Jane announced in a clear voice, her fingers gripping his hard. "I asked him to meet me this morning so I could tell him of your wishes. Wishes that I cannot agree to."

"Last night, you agreed," Mrs. Richards insisted, though there was not much fierceness behind her words.

Jane shook her head. "Last night, I agreed that you made yourself clear, which is all you asked of me. I am free to act for myself, Aunt, and so I shall. Simon is a good man, and he loves me." She broke off and looked at him then, her smile so sweet, it nearly removed his kneecaps. "He loves me so much, as I do him."

Simon winked at her, unable to keep from returning her smile.

"We are going to be married, Aunt," Jane went on, facing her once more. "We are not engaged yet, but we have an understanding, and Simon is a man of his word. So you may cut me off if you choose, but I choose Simon. As he chooses me."

Mrs. Richards blinked and looked at him, her eyes calculating. "Is this true, young man? You choose my niece in spite of your aunt? In spite of my forbidding it?"

Simon bowed from the neck only. "Mrs. Richards, I have the greatest respect for you and have no wish to cause you distress or offense. But I love Jane above all else, and I am prepared to act in defiance of your wishes for her. We will marry, and we would wish for your support and blessing, if you can give it."

Her aged lips pursed, creating more lines in her face as her attention flicked between the two of them. "Hmm," she said slowly.

They waited, and Simon, for one, was holding his breath.

"Well, that is a great relief."

Simon was positive his ears were deceiving him, and he stared at the elderly woman in shock. "I beg your pardon?" he coughed.

Mrs. Richards all-out beamed, seeming to dance a little in her bed. "Do you have any idea how much went into throwing the two of you together? My word, we are exhausted."

"We?" Jane repeated.

"Come on out," Mrs. Richards called. "It is time they knew!"

The door to her dressing room opened to reveal his aunt Louise, Ellis, and, shockingly, Miss Wyant, all of whom were grinning unabashedly.

"What the actual devil?" Simon looked from his aunt to his friend and back to Mrs. Richards.

"You did not think this was all happening by accident, did you?" Mrs. Richards chortled and tossed her bedcovers aside, swinging her legs to the side of the bed. "We've been planning this for weeks!"

"All of you?" Jane asked, fumbling for a chair and sinking onto it, still clinging to Simon's hand.

Miss Wyant giggled, clapping her hands. "Did you really think I was that hopeless in the company of a man I admired? Heavens, Janie, you are a dear." She looked up at Ellis, beaming in delight. "George and I met months ago at a soiree in Bath and formed an attachment. I was in the vicinity of your aunt's home and paid her a visit, during which I told her about him."

"And she told me everything," Mrs. Richards said with a laugh. "Including that he had grown up in Derbyshire, rather near to Brockton. And I know someone who also grew up near to Brockton, so I wrote to my dear friend Louise right away."

Louise nodded, her nightcap bobbling a bit unsteadily. "And I confirmed that I had known dear George since he was born and that he was friends with my nephew Simon, and thus . . ." She gestured to Simon and Jane rather fondly.

Simon had lost the power of speech and could only gape. He moved his attention to Ellis, who was the only one who seemed a trifle sheepish.

"We knew that you and Miss Richards would not be able to resist intervening if Beatrice and I were complete rubbish at courtship," Ellis told them, scratching the back of his head. "You may not like love and romance, Appleby, but you are a good friend. Well, you may not have previously liked love and romance, anyway."

The entire room managed to laugh there, including Simon and Jane.

"So this was all . . . a plot?" Jane managed, beginning to smile.

"A scheme, my dear," Mrs. Richards corrected as she approached her niece and gestured for her to rise. "A delightful match-enabling scheme. Why else do you think I insisted you come with me to this house party?" She opened her arms for an embrace, quirking her brows as she laughed.

Jane's jaw dropped and she hugged her aunt, finally releasing Simon's hand to do so.

"What was yesterday, then?" he demanded, not quite ready to forgive everyone yet. "You contrived to keep us separated the entire day? And then engineered a feud to . . . to what end?"

Louise tsked and made her way in his direction, her walking stick rapping on the wood floor. "To make you decide, dear boy. To solidify your feelings. You overthink things entirely too much and might have tried to rationalize your way out of your feelings. And after your little hiding from the others in the green the other day . . ."

Simon stared down at his aunt, his eyes wide. "You knew about that?"

She cackled and patted his arm. "Look where we are, dear. And remember where my room is. Anne-Marie and I have perfect views of the green. I must say, bad form not to promise just now. It was a perfect opening." She held her cheek up for him to kiss, chuckling softly to herself.

Feeling rather shaken, Simon gave her a perfunctory kiss, then looked at Jane in disbelief.

"Was any of it real?" she asked, more for him than anything else.

"All of it was real, darling," Mrs. Richards told her, patting her arms. "We simply provided the opportunity. We did not tell you what to say or how to feel. Look at that man there. How do you feel now that you know?"

Jane obeyed, staring at him for a long moment.

Simon stared back, and somehow, his heart swelled, his legs gained strength, and his mouth curved into a warm smile.

He saw Jane's shoulders move on a sigh and saw the delicious curve of her lips. "I love him," she murmured softly, so softly he barely heard her.

"I love you," Simon told her, sliding his hands into the pockets of his great coat and shaking his head. "We are well and truly matched, are we not?"

Jane nodded as she beamed, laughing to herself. "So it would seem."

He'd have kissed her then, if there had been a chance.

"Now," Mrs. Richards said firmly, clapping her hands, "I absolutely agree that no engagement can come at this party. We will not give Delphine the satisfaction."

"Indeed not," Louise agreed, thumping the ground with her cane. "George, you and Beatrice should be engaged, however. Simon and Jane will become engaged next week, and we will have the banns read sometime after that. Anne-Marie, what do you think of St. George's in Hannover Square?"

"Perfect. We must outshine Delphine's quaint little castle wedding."

Simon ignored all of them and kept his focus wholly on Jane, who was smiling at him in return.

Matched they were, both in their courtship and in their life. And so, they would continue on, well matched, well loved, and well and truly happy.

In spite of everything.

EPILOGUE

"I do not see why I cannot give the bride away. It is most unjust."

Jane rolled her eyes and looked at Taft Debenham, Earl of Harwood, with all the impatience others used for brothers alone. "Because I have a father and he is living."

Taft scowled at that, shaking his head. "It makes no difference. I look better beside you than he does."

"But then people might think that I am marrying you," Jane countered, plucking a small leaf from the stem of a flower and casting it to the floor.

"Ergh." Taft shuddered and crossed himself. "No, thank you. Appleby is a good sort, he'll do much better for you."

Jane smiled at the thought and nodded. "I know."

Taft chuckled and put his arm around her shoulders. "Your happiness is sickening in its sweetness, Janie. But if I have to give you up, it might as well be to a man you love. Not to mention one who can defend your honor. I have never seen a man box so well as him, and that is nothing to sniff at."

Jane shoved Taft away with a snort of a laugh, looking down at her lavender-and-lace bridal gown as though it needed adjusting. "Go away now, Taft. I must prepare for my grand entrance."

"Very well, I shall join the other guests." He kissed her cheek quickly and moved to the door, cracking it open ever so slightly. "Gads, there are so many in there. I did not know Appleby had this many friends."

"Neither of us do," Jane replied as she shook out her skirts. "Our aunts made sure everyone from Society was invited. The Roths should be there somewhere, if you need a friend."

"Are they, indeed? Most excellent."

"Or," Jane went on as though he had not spoken, "there is always Alexandrina."

As she'd anticipated, Taft's entire body cringed. "Absolutely bleeding not," he spat. "The last time I saw her, she snarled at me like a feral dog."

"She did not!" Jane laughed, turning to scold him.

Taft held up his hands and nodded. "She did, I'd bet my life on it. There is something wrong with her, Janie, and it is time someone told her. Someone who is not me."

Jane waved him off, and this time he left, leaving the door partially ajar.

Alone at last, she sighed, the butterflies in her chest and stomach roaring to life again. Not that she was dreading what was to come, but she was excited. So very excited.

And happy.

Her wedding day. It seemed such a strange thing to say. Weeks of waiting after knowing each other for less than that, all leading to this. And yet . . . those weeks had been so dear to her, so tender and filled with joy and hope. Simon was everything she could have ever wanted, including a witty companion and friend even when they were not being romantic. She had always wanted a husband she genuinely liked, even if there was no romantic love, and now she was getting one.

One she also happened to love more fiercely than she

thought a human heart capable. One who saw her as a person, not only a woman. One who respected her mind and her opinions. One who was not afraid to defer to her. One who made her pleased to be precisely who she was.

That was what she loved most about Simon. He wanted her just as she was and wanted her to be herself in any situation or circumstance. He made her feel like the very best version of herself and gave that self wings to fly and to soar to its fullest abilities.

She could only hope she offered him something of the sort in return.

And to think—they had gone from matchmakers to a match made themselves.

No one would fully believe that story, should it become known.

The aunts, however, were of the mind that no one should know the truth. That was perfectly well and good, as far as Jane and Simon were concerned. They simply wanted to start their life together and remove to Geigle as soon as possible.

Jane, for one, could not wait to see it.

There was a soft knock at the door. "Jane, dear?"

"Come in, Papa," she called, holding her flowers close.

Her father, sweet man that he was, seemed to tear up when he saw her, in spite of his smile. "You are so beautiful, my girl. I am delighted to see you so happy."

Jane reached out a hand for him, which he took and kissed. "Thank you, Papa."

"And I must say," he added with a faint sniffle, "I already like your husband more than your sister's. We shall keep that between us, shall we?"

"I think so, yes," Jane laughed.

With a wink and a nod, her father kept hold of her hand and led her to the door, then out into the vestibule, where they paused and waited for their cue.

Jane could see Simon up ahead, his back to her, as tradition dictated, Mr. Ellis by his side. She could see Simon's left leg bouncing just a little and smiled at the pure sign of his nerves as well.

Her heart was going to burst when she saw his face, of that she had no doubt.

And if she knew her soon-to-be husband at all, his heart would do the same.

And they would make each other ticklishly uncomfortable for the rest of their days.

"Are you ready, Jane?" her father whispered, her hand still in his.

A wave of calm washed over Jane, her eyes still fixed on Simon, who suddenly glanced over his shoulder, his eyes fiercely blue and fiercely hers. She smiled at him and caught a glimpse of his own smile before he turned back around, his bouncing leg now still.

"Yes, Papa," Jane told him, exhaling in sheer delight and certainty. "I am ready."

NEXT IN THE CASTLES & COURTSHIP SERIES

A Suitable Arrangement

By

Martha Keyes

THE CASTLES & COURTSHIP SERIES

An Amiable Foe by Jennie Goutet

To Know Miss May by Deborah M Hathaway

A Heart to Keep by Ashtyn Newbold

A Noble Inheritance by Kasey Stockton

The Rules of Matchmaking by Rebecca Connolly

A Suitable Arrangement by Martha Keyes

An Engagement with the Enemy by Sally Britton

Charming the Recluse by Mindy Burbidge Strunk

Each book is a stand-alone romance and they can be read in any order.

ABOUT THE AUTHOR

Rebecca Connolly is the author of more than two dozen novels. She calls herself a Midwest girl, having lived in Ohio and Indiana. She's always been a bookworm, and her grandma would send her books almost every month so she would never run out. Book Fairs were her carnival, and libraries are her happy place. She has been creating stories since childhood, and there are home videos to prove it! She received a master's degree from West Virginia University, and is a hot cocoa addict.

Want to hear about future releases and upcoming events for Rebecca Connolly?

Sign up for the monthly Wit and Whimsy at: www.rebeccaconnolly.com

Made in the USA
Coppell, TX
03 October 2023

22349585R00155